ON THE WAY HOME

ON THE WAY HOME

Robert Bausch

ST. MARTIN'S PRESS
NEW YORK

Copyright©1982 by Robert Bausch
For information, write: St. Martin's Press,
175 Fifth Avenue, New York, N.Y. 10010
Manufactured in the United States of America

Library of Congress Cataloging in Publication Data

Bausch, Robert.
On the way home.
  I. Title.
PS3552.A84705   813' .54 81-18227
ISBN 0-312-58459-8   AACR2

10 9 8 7 6 5 4 3 2 1

First Edition

This book is for the women
in my life:
Geri,
Sara,
and Jules . . .

To go mad, one must have a terrific accumulation of sanities. . . .

Henry Miller

PART ONE

I. THE TAPES

Fireworks went off behind me and I jumped into a construction ditch. Children on their way to the fireworks laughed and pointed at me. I think I was crying. I was making this noise, like a horse, and shaking. A man shooed the children away and picked me up out of the ditch. He had gray hair and a kind face, and I was afraid for him. He brushed my clothing off. I was still shaking and crying. I couldn't stop.

"Are you all right?" the man said.

"I don't know."

He looked into my eyes, as if he couldn't find something and thought it might be there. Then he said, "How long you been back?"

It was hard to talk. I told him I had been back three months. I really don't remember, though. Not even now. I thought it might be two, three months. "I'm all right now," I told him.

"I know how you feel," he said. I felt as if I was hearing his voice just after a dream. His eyes were impartial, staring at me. I was shaking inside. I felt as though my heart had come loose, and it bounced around in my chest looking for a place to attach. It would stop if I concentrated on it. Sometimes it's like the water on your windshield when you drive in the rain. The wiper clears it away and you can see for a second, but then the water just comes running down again. The wipers never clear it all away.

"You sure you're all right?" the man said.

"Yes," I said, but he knew I wasn't. He was much older, and I wished for a crazy, calm moment that he was my father. His hands rested on my shoulders, holding me down. I knew the moment he took his hands off I would go up. I would soar over the park and the fireworks would explode all around. There wouldn't be anything left of me after

3

that. I felt the man's hands move, and I said, "Don't let go of me." One hand moved down my arm and the other tightened.

"I won't," he said. "Don't worry. I've got you."

I tried to relax. "I'm a little nervous," I said. My teeth chattered, I couldn't stop shivering.

I thought I had been pretty calm before the fireworks went off. I wanted to get back to that feeling. I was walking toward my parents' house. I'm new in Florida, having just gotten back, and I'm not used to their house yet. They moved here while I was away—I was missing, but the army reported me dead. So my father wanted to come here. I never have gone home. Not really home. I'm only visiting my parents. I've been staying there since I got back. I can't remember how long, two, three months. I'm not really back yet, I guess. I was in and out of hospitals in my last year of the Army, and once since I've been here. I don't like the hospital. I feel like that's what has become of my mother and father's house. My bedroom is white. My parents don't know who I am. My father said, "I'd rather he lost an arm or a leg than for this to happen." I heard him say that to my mother one morning. He'd never say that to me. We don't talk to each other very much, now. I don't know what I should say, and he tries to avoid asking me too many questions—since my last trip to the hospital.

I was on my way home when the fireworks went off. I didn't even know it was a holiday. I'd been out walking around again. Walking around the town, and down along the beach, helps me not to think about myself. It's a peaceful town, Englewood. Except for all the cars and lawn mowers and trains. I like the palm trees, the green pines—and being near the water.

"Where are you going?" the man said.

"I'm OK. I was just going home."

He blinked and said, "Want me to walk with you a ways?"

I felt his hands coming loose. "Don't take your hands off!" It was a scream. A cry my mind made without me. "Please. Don't take your hands off." I grabbed his arms.

"Hey," he said. "You *do* need some help."

"If you would just hold on for another minute."

He had his eyes out, airing them, letting them dry. He was afraid of me too.

"I'm sorry," I said.

"It's OK," he said. He covered his eyes with a brown hand, wrinkled his brow the way my father does when he is sorry, or impatient, or confused. "I know what it's like. I know. Take it easy now."

We were touching. We didn't say anything for a long time. He was breathing there, holding me. His eyes were dry and they stared at me. People walked by. I heard their feet on the asphalt, the gravel. I saw a lightning bug go down behind the eyes of the man and I screamed.

"Hey," he said. I scared him.

I tried to calm myself. "H-hold on," I said.

His eyes widened, moved toward me from the sockets in his head.

"You're shaking like an engine," he said.

"I know."

"Look at you."

"I'm afraid," I said.

"You've got to have some help." He put his eyes away. There was only a face there, and he removed his arms and moved back from me. "I'll get you some help. Stay right there." He went away so I couldn't see him. I hadn't started to rise yet. I started screaming, waiting for it to happen. People stopped. Young boys, eating popcorn out of little white bags, laughed, pointed at me. I saw popcorn chewed in their mouths as they laughed. Lightning bugs were all over the place. If I held my head still and stared at the trees behind the boys I could see the little tiny winks of light. I thought of summers long ago, when I was a little boy and everything was firm, and I lived in a permanent house on holy earth and chased lightning bugs into darkness with a glass jar and a lid with holes in it. My father punched the holes in the lid with a screwdriver and said, "They got to breathe, son. Everything's got to breathe."

I watched the lightning bugs. I don't think I screamed again. The man came back.

"I've got some help coming," he said, but he didn't talk to me, he tried to assure everyone standing around. I wanted to tell everybody I was all right. Just a little nervous. I couldn't hear the fireworks anymore. They reminded me, that's all. They went off suddenly, and I didn't have time to realize what they were.

"Why don't you come over here and sit down?" the man said. His eyes were fine now, and relaxed. He took my hand and we walked to the corner, sat on a public bench there. Some people followed us. He put his arm around my shoulder.

"Calm down now," he said. "It's just a little celebration. That's all."

"I remember those," I said.

He leaned back and said, "You don't have to scream. I'm right here."

6

I tried to whisper to him. "I'm sorry. I can't hear myself."

"You cold?" he said.

"I'm just afraid."

"You're all right now," he said. "You're home. This is home. No one's going to hurt you."

He kept saying that to me, over and over in the same voice. People stood silently around, trying to get a look at us without moving. They shuffled in the same space, inhaling and exhaling, perspiring into the white evening air.

"This will go away after a while," I told them. "It usually goes right away after a while." But I couldn't make it stop.

"Do you have any medicine?" the man said.

"No. I have a doctor. I have a man who is my doctor."

"I hope you don't mind," he said. "I've called an ambulance."

I felt the word "ambulance" spread out under all my flesh. I was cold, very cold. "I don't want that," I told him. "I'll be OK pretty soon."

I heard the wail of a siren. It was behind the trees, inland. The quiet people stirred the way the top of a tree does when the wind hits it. Someone put a jacket over me. The man said, "Thank you."

I looked around but I didn't see who it was. There were so many people behind us. I said, "Thank you." A woman with dark red lips and blonde hair leaned toward me and smiled.

"That's OK, honey," she said. She was chewing gum. I saw lipstick on the edges of her teeth. When I was a boy, and happy with all the world I knew, I saw a woman like that rescued from a burning house. Her face was cracked open, like a coconut, and she screamed, "Honey. Honey. Honey." She called her husband, or somebody who loved her, to help—as if just by his being there she wouldn't be burned anymore, the pain would stop. Two men had her. They laid her down on a sheet near the front wheels of a car. The two men were disgusted. Couldn't stand the sight of her. She kept screaming, "Honey. Honey." And after a while, all the kids who had come to watch the fire started screaming too. They mocked her. Each time she screamed, they laughed and hollered with her. "Honey. Honey."

"The ambulance will be here soon," the man said. His eyes stretched and gave a blue sigh. "Hold still now."

I could hear the siren, a human scream, coming closer. It shocked the trees. The breezes settled cautiously around all the houses and listened.

"I'm afraid," I said.

"Hold still now."

"You're not my father." I started crying. I grabbed his shirt and pulled him close to me. "Are you?"

"No, son. I'm not your father."

I saw the collar of his white shirt begin to turn yellow around the edges, and I let go. I saw fire. I was beginning to burn. I felt it on my legs. I screamed. I tried to get out of the fire, but the man held me there. He wouldn't let go of me. His shirt turned black.

"Calm down," he said. "It's all right." He kept saying that.

The smoke was terrible around me. We struggled.

"Help me," the man said. "He'll get away." I got free. He stared at me through the smoke. "Don't go running off. I'm trying to help."

He reached for me. I touched his hand, tried to pull him from the fire, my fire. He was lost. I saw his eyes go down into the fire and I ran. I ran toward water. I ran out into sand and more sand. I kept running, straining for the water, the fire burning me, burning me. I went into the ocean, spread my arms and collapsed in the stronghold of the sea. I floated on my back, felt my skin in the water and the air above me. I felt water in my ears, in my hair. There was no more fire, and the shaking was going away. I felt it wind down until it was only a tiny murmur in the center. I was going back, going back. I was peaceful finally. I would be the first. The first of the race, the species, to go back to the sea. I would be a fish. A fish.

I lay back and rested in the water, the night-blue ocean, the cold water, the holy water.

II. MICHAEL

"Do you still want to be a fish?" Kessler has his hands folded in his lap. His bald head shifts, eyes glare at me like soap bubbles. Tiny winks of light which don't change unless his eyes move.

"I don't know," I say.

"Why did you come out of the water?"

"My eyes." I want to think about each word before I say it. I feel calm now. I know my fire was imaginary, the water only salt and seaweed, and fish. I lost control of myself.

"Go on," he says.

"So I came out."

"Your eyes, though. What about them?"

"I can't keep them open."

"You're tired? You want to sleep?"

"No. I can't keep them open under water. Fish have to keep their eyes open. I've seen them."

"They have to breathe, too." There's a look on his face I don't like. A half-smile, as if he is sharing something with himself, privately, in front of me—something he will laugh about later.

"I know it was silly," I say.

"You do?"

"Of course. I guess so. But I believed it when it was happening."

"And you came out of the water because your eyes hurt?" He bites his lower lip, touches the silk hair over his ear. He is my doctor, a man my mother and father believe will be able to stop the fear.

"Yes."

"Then what did you do?"

"I went home. To my father's house."

"Did you tell them about it?"

"I only saw my mother. I went right to my room."

"You didn't say anything to her?"

"Sure. I said, 'Hey mom, I just thought I was a fish.' " Kessler has the half-smile again, only this time he's amused at me.

"Why do you want to be a fish?"

"I don't."

"You said you did."

"I thought I did."

"You don't anymore?"

"The sea is peaceful."

"OK."

"If I could go back, I would."

"Go back?"

"That's where we all come from. The water. It all began in water."

"That's too easy, Michael." He folds his hands in front of him like a man holding cash, waiting to make a bet.

"I have to get out of the world. I want it all to go away."

"Were you trying to do that last night?"

"Yes."

"But the water hurt your eyes?"

"Yes."

"What about breathing?"

"I held my breath."

"Didn't that hurt?"

I think of the phrase "a world of hurt" and feel numbness spilling down my arms, as if my blood suddenly begins to thin out, dissolve into some sort of gas. I feel light and my fingers begin to tremble.

"I think so," I say, but I don't remember it. The water was green, and my eyes burned, so I came out.

"You don't know."

"I didn't feel anything but the coolness of the water, and then my eyes."

"How long were you under?"

"I don't know. I guess not long."

"Were the fireworks still going on when you came out?"

"Yes. But it didn't bother me. I knew what it was."

"You weren't scared anymore?"

"Not like before."

"And now?"

"Yes."

"You're scared now?"

"A little."

"Why?"

"I don't know. My fingers feel like there's no blood in them."

He gets up and walks over to his desk. The top of the desk is always clean, he never works there. He has a table in the corner of the office cluttered with notes and memos and records of all his various conversations. He seems to study the calendar on the desk. Still his eyes don't move. It's like his head carries them from place to place, moving them into position to gaze at the world.

"Would you like something to calm your nerves?" he says, still looking at the calendar.

"I don't know."

"I can prescribe something." He turns, leans on the desk.

"If you want to."

He moves his head slightly, as if throwing back a wisp of hair, although he is bald, and says, "Can you come back tomorrow, say at three?"

"OK."

"I don't think I will prescribe anything for you, unless you want me to."

"OK."

"Go home and try to get some rest."

"Sure," I say, standing up. "Some R and R."

He comes over, like a priest, and places his hand in the middle of my back, moves me to the door, talking about tight schedules, other patients to see.

"I'll see you tomorrow," I say at the door. He smiles, only his mouth spreading, the rest of his face passive, frozen.

"I don't have to go back to the hospital." I feel stupid when I say this.

"Of course not. Stay out of the water, though," he says with that lonely smile.

"Sure," I say.

"And next time you get so—so nervous, call me."

"Even if I'm dreaming," I say, trying to be funny. I feel so elated that he's not going to put me in the hospital again I forget about the lightness in my fingers. "You know," I tell him, "I really think I'm beginning to get better."

"See you tomorrow," he says.

Outside, the world takes me by surprise. I like the air here. Florida is warm and very bright. I am in paradise and I shouldn't let myself go so often. I can live. I can be like my father, comfortable and very careful and even. I have to make myself normal.

My parents live only two blocks away in a white house that sits up on a small green hill off the road. Their house is on the main road into Englewood, right inside the city limits. Englewood is a flat city, full of row houses, shopping centers, gas stations, movie theaters, banks. My father's house is on perhaps the only hill in the town, a long hill that runs from just after the city-limit sign into the center of town, where it dies hard by a white brick wall which borders a drive-in bank. In the evenings my mother and father like to sit on the smooth grass, or on the steps leading up the hill, and watch the cars entering and leaving the city. My father is retired. My mother never worked. They sit in that house and wonder what to do next, although my father would never admit he is bored.

I could go down to the corner from Kessler's office, cross the street, and go on up the road by the park which sits between my parents' house and where I am standing now. Or I could cut through the park. I can almost see their house from here. Cars pass carrying the sun on clean windshields. I look down to the corner. A dog prances up to a mailbox there and sniffs around the iron legs. I wonder what the dog thinks of fireworks. An old woman, with a walker gleaming in front of her, as if she is carrying with her her own front porch, leans toward the curb by the dog. She waits to cross.

Fireworks. Yesterday was so long ago. I want to wear a tie and adjust it in front of a mirror.

I cross the street and start through the park. I am in a grove of pine trees which blot out the sun. I get partway through and discover that I'm moving quickly and erratically from one spot of light to the next. It's like skipping cracks in a sidewalk. That's all. Nothing to worry about. I begin to notice my breathing. I wonder if my movements are causing the vibrations I feel in my chest. I can't be shaking again. A man sits on a bench near a set of swings, watching me. Bald head in the shade with two little eyes following me through the park. He wears a tie, loosened at the neck, a white short-sleeved shirt. If I talk, it will be all right, but when I leap toward him through the dark air he gets up and moves away.

"It's OK," I say. "I'm just trying to stay in the sunny spots."

"What?" he says. His voice is old and used up; full of smoke and food, and years of yawning, laughing, talking.

"The light. Remember when you were a boy—"

"Stay away from me," he says. He is not afraid, not even wary. He is going to defend the light he occupies. I don't want to take anything away from him.

"It's all right," I say.

A breeze moves through the trees, lifts the hair by his ears.

"Goddamned people," the man says. He moves away, walks toward the street, talking to himself. I jump to the spot he was standing on. The bench in front of me is green, worn at the edges, paint peeling away. I take a deep breath. Everything slows down. I walk past the bench toward the other side of the park, and I make myself move through the shade the way the old man did.

When I get to the other side, I stand still by the edge of the grove and study my parents' house across the street. I feel as if I've just played a game of basketball. Walked through a vacuum, unable to take in air. My head burns. The house on the hill, white and in between two other houses, with a black driveway going up the side, looks peaceful. As if it has been there since the beginning, since before man. There are mirrors in there. Mirrors.

I'm not shaking. I am tired and I know I've been silly, playing a childish game with spots of light on the ground in the park. That's all. I'm fine. Fine. I will go into the house and try to find one of my father's ties.

III. DALE

Michael's father turns from the window and looks at his wife.

"Anne, he's just standing out there looking at the house."

"Get away from the window, he'll see you."

"I don't think he sees anything anymore." He moves from the window and sits on a long green couch which rests against a bare wall to the left of the window. The room is large, with high ceilings and very little furniture. It is the largest room in the house and it faces the dining room, which leads to a small kitchen and a back door that is always open, a tight screen keeping the Florida insects at bay. As he sits on the couch, there is a stairway in front of him to his right with wood rails smoothly polished. It is one of the things he loved about the house when he first saw it. *Why build when you can have a house so beautiful?*

"You don't know what he's going through," Anne says.

"He doesn't know."

"He needs time."

"We've been over this before."

"The doctor says we shouldn't pressure him."

"So we just go on like this? He comes and goes, doesn't talk except to say hello? Wanders around town like a zombie?"

"Stop it, Dale." She moves to the window, her feet barely sounding on the carpet. When they first moved in she complained that the carpet was oppressive and made her hot. "The weather's too warm for such a thing," she said. He refused to take it up, because he liked it so much when he first saw it, and even now in the early morning, he loves to walk across it, feel the texture of it on his bare feet.

Anne stares through the gauze curtains, and Dale studies her face. The lines by her eyes amaze him, make him think about change, growth time. What a movement it all is. A month ago, he was rooting through a drawer, looking for a T-shirt, and he found an old driver's license with her picture in the upper right-hand corner staring blankly out to him through the yellowing lamination. She looked so young, indifferent, unmoved by the earth and its passions. He had not noticed her age until he saw that picture. And how old was she then? Twenty? Thirty? They have settled into the seasons, let the earth take them beyond dreams and wishes and desires. He runs his fingers through his hair, a gesture which, for a man his age, used to provide a certain amount of satisfaction. His wife stands next to him staring out the window at their only son, and he is filled with a terrific sense of loss, a feeling that strikes him like a cold wind from the surf and whirls around him, passing him as if he is not there. Nothing in his life grows anymore. It is all ornament; the vegetable garden he tends in the early morning during the long season satisfies him only when the plants are half-grown, and the ground is well weeded, and the greenness mixes with the brownness of the dirt in patterns, perfect patterns. He plants in rows, neat rows. Near the end of the year, when it's so hot the plants turn the color of the dirt, and weeds begin to grow faster than cancer, choking the delicate vegetables until they disappear, he cannot make himself go into the garden. He lets it go, pays a friend to till all of it in, until it's only a patch of brown dirt again. Then he feels anxious, impatient, even though he knows that here, in Florida, he will be able to start all over again in only a month. The vegetables he does eat taste thick and hot, as if the Florida air has seeped into them. And each time he has the garden tilled, he is conscious of another year, another frame of time flipped by like the pages in a book. Where is Michael? His salvation? What has happened to the son who would grow up and be friends with his old man?

Anne moves the curtain aside.

"What's he doing?" Dale asks.

"I can't see him very well."

"Is he—"

"I think he's coming in."

"Well, don't be standing there," he says, but she has already moved. She comes to the couch and sits down. "Read a magazine or something," he tells her.

Michael comes in too slowly—as if he is on some solitary voyage of crime. There is no sound in the room. He stands by the door staring at them, his hands in front of him, motionless. He lowers his head and says, "Hi." It is almost an apology. Anne murmurs a response, and he stands there in front of them, waiting. Dale thinks perhaps they will have a conversation now, but he doesn't know what to say. "Have you been out walking?" Anne says. Michael stutters something, then falls silent. Dale wants to cut through the quiet formality and find out what his son is thinking, what is going on in his boy's terrible mind. This is not the boy he made.

"What's the matter, son?" he says as gently as he can.

"Nothing."

"Well, it's sure a nice day out there for a walk, isn't it?" Anne says hopelessly.

"I've been to see Kessler," Michael says.

"You weren't supposed to see him today, were you?" Anne's voice is calm, full of moderate interest, conversational.

"He said he didn't have time. I'm supposed to see him tomorrow at three." Michael avoids their eyes. His hands are trying to hide someplace but his pockets are too tight.

"*We* have time," Dale says. "Want to talk?"

"Dad?" he says. "Can I borrow one of your ties?"

"You going to look for a job again?" Anne says, and Dale almost blurts out, "When did he *ever?*" But he studies his son and waits. Anne leans forward, expecting the right answer because she believes that this will be the natural course of events—she has predicted this as one of the sure signs of Michael's recovery, but Dale only half believes her. She has often said that a job isn't crucial, but it would help. Yet she won't let Dale force the issue. She waits, as she is waiting now for it to happen. She has often said that they must wait, have patience. She has often said everything will be all right.

"I just want the tie."

"What do you want it for?" Dale says, a little too suspiciously, and he feels Anne's hand on his arm. He sees himself jerking his arm away, getting up and slapping Michael, screaming for him to come back, to come back. But he doesn't move; he sits there feeling the weight of her hand as if a mouse has crawled up his arm and rested there. He looks directly at his son now, waiting for an answer.

"Can't I just borrow one of your ties?"

"What are you going to do with it?" The mouse moves on Dale's arm. He wants to turn to her and tell her to leave them, force her to get out so he can be alone with the boy, fix him.

"What do you want it for?" Anne says with true care in her voice.

"I think I might look for a job," Michael says, staring at his feet. Dale knows all the lies of his son and this is one of them. But he gets the tie anyway. The first conversation is over, because it had nowhere to go. They have not had a sustained discussion with their son since he returned. At first they tried to restrain themselves because the Army had informed them that Michael was "troubled" and even "slightly unstable." The Army had said, "He's had a terrible experience. It will take time and patience." His disability was not something one could treat with drugs. The boy would have a steady income. His disability was a source of income, would always be until Michael died. It would be his second death, officially. Dale couldn't understand why the payments would be permanent, if Michael's condition was only temporary. But he restrained himself, and Anne walked around as if she were trying not to wake the baby.

Upstairs, Michael takes the proffered tie as if it is something the body needs; then clutching the tie, he retreats, small and trembling, into the bathroom. Dale walks over to the king-sized bed he bought when they moved to Florida and stretches out on top of the covers. He does not even remove his shoes.

He can't go back downstairs to Anne, so he stares at the ceiling, his hands at his sides. From his place on the bed he can see the bathroom door, but he avoids it, keeps his eyes above him, thinking that behind the new door with its shiny brass knob is a stranger claiming to be his son. A person, from somewhere in the dark, who has brought about the only unbearable change in a life of changes. It is a change so profound that it has not really altered the course of Dale's life. He is still the same man, with the same woman and the same memories. All the canceled checks are still the same, the furniture is his furniture, some of it new, some of it with him since his marriage. Arrayed on the shelf next to his bed are his books. The same books. But the pages are blank and the room, the house, the whole present, and all the past are empty. It is as if the boy's return, the coming of this stranger, has caused a plug to be pulled somewhere in the center of all the chemical processes which make Dale a living man—and everything important to him has leaked out. Comfort means nothing to him; there is no joy in anything.

Outside the sun is getting weak. He thinks about the end of another day as if it were a mathematical problem that can only be worked out on paper. A problem he must solve, a complex mental equation which does not balance. He was a policeman for twenty-one years. In the twenty-first year, he was told his son was dead. Killed in action. He waited for a body, a silver coffin, for nearly three months. He heard nothing from the Army. Nothing. When he called, they told him they couldn't explain the delay. No one knew where Michael was. He could not wait anymore, so he retired, sold his house in Chicago, moved to Florida, bought a new house on a smaller plot of land. A house already built, which subtracted half his dream of twenty years; a dream he made notes about on blank sheets of paper when there was nothing to do at work. But the house was paid for, and his pension was enough to allow them comfort. When he was in Florida, starting over, for only three weeks, the Army told him Michael was alive. They kept him for another year, sent infrequent letters explaining that Michael had been through a shock and that he would be coming home soon. There was only one letter from Michael, in the beginning. It arrived the same day as the letter from the Army. Then Michael came home, and he was someone else. Someone else.

The house is quiet. He lies on the bed, trying to make the equation balance. Count all the days and nights, divide by moments like this—everything he has experienced, but failed to collect in peace and remember—add Michael, a changed being. This will reduce all of life to a finite number, the numerical value of existence. The thing he has lived for.

IV. ANNE

Alone in her new living room, Anne Sumner watches the window lose its light. She is afraid that her voice in the quiet house will sound loud and false. *Ridiculous. No one will answer.* Yet she wants to be cheerful, to carry on normally, make the house a place of comfort for all of them. She is the only one holding on anymore. She is tired of these evenings, these quietly arresting evenings when all the rooms fall silent, and each abides in a private corner away from the others and the responsibility of talk. They all know each other too well, after all these years. There's really nothing to talk about, because Michael has been to the other side of the globe and something happened to him there that robbed him of speech. And Dale is unhappy in retirement, a retirement he rushed to, couldn't wait for. So they are their private selves, away from each other and *what is there? What is there?*

It is nearing supper time, and she is hoping her son will come down and announce his hunger. Dale will holler from the bedroom that they ought to go out and eat: "Maybe that Mexican restaurant on Winover." Michael will say he doesn't feel like Mexican food. And Dale: "You don't look like it either, sport."

She feels a soundless breath of laughter at the thought of this.

Michael doesn't laugh anymore. When does he laugh? Oh, he chuckles now and then, but only when he is embarrassed, during one of the many silences that build up like dead leaves blown by the wind against a fence. And even then—it is hard for her to acknowledge this—it is brittle and short and insincere. Not really laughter at all. A sort of apology for being there and not having anything to say.

The room is darkening now, almost perceptibly, and she knows she will have to move soon. If only to turn on a light, for she does not like a dark house. Yet she does not want to be the only living thing in the house. She must do something. The television would be an invasion, and she cannot stand the screaming voices of the radio. Dale is upstairs, lying on the bed more than likely, and Michael? In his room? With his horrible living dreams, and no idea what to do with himself. His problem is not going to go away, and neither is he.

A part of her wants Michael to go away. He has been unknowable since his return. She cannot get close to him, get him to talk. She fights the thought whenever she discovers it, but she knows it is there. If he would just go away, *be dead.* The words shudder through her, and she feels a low ache in her throat. *Michael dead.* It is a face she suddenly recognizes in the shadows, and she cannot sit still in the same room with it. She has never been so threatened. When she thought Michael was dead, she lived in the world for three months as if she had gone on living after her own death. She could not speak her grief; no one could break into her quiet and senseless existence to console her. She could not eat, and all night she saw him dead in some yellow field, alone, baking in the sun. Dale was useless, almost absurdly comical in his efforts to get her to accept what he himself did not yet fully believe. She caught him writing a letter to Michael, a few days after the news came, crying over the paper like a child being forced to write something a thousand times, as if he were being punished.

She hears Dale moving upstairs, gets up, walks to the foot of the staircase. There is no more sound. She starts up, stops. Her shadow lurks on the wall. She holds the banister, the cold wood, polished smooth by years of careful hands other than her own. Someone else's years, years when Michael was young and hers and alive. She holds the shiny wood, studies its texture, the lines in it. She cannot hear anything but her own breathing. Metal won't survive in Florida. She had to buy new furniture when she moved, but she saw this as a blessing at the time. Michael was dead, and she wanted nothing to remind her. Florida was to be another life, a retreat.

She returns to the living room and stands before the couch. It is nearly dark and the white air outside seems artificial, as if the world is lit by neon. She cannot believe it is the end of another day and the three of them, Michael, Dale and Anne—this Anne she barely knows—are all once again existing in private. Three strange vessels in this cold darkening house.

She is conscious of her movements, and realizes that she is nervous and restless and doesn't know what to do. She sees herself walk to the stairs in the eye of memory and wonders what she was thinking of, what she might have been about to do. Go up to see Michael? Stand at the top of the stairs and scream, "All right everybody, out into the hall." And then what would she say? Would they come out at all? Laugh? *Let's eat, what do you say? Let's be alive again. Alive.*

Each day she tries to make things normal, approaching Michael with love and care, letting him be alone when he wants to, being there for him if he should decide to share what he's going through. She knows it is time to be another person, not his mother. But he needs a mother —a source of strength. She has never had any stereotyped idea about motherhood, but she has always believed in the importance of affection, and she wants to hear him, to listen to him and understand what he is afraid of. It is a way of caring which she knows is the only thing one person has to offer another. Her son is a person and so is she. There is no other connection, no other governing idea or diverting traditional expectation which moves her. She wants to bring him back to her so her life can go on, so she can return to the seasons.

But he is not home. He lives in the house like a pet. And he does things she cannot understand. In the middle of a conversation, he hides. He talks to her as frequently as a stranger asking for directions. He seems to listen, turns his head and nods, acknowledges her with his eyes. But his voice won't come, and when he does talk the sound is out of sync with his lips, like a film with the sound running a few frames behind. And he repeats himself. Or he talks in short and fearfully monotonous sentences, as if there is some technological miracle going on inside a mechanical device which looks human. And each day he does exactly the same things, as if the device were programmed to carry out each act in sequence. He gets up and sits by the window in his room for an hour. Then he comes downstairs and sits at the breakfast table while she cooks him poached eggs and toast. Sometimes he pushes the eggs to the side and eats only the toast—but he always asks for both. Then he leaves the house. He does not return until later in the evening, and unless he has an appointment with Kessler, she has no idea where he is until he appears in front of the house. When he comes in, he goes to his room. He does not come down for dinner unless he has been to see Kessler.

And Dale gets more and more furious.

"He ought to at least talk to us," he says. "What's he doing all day?"

"Walking around the town, I guess," she says, but she doesn't believe anybody would do that. Not all day.

"Maybe I should follow him one day," Dale says.

"That would be wonderful. Suppose he saw you. What then?"

"What is he, a bomb? Are you afraid he'll go off or something?"

She never knows what to say to Dale when he gets sarcastic and points out the absurdity of everything. Maybe she believes his vision and cannot answer it.

Michael's first day home was like a play in which everyone forgot the lines. The long silences on the ride from the airport—a ninety-mile drive from Tampa to Englewood—seemed almost lethal, as if one of them might die from lack of words in the air. She had turned on the radio, after a long silence, and Dale emphatically reached over and snapped it off. He was stewing as he drove, and Michael stared out the window as if he were mad at them for something—as if they had all just finished screaming at each other. When they finally pulled into Englewood, Dale seemed to revive—he got all excited again. Michael was alive, and they were home. She felt it, the euphoria, the sense of time easing things, of peace waiting for them in the weeks ahead. Dale drove around the town, talking about all the spots: the water, the sea wall where they would fish, the shops on Main Street that sold pipes, and incense, and hardware, and cheeses from all over the world; the restaurants they would eat in. He talked about all those things and Anne felt the importance of the silence from the backseat diminish, although she was afraid to turn around and see if Michael was listening. When they got to the house, Dale wanted to show it off too, but Michael went to the bathroom, then came out and asked them if he could see his room.

"Don't you want to see the house?" Dale said. He was like a little boy, proud of something he had done, and trying to get his father to admire it. An odd sort of reversal which caused her to remember the two of them in similar rooms years ago going through the same expectation and disappointment. She used to tell Dale, "You've got to pat him on the back once in a while—admire something he's proud of." And Dale said he would try, but he never could bring himself to compliment the boy—"We could spoil him," he would say. "Make him an under-achiever who gives up. You want to do that?"

So Michael wasn't interested in the rest of the house, and Dale had been hurt and then angry. But he tried not to show it. And Michael went to his room and closed the door.

She is in darkness now and it surprises her. She goes to an end table by the couch and turns on the lamp. It is still quiet in the house. She goes to the staircase again, places her hand on the wood and listens to Dale's faint breathing. Above her, she can see light under the bathroom door. She ascends the stairs, her eyes on the light, holding herself erect. She touches the wall and braces herself, trying to be quiet, as she rises toward the slot of yellow light, as she rises in fear toward the room where her son hides.

She stops in front of the door. "Michael?" She talks to the yellow light at her feet, her hand out, nearly touching the door. She cannot hear anything but Dale's steady breathing.

"Michael?"

She hears something moving behind the door, and then it opens, just a crack, and stops. It's as if the door has come ajar by itself. She places her hand like a spider on the center panel and pushes the door open. Michael is sitting on the side of the tub looking right at her. He is short, with a wide nose and mouth and very close-cropped light brown hair which covers his head as if it were painted there. His eyes are light green and they seem to have unusual depth, as if they look out at the world through some sort of clear glass. His eyelids grow tight toward the bridge of his nose, a suggestion of Oriental genes which has always puzzled her. He is wearing Levi's, tennis shoes, and a green undershirt. There is a gray tie around his neck that has been knotted absurdly in a half-Windsor. The back piece is longer than the wide front. His hands on his knees, he sits in front of her and watches the air in the room as if she is no longer there.

"What are you doing?" she asks with polite curiosity.

"Getting dressed." His voice sounds as if it is emerging from sleep.

"Dressed?" she says, and in the back of her mind she discovers fear —she does not know what he might do, what she might cause with this intrusion.

"I was putting on my tie."

It is as if she has caught him at something—something private—and he has resigned himself to whatever punishment she might wish. She realizes that he has recognized her fear and it shames her.

"I just wondered what you were doing, that's all."

"I'm adjusting my tie."

"Don't you think—" She pauses, afraid to finish.

"What?" His eyes widen.

"Nothing."

"What?" He looks into her eyes and for the first time she has the feeling that he is seeing her.

"Shouldn't you have a shirt on?"

"I have a shirt."

"No. I mean—a dress shirt. Are you going out tonight?"

"I don't know."

She leans against the sink to his right, determined to begin again. "I'm sorry, Michael. It's none of my business. I just wanted to talk." She reaches out and rests her hand gently on the crown of his head. He raises his arm and takes her wrist and moves her hand away, a motion slow and deliberate, without emphasis, as if he is removing a hat.

"I'm not going anywhere. I just wanted to adjust my tie."

"Stop it," she says, and she cannot get the words back. The absurdness of the tie with the undershirt and his bare neck forces her to deny him. She does not want him to be this way in front of her. He reaches up, touches the tie at his throat.

"I can't get it right." He struggles with the knot.

"Wait a minute," she says. "Wait a minute, son."

She kneels in front of him, looks into his green vacant eyes.

"Talk to me, OK? Just talk to me. Tell me what's bothering you. You can talk to me now. I'll listen. I'll listen. I won't interrupt. Just— talk to me." She is beginning to cry under her skin, but she holds it in, her throat aching, trembling.

He drops his hands. His face is expressionless, although he is seeing her now, as before.

"I'm, I'm—" He stops.

"Go on."

"I can't talk just now."

"Why? I want to help you."

"Everybody wants to help me. Yesterday a whole crowd tried to help me. But they were just looking at me."

"What happened yesterday?"

"I went into the ocean. I ran from them."

"From who? Who was chasing you?"

"The people. They called an ambulance."

"Why?"

They lean toward one another now, her hands on his knees. She can see her reflection in his eyes, a tiny Buddha squatting in a green temple.

"Did you know yesterday was the Fourth of July?" he asks.

"Yes."

"Well, I didn't. And when the fireworks went off, it—it scared me."

"You were frightened?"

"No. I was terrified. I started shaking again."

"Shaking?"

"Mom, I'm afraid—I don't know, sometimes I'm—I'm just afraid."

"Why? Of What?"

"I can't talk about it—when I do, I get to shaking again, and then I—I get—I get—" He closes his eyes, and his face seems to lose elasticity, as if it is turning to stone right before her eyes.

"Michael," she says. "It's all right, son. You're home, you're home."

He opens his eyes. "That's what my friend kept saying to me."

"What friend?"

"A man who tried to help me last night."

"During the fireworks?"

"Yes. He tried to help me but all these people were staring at me. When I heard the ambulance—that siren, that siren—I thought—I thought I was on fire."

"Michael."

"Honest. I felt it burn, smelled the smoke."

Anne tries to believe. She listens to him completely now. She knows he will not accept anything else from her but this; that he will tell her what he saw and felt only if she is willing not to deny any of it.

"So you ran?"

"I went down the beach into the water."

"Into the water."

"Yes."

"Michael, that's so dangerous, especially at night."

He tilts his head and looks at her as if she has changed colors, a look that has a smile on the edge of it. She feels ridiculous, motherly. She says, "I'm sorry. I guess it's silly for me to talk about danger to you after—"

"I tried to stay there but it hurt my eyes."

She thinks of suicide, Michael and death, courting each other in the water, and she is frightened again.

"You weren't thinking of—you weren't thinking of—" She hesitates, considers what word she can use—"hurting yourself?"

"I wasn't thinking of anything—that's what I liked about it."

Anne reaches up and puts her hand on the side of his face, and he does not take it away this time. His face changes, a look of puzzlement appearing there, almost as if he has willed it.

"I want to be very tender with you," she says. "I want to care for you."

"I'm not right, yet," Michael whispers. "I know it."

"It will take time, son. And we'll hurt. We may hurt each other. We may never get all the way through this. But I love you, and I hurt with you and I'm afraid too."

"Are you? Are you really afraid?"

"Yes. I'm as scared as you are."

"Are you afraid of me?" These words pierce her flesh.

"No. I'm afraid *for* you."

"Don't be afraid of me. OK? I know what's wrong with me. When I'm losing control I can feel it happening. I know it's coming, but I can't stop it—it's like a drug."

"What is it, Michael?"

"It's—it's just—fear. That's all. Nothing I can put into words."

There is a pause, and Anne hears the insects outside. She notices a drop of water hanging on the spigot in the bathtub, gathering weight, ready to fall.

"Michael?"

"Yes?"

She looks into his eyes, trying to gain courage from what she sees there. "What happened to you over there—when you—" His face contorts again, turns the color of a fingernail, and he begins to breathe heavily through his nose, his mouth tightly closed and folded in upon itself. She hears something rising in his throat, and she moves her hand to the back of his neck.

"Thethethethethethethethe." He sounds like an electric motor.

"Michael. Michael." Her hand comes around to his mouth and she stops the flow. His eyes are closed. He still breathes rapidly through his nostrils.

"It's all right," she says, to herself.

He opens his eyes, looks at her as if he is checking to see if she is still in front of him. He blinks and says in a whisper, "I'm OK. I'm OK."

"I'm sorry. I didn't mean to remind you."

"I'm all right now."

"Are you sure?"

"Yes. It helps that you were here."

"That's all I want, son. Spend more time with us. We've got to go through this together."

He reaches up and starts to pull on the tie. She stops his hand, kisses him gently on the forehead and, looking into his eyes, tries to smile. She still wants to cry, but part of her is unwilling now. She takes the tie in her hands.

"Let me do this for you," she says.

He leans his head back, his hands rising up to her shoulders, and she begins to fix the tie.

V. DALE

He hears the morning gathering at the window and sits up in his bed, feeling as if his eyes have been skinned and sliced. Anne is not in the bed, although he can see where the covers have been disturbed by her sleep. He lies on top of the bedding, still in his clothing of the night before. His nap has turned into a full night's sleep, the first in a long time. He lies on his back and counts the hours he has been asleep. He doesn't think of Michael until he glances to the bathroom door, which sits open now, surrounding the sunlight as if the burning gases resided there. The house is quiet. He does not want to see himself in the mirror by the bed; he knows he is alive.

He goes downstairs, past Michael's closed room and into the kitchen. Anne is sitting at the table in her bathrobe. The table is set off from the rest of the kitchen and surrounded by what the real estate agent called "Florida Windows." It is really just a cozy little breakfast nook with too many windows—similar to what the Sumners had in Chicago, except that snow is never painted into these frames.

"Good morning," Anne says.

"Where's Michael?"

"Still asleep."

"Not surprising." Dale goes to the refrigerator.

"Want some eggs?" Anne says.

"No, I'm not hungry." Dale notices something about Anne's voice which intrigues him. She is happy about something and can't wait to tell it. He peers into the refrigerator at the stained racks, but he doesn't touch anything. "Goddamned air even gets into the icebox," he says.

Anne sips her coffee. Her lips make a sound that pleases him, reminds him of cold winter mornings and cigarettes, and forays into the snow.

"That coffee any good?"

"Best I've had in a long time."

He closes the refrigerator and moves to the stove. "You wouldn't think rust could grow in a refrigerator."

"What are you looking for?"

"Cups. Where are the cups?"

"There's one in the dishwasher."

When he has the coffee he sits in the chair across from her. She is not looking at him, but there is a smile on her face.

"I'm going fishing again today," he says.

"With Eddie?"

"Yes."

"And Michael?"

He looks into her eyes and waits. She lets her cup down and says, "If you—if you think—"

"If I think what?"

"He might enjoy it. You haven't asked him in a long time."

"He said no every time I *ever* asked him." He raises his cup, sips the hot liquid, watching her expression. It puzzles him. The light from the windows crosses Anne's face, her eyes in one of the lines of shadow, so all he can see is her mouth and the smile that plays there.

"What happened last night?" Dale asks.

"We talked. We actually had a conversation."

Dale has both hands around the cup, holding it up just off the table. She couldn't wait for him to ask her, so he feels manipulated.

"And?" he asks, after a pause.

"We had a good talk—about—about his problem."

"What did he say?"

She tells him the news in a voice that is so full of optimism it angers him. Michael is going to be all right, all he needs is—time, and patience and a little love. Understanding. As if all these things were some remedy to a scientific problem, a chemical reaction guaranteed to produce the desired response. Just mix in the ingredients, stir, wait, and Michael will come back as before. Michael even knows there is something wrong with him, that he is not normal, and we're all going to work together to overcome it. This is the beginning, the beginning. She sounds like a commercial message, as if she is telling him he will no longer have to worry about chafing hands, athlete's foot. He cannot get over how stupid she sounds. It embarrasses him to look at her. He drinks his coffee, listens quietly. When she is finished, she gazes into his eyes, waiting for the good news to register.

"What's the matter?" she asks.

"Everything's going to be all right."

"You've got to believe now, Dale. You've got to believe in him."

"He thought he was on fire? He ran into the ocean to put out a fire on his body, and you think everything's going to be all right."

"He knows he wasn't on fire."

"That's good."

"You're going to get sarcastic now," she says, disgusted.

"No, I'm not. I just want to express my thanks he didn't become a two-alarm."

"I can't talk to you." She looks down at her cup, traces her finger around the edge of it. He studies the hair which lies over her brow, hiding her eyes, and thinks about its grayness, the time it took to change her hair to thin strands of wire. It was such fine hair when he first met her, and it gathered in sweat around his loins when they made love. They were such a trembling body together in their youth, full of discovery and warmth and time. Especially time. On cool summer nights they would lie in bed, the night breezes moving through the room, and he always felt as if he could lift a light beam, play with it for her amusement. Now there is a plan to their lovemaking, as if they have joined some sort of tennis club. And although there is still passion, and love—although he still holds on to her as though she were the last promontory over a vague black sea—he misses her when she was young. When they didn't know so much about each other.

"You want some more coffee?" he asks.

"Dale, he can't do this without you." She is looking directly at him again, her face wrinkled with concern.

"He doesn't need me, or you. He needs the hospital."

"No." She almost yells this. "I won't stand for that. Not again."

"They calmed him down once. They can do it again."

"They pumped him full of valium. He sat around in a bathrobe and watched soap operas all day with the rest of those drooling—"

"The *rest* of them?"

"I'm not including Michael. You know what I mean."

"He's going to do something, I just know it."

"Not if we help him."

"That's bullshit."

Her face does not change, but he notices a faint tremble by her eyes, a reddening over her brow.

"No, it is not," she says.

"Anne, it's the mind. The *mind!* You can't unburn toast."

"We're not talking about toast."

"What we're talking about is whether he should go to the hospital or fishing with me. I think the hospital is a better idea. Let professionals take care of it."

"So we just give up?" She blinks her eyes and water appears there, as if she has called for it.

"I want to go on living. I intend to go on living."

"I felt so good this morning." She is crying now, staring down at the table. "He talked about it last night. He said, 'I know I'm not right.' We're getting somewhere."

"He's had enough people tell him in the last three months that he's not right. He ought to know that by now."

Dale gets up and pours more coffee in his cup, leaving Anne to her tears. He walks to the back door and stares out into the yard, to the houses behind his own, drinking the coffee, thinking about Michael's last trip to the hospital. He was there for three weeks, and he never spoke to them on any of their visits. He didn't speak to anyone as far as they knew. He had only been home for six days, when he stopped eating and began crying: moaning for hours, in spite of Anne, Dale, the doctor, time. He was like a motor for which no one could find the switch, running on and on. Dale marveled at the energy of it, the power and strength it must have taken. But while his son was in the hospital, the crying stopped. Michael watched television all day in silence, laughing when the crowd on the TV laughed, or when the others in the room saw something funny and howled at the blue screen like apes around a fire. But he never said anything. They did something to him in the hospital to calm him down, bring him back, and they would probably have to do it again. But they didn't really bring Michael back; they only calmed him. What Dale wanted then, and what he wants now, is for them to *bring Michael back;* the boy who left home for the Army in that other life back in Chicago. Not this alien who comes into rooms like a criminal, who breaks into tears at the sight of an insect, or a funny-shaped cloud.

"I think he's coming down," Anne says, drying her eyes. "Try to talk to him, will you?"

Michael is moving on the stairs. Dale finishes his coffee, a final gulp and—as Michael enters the kitchen—he walks over to the table and says to Anne, "Want some more?"

Anne looks at Michael and greets him with that commercial voice, "Good morning, son."

Michael stands in the doorway in his underwear. His legs are short and bowed. He has a look on his face of shock, and a curious sort of contentment, the way a man looks when he has been shot and he finally knows that this is death: a look which plans to study every detail of this death, since it is his own, his very own. He has a tie around his neck, and no clothing on save his undershorts.

Dale cannot take his eyes from the tie. "Do you want some coffee?" His voice is strained, almost as if he is hearing the sound of his words under water.

"I'm hungry," Michael says, too loud.

"How about some eggs?" Anne says.

"Want some eggs?" Dale says, thinking: *Of course, he'll have what he always does, poached eggs and toast.*

"You don't have to be afraid—I slept funny."

"Nobody is afraid," Dale says slowly.

"OK. Yes. I'd like some eggs."

"Poached?" Anne says as she gets up from the table.

"I guess. Whatever way is most easy."

Anne pauses by the counter, looks at Michael, then to Dale, as if to say, "See?" She takes out a frying pan and goes to the refrigerator. Michael moves to the table and sits down.

"I'm going," Dale announces.

"Aren't you—don't you want to see if—" Anne pleads with Dale by the use of the silence after the word "if," and he knows what she wants him to ask.

Dale looks at Michael and says, "I don't suppose—"

"Where're you going, Dad?" Michael's voice is loud.

"I thought maybe you'd—"

"Going fishing again?"

Dale is surprised at Michael's willingness to talk, to say the word "Dad."

"Yes. You want to—"

"With that friend, Eddie or whatever his name is?"

"Yes. Will you stop interrupting me?"

Anne says, "Dad thought you might like to go, too."

"I haven't been fishing in a long time," Michael says. He turns and looks out the windows, his hands folded in front of him. Anne breaks two eggs into the frying pan and says, "Two over easy, OK?" Michael stares through the glass at the yards and houses, the black driveways. What else could he see out there? Dale watches him, sees the view of the window, and waits. The eggs begin to sizzle in the pan.

"Michael?" Anne says, glancing at him with her head slightly tilted.

He turns his head slowly back to the room, as if he is pulling against some power, some restraining force in his neck. His eyes are wide and have that awed look about them, as if he has just been rescued from a fire or a plane crash and cannot believe he has survived.

"Two over easy?" Anne says, with infinite patience.

"You're doing that on purpose," Dale says too loud.

"What?" Michael sits at the table in his underwear with one of Dale's ties around his neck.

"Why don't you go get some clothes on?" Dale says.

"Your father wants you to go fishing with him."

"Put some clothes on! That's what I want."

Michael rises from the table. His loins bulge absurdly and his thighs, looking blue and full of thin capillaries, shake as he moves.

"OK," he says, his eyes becoming senseless, empty. "I'm sorry, Mom. I'll go get dressed. I'm so used to life in a barracks."

"Barracks!" Dale yells. He cannot help himself, nor can he get the scream back. "You haven't been in a barracks for months," he says quietly, trying to explain himself. He is conscious of Anne's eyes on him.

Michael starts out of the room with his head down, just the way he used to leave a loud room full of his father when he was a boy. Dale recognizes his son in the tight-stretched body of this man, and he stops him.

"Wait a minute, son," he says.

"Michael?" Anne says, turning from the stove. "Your eggs are ready."

Michael turns in the door frame, his hands at his sides. "I'm just going to get dressed," he says calmly.

"You want to go fishing with me and Eddie?"

"OK."

"Do you really want to go? I'll wait for you if you do—but you don't have to."

"OK." Michael looks directly into Dale's eyes.

"So I'll wait then?"

Michael turns and disappears around the corner into the dining room.

"You shouldn't have yelled at him," Anne says, putting the eggs on a plate. The smell of the eggs makes Dale hungry.

"Put me two of those on," he says, going to the table.

"You shouldn't have yelled at him."

"I heard you. You saw what it did for him, didn't you?"

Anne sits at the table and starts to cry.

"Stop it," Dale says. "Just stop it."

VI. MICHAEL

Water slaps the sides of the boat, a sound like a film breaking. Eddie fishes out of one end, my father out of the other. I hold one of my father's rods and my line runs out into the water but I'm not fishing. I feel as if I'm on a ledge, far above the world and if I do or say anything, I will fall. Eddie is an old man, older than my father. He wears a shirt that crawls with little fishes, green and blue, but they don't seem to bother him. He studies the blue water, the white sky, as if any minute they might make a sound, utter words for him to remember. Hair sticks out of his nose like the blossoms of a weed. His skin is dark brown, and full of lines, white hairs. He was disappointed to see me when my father and I arrived. He didn't expect to be fishing with a novice, and it was clear to him that I'd never fished from a boat. "You just sit in the middle and don't talk," he said. My father said, "Mike's a good fisherman, right, son?" I climbed into the boat and studied the water, the green water with seaweed and algae swirling in it like tea.

Now, Eddie watches the water hit the boat and says, "Goddamned speedboats. Scare the fish away."

I can't stand all the light. The sun is above me, burning the air.

"Maybe we should move," my father says.

"They'll just follow us," Eddie says. "They like to disturb good folks."

I know I am beginning to get afraid. I hold the rod tightly. *As long as I have the rod, I'm OK. As long as I have the rod, I will be OK. Nothing will happen.* I think of my mother, the eggs for breakfast, the smile on her face when we left. She said, "Have a good time. See you for lunch." I could not think about lunch; it didn't seem like something time would get to.

"Not a nibble," Eddie says.

"You cold, son?" my father says, looking at me as if I might jump into the water.

"This goddamned wind goes right through you," Eddie says.

"It's not that bad. Are you cold, Michael?"

"The sun's bright," I say.

"It's enough to keep me warm, but you looked like you were shivering."

"Want a drink?" Eddie says. He reaches down under his seat and retrieves a bottle. The fishes on his shirt seem disturbed; they swirl and stir.

"Give some to Mike," he says. "He looks cold."

Eddie hands me the bottle. "Drink up."

"I got something," Father says.

I hold the bottle up and look at the sun in it. My father stirs the water, moves slightly forward, then winds his rod. It whirs like an insect.

"Well, drink it," Eddie says. He doesn't seem to understand that my father has one. My father has something on the line.

"Give me that."

The fish eyes bounce on the floor of the boat in front of me. Even in water a fish's eyes look dead, like the eyes of a corpse. On the floor of the boat the fish's body flaps but the eyes don't move.

"Not much of a fish," my father says.

Eddie takes a drink, tends his line. "It's a start," he says.

"Red tide'll be here soon," Father says. "Won't be any fishing for a long time after that."

My father turns and puts his line back. The fish stares up at me, the eye not moving. Only the tail has life. It flaps against the floor like a loose shingle stirred by the wind. My eyes burn. In the distance

I hear the gradually increasing drone of an engine.

"Here comes another motorized fool," Eddie says. "I swear to Christ, I wish they'd burn or something."

"This ain't no golf course," my father says. "I guess people got a right to make noise."

The fish stares up at me, a shield with a curious crest.

"Want to go in to the sea wall?" Father says.

"Nah."

"Maybe it'll be less populated."

The wind cuts in front of me, my hair moves.

"Wonder if I've still got bait on this line," Eddie says, reeling his line in. The reel sounds like the alarm on a wristwatch. I can smell rotting seaweed, and dead fish, and gasoline. "How about you, Michael?" he says. "Ought to check your line."

"I guess I'll get this fish out of the light," my father says.

I watch the eye disappear in the cooler. It is dark and cold in there, but I hear the tail flapping against the ice cubes for a while. *The eye, the eye.*

Water slaps the side of the boat again, full of seaweed, and small black flecks of sewage.

"Still there." Eddie throws his line back. The fish on his shirt whirl and flip. My father turns and looks at me: his eyes are the color of the water.

"How are you doing, son?"

"OK."

"You're bored, aren't you?"

"No, sir."

"You're not much of a fisherman," Eddie says. "Look how limp that line is. Why don't you throw it out again?"

The air burns my nose. The sun comes lower, seems to sink into the boat.

"I'm having fun," I say.

"You're shaking, son." My father leans toward me, holding his rod steady in front of him. He reaches out and touches my arm. "You're cold."

"I'm OK."

"The sun's burning the hell out of me," Eddie says. "How can he be cold?"

"Are you all right, Michael?" my father says.

"I was thinking about this morning."

"What?"

"I was just thinking."

"A fellow has a lot of time to think when he gets out in a boat on a day like this," Eddie says.

"It's a nice day," I tell him.

"You thinking about the war?" he says.

I look over at him, but he's staring out at his line.

"Eddie, Michael doesn't talk about that."

The voice of my father comes softly on the air around me, like the first word after silent prayer.

Eddie turns from the water and looks at me. "Why not?" he says. "What'd you do?"

"Time for a bite," my father says. He is turned away, and I see his ears, red and long, and the hair on his neck with little white bare spots patterned there as if by design. The breeze is cool and smells of gasoline and salt water and trees. I hear a tractor in the distance, somewhere inland, pushing land out of the way, making holes.

"I remember the big one," Eddie says. "And I talk about it, too. I'll never forget it."

"We're all veterans," my father says. "If we keep talking, we won't catch any fish."

"I saw a guy right next to me lose his intestines," Eddie says. "Swear to God. It was the worst thing I ever saw."

A sound escapes from somewhere, and I can't identify it. A bird sound, only it seems to have vowels and syllables. Both Eddie and my father look at me, wait for me to say something, but I'm trying to identify the sound.

"Goddamn it, Eddie. Shut up about the war," my father says.

"OK. OK. I'm sorry. Jesus," he says.

My line moves, I feel the fish take the hook inside my hand. The fish is quick, not very big, nothing but a tiny murmur which registers under the flesh of my hand. The sound I heard seems to have risen up into the wind, like a balloon full of helium.

"You got something, Michael," Eddie says.

"I didn't want one."

"Reel it in," my father says.

"I didn't think I would catch anything." I turn the reel: it winds smoothly, quietly. The line moves in tight circles in the water. The line moves—it is so thin I can barely follow it. It makes little ripples where it enters the water. The line is taut and it moves. . . .

. . . We stand around watching a tank sink in the brown mud. Rizzolo jokes about the wrong machines for this war. Caswell is high, chewing gum. He spits through his teeth with a high whistling sound. Brinkman leans next to me, his arms folded. I feel his breathing. The sky is white, but there is no sun yet.

"Here comes Niles," Caswell says. "The golf pro."

Captain Niles comes over clutching himself, almost as if he is cold, although it is already very hot, and the air is thick with green water. He lets out a short laugh.

"What's so goddamned funny," Sergeant Hall says. He stands in front of us, his hands on his hips, shaking his head. He is the only one of us who has been to war before. Captain Niles is younger, and new at this.

"Hall's pissed," Caswell says. He wears his helmet way back on his head, like a traffic cop, and his eyes are always heavy, half-closed, as if any minute he might fall asleep.

"Did you say something, hippie?" Hall is looking at Caswell, his eyes frozen in his face.

"Not a thing, Sarge."

Brinkman crosses his legs in front of him, looks over at Caswell. "Leave the good sarge alone," he says. "It's a rotten morning."

Niles walks down to where Hall stands in mud up to his knees. The rest of us are on higher ground, a few feet away.

I have never seen a tank in the jungle before.

There is a cable attached to the tank, and a winch—a machine which reels in the cable like a fishing reel—groans under the soaked trees. Captain Niles stands next to Hall, talking. I watch the back of his head, the thin blond hair which bulges out from the bottom of his hat.

"They'll never get that thing out of there," Caswell says. He is always the one who is in trouble, who gets Sergeant Hall screaming at him like a father. He loves to tell jokes, play his guitar late into the night. All of us listen to him, watch the movements of his thin, white hands, as if he is a priest—a man who gives absolution. Hall cannot stand Caswell's willingness to talk, his refusal to stand at attention and take it. "This is a fucking lousy war," he says. Hall tells him to wait until he gets into it. Wait until we all get into it. "You haven't seen anything yet."

"You're going to get court-martialed one of these days," Brinkman says to him. Caswell smiles. "They need my body here so they can count it later," he answers. Then he goes on talking until Hall is furious and wants to punish all of us.

I watch Niles talking to Hall, and I hear him say, "Nowhere for a tank, is it?"

"No, sir," Hall says.

" 'Sir.' Did you hear that?" Caswell says. He flicks a cigarette down into the gulley. It smokes there in the mud for a while, then dies. The winch pulls on the wire, but the tank doesn't move. The machine groans, like the cry of a great bird, except there is no pulse to it. It goes on and on. My ears begin to recreate the sound deep in my head. The cable is taut. It is absolutely tight. The tank sinks a little more, as if it has breath and lets out some air. Suddenly the wire moves. I see Hall crouch down, eyeing the wire. Everything seems to pause. I hear a high wail, a sort of cry in the distance, a siren. I don't know what it is. It gets louder, and Hall yells something at Niles.

"No," Niles says. He shakes his head, turns to Hall, a smile on his face.

Hall comes running up out of there.

Niles watches him, turning his body until he is facing us.

"Better get out of there," Hall says.

Caswell kneels down, folds his hands over his knees. Brinkman touches me with his elbow, points to the winch.

I look at the machine, and as my eyes move, the sound stops. A small cloud of dust erupts right at Captain Niles's waist.

"JESUS!" Caswell screams.

Niles looks down at himself, a surprised look on his face, as if he has just won something, and then he topples over. He is a pair of dominoes, balanced one on top of the other, and he just topples over.

Brinkman screams, pulls my arm.

"I told him," Hall says. He walks down into the gulley, stands next to Captain Niles, the heap of clothing and flesh that a second ago was Captain Niles. Hall asks for a cigarette.

"Get your own fucking cigarette," Caswell says, crying.

I stand in the whispering crowd, staring at the Captain's boots, at the shoelaces tied neatly, the mud caked on the soles. I listen to airless dry voices surrounding this first death, this first death for all of us. . . .

. . . "It's a blowfish," my father says. He holds the fish down with both hands, and it sucks in air and exhales hard, like an athlete. It breathes. A breathing fish. I hear a cry again, high overhead.

"Listen to him," Eddie says.

"Michael, please," Father says.

"What the hell's wrong with him, anyway?" Eddie is looking at me.

"It's just a fucking fish, son."

"It's legal to eat them too," Eddie says, trying to laugh.

"Stop it." My father holds the fish and looks up at me, his eyes like marbles in a glass jar. The fish is swollen, and it has round eyes and a round mouth. A mouth like the mouth of the long dead.

"What's the matter with you?" Eddie says.

I try to hold on. "Nothing. I'm looking at the fish."

Under my father's hands is the green fish with the mouth of the dead, and I feel my body losing all of its warmth, its air.

"Let's go in," Eddie says. "This is ridiculous."

Tractors push dirt beyond the horizon. The water is clear and quiet. Clouds move up along the beach, shaped like great white rabbits. The sky is unbelievably blue.

"What the hell'd you bring him along for?" Eddie says. His face is cold. It has the texture of stone. He is a tombstone, a mouth. My father leans over and takes the fishing rod away from me.

VII. ANNE

Dreaming, she sees them drive up the driveway, talking loudly, laughing—both sweaty and a little sunburned—fish hanging in a bunch from Dale's hand like silver fruit from a red branch. Dale gives her a knowing glance to let her see that he is with her and all went well. Michael smiles, talks of the water, the fish, the long day in the warm, benevolent sun. She holds this blue vision frozen, on the tattered edges of sleep, until something cracks its thin membrane and she begins to hear noises swimming around in the air, the clouds, Michael's smile. The noises become quite distinct, and she sweeps out of bed thinking, "They're here," but as she gets to her feet she realizes it is too early, and the noises are the loud and insistent knocking on the back door of some rude intruder.

She puts on her robe and goes down the stairs into the kitchen, a little afraid, feeling as if someone has consciously troubled her sleep, as if a bucket of water has been thrown into her face. She hesitates by the door, trying to make out the shape that she sees through the white lace curtains over the window.

"Hello-o?" a young voice says, a girl's voice.

Anne opens the door and says, "I'm sorry, I was resting."

"At this hour?" the girl says. She smiles, pouting as if she has done something evil but ought to be forgiven because she is so young and innocent and lovable.

"You're—" Anne pauses, trying to remember the name.

"Lucy," the girl says. "I talked to you just briefly the day you moved in. Remember?"

"Oh, yes. Lucy. Come on in." Anne steps back and allows her to pass into the kitchen.

"It looks very nice," Lucy says.

"Want some coffee?"

"No. Not really. I just came over to see how you were doing. I'm so bored over there by myself all day." Lucy lives in the house behind Dale and Anne, and she was standing by her fence watching them when they moved into the house. Her backyard is larger, and she spends a lot of her time lying in the sun on a blanket just off a small patio, which contains several lawn chairs, and a kettle grill. She and the man she lives with often have people over, cluttering up their yard in the late evening, standing around the barbecue grill, talking, drinking, laughing. They are quiet only when they eat. The man she lives with seems much older, much more staid in his activities during the day. He often sits by her blanket in the afternoon, and they coo at each other like a couple of pigeons. Anne has only rarely given herself over to the temptation to watch them. There is something about both of them—she has never talked to the man, doesn't even know his name—there is something about them which seems faintly illicit. She resents them at times. They seem to enjoy each other so much.

"I like what you've done with the Brenners' house," Lucy is saying. "It's such a nice place if it's taken care of. I really hate sloppy people, don't you?"

Anne puts water on to boil and offers her guest a seat at the table.

"Sure you won't have some coffee?"

"No. Really. I just thought I'd see how you were getting along."

"Fine." Anne doesn't know what to say. It's nearly twelve, and she has been asleep all morning again. Sleep. Her one drug. When

Michael is gone and Dale off to his fish, she sleeps.

"The Brenners were such slobs," Lucy says. "Really."

"They seemed nice enough to me."

"They cleaned the place up for you. That's why."

"I guess they wanted to sell it."

"Really."

"Did you know them very well?" Anne is looking vaguely for her cigarettes, standing in front of the table where Lucy watches her as if she is in the first row of some audience and the show has stopped.

"What are you looking for?"

"My cigarettes."

"You smoke? You don't look like the type."

"Here they are." She takes them from the top of the stove. "I only smoke once in a while. Not all the time. That's why I keep losing them."

"Really." Lucy says this with the same tone other people use when they say, "I agree." But Anne doesn't know what she means. In a way it angers her to be made to feel alien by the use of one English word.

"I suppose you don't smoke?"

"No. Never. I like to keep my body pure."

Living with an older man? Lying in the sun until her skin boils? But this is youth—so full of the idea of living she's unconscious. Anne lights her cigarette, sits down across from Lucy. "If you don't mind I'm going to sully mine a little bit."

"I'm sorry," Lucy says with surprise. "I didn't mean to imply—I wasn't saying anything about you."

"You were," Anne insists. "You didn't know it, but you were."

"I've insulted you." She gets that smile with the pout on her face again. Her eyes seem far apart and individually they contain thin curving layers of color, like the outer surface of a soap bubble. But the colors don't seem to match. It's almost impossible to look at both her eyes at once. Her face is round, and her nose is just a touch too large, the only slight distortion in a face that has the structure of polished glass figurines —smooth and round with very delicate shading. She is tan and wears white jogging shorts with a navy blue sleeveless blouse. She watches the cigarette smoke swirl around the lamp now, while Anne drinks her coffee, and neither has spoken since the water began to boil. Anne waits, feeling embarrassed, and she holds in her mind a vision of this girl twenty years from now. *What will life be like for all these perfect people? For all these clean, pure people, who think nature is anything not manufactured?*

"So you knew the Brenners well?" Anne says, finally.

"Not as well as some of the other folks around here. But we saw them sometimes. We talked over the back fence—you know—that sort of thing. But they were pretty private people."

"Why did they move?"

"Their daughter married a Negro. That's what I heard. And they went back to New York, I guess, to be around in case she had to leave him or something."

Anne draws on her cigarette, sips the coffee. Behind Lucy she can see through the windows to the tall green pine trees which stand in the blue air over all the houses like algae in an aquarium. Nothing moves. It is clear and hot and all the yards are filling with pine needles. August is coming and with it will be heat and humidity and long days with Dale complaining that there is nothing to do. The red tide will come in and stay until Thanksgiving—thousands of dead fish washing up on the beach like the first snouts that must have crawled up out of the oozing mud that was once earth. Everywhere will be the smell of dead fish, and the hot thick air, and where will Anne sleep? What will she do then?

"People get so upset over nothing," Lucy says.

"Maybe they can't help it."

"Is that young man, that guy who stays with you, is he your son?"

"Yes."

"What does he do?"

"Nothing. He's just back from the war."

"Was he over there?" Supremely excited, Lucy leans forward as if she has been told about somebody's impending wedding.

"He was captured, more than a year ago."

"God. That's horrible."

"He escaped. All by himself. He was the only one. The Army told us, when he was first missing, that he had been killed in action."

"Oh, that was—that must have been just awful."

"My husband and I moved here then. We didn't know he was alive until we got a letter from him, about three weeks after we came here." Anne tries to remember how she felt when she got that letter. At first she thought it had been delayed, and she was holding in her hands the last letter her son wrote; that he would be speaking to her from his time in life months before. She wept, silently, leaning against the mailbox, and the world seemed to settle into a sort of quiet audience, waiting for the curtain to drop. There didn't seem to be an end to her weeping, however, and she became conscious of herself, leaving the walk in front of her house and floating like a spirit high up over the houses and cars and trees, toward the top of the sky and Michael. When she got into the house, she opened the letter and found that Michael was in a hospital in Japan, had escaped and survived. And there she was with her tears, laughing at the opposite wall, laughing and crying, all at the same time. Her grief and joy blended in a mixture she did not recognize, as if she were turning into another person, another beast. She was not sane then. Not even remotely rational. She was only an exposed nerve, being caressed and tortured all at once.

"I'm against the war myself," Lucy is saying. "So is Ben. My husband."

"I don't think about it. Michael had a horrible time, and I wonder sometimes if it is worth it, if we aren't making a mistake. But I don't think about it."

"So many young men," Lucy sighs.

"What does—is it Ben?"

"Yes."

"What does he do?"

"He's retired." Lucy looks down at the table. "A lot of people didn't think much of me marrying a man so—a man Ben's age. But we love each other very much."

"Good," Anne says. She dips the cigarette in the ashtray, plays with it until it goes out.

"Benjamin was a lawyer. He saved my life, I'll tell you."

Saving lives. That's what it must be all about. The world has too many victims.

"I was married to a marine who was over there, and he came back so fucked up he didn't know who I was. Really."

And who are you? A natural, a pure one with a clean body, who throws words around like a man.

"He beat me. He drank. He hated everyone." Lucy toys with one of her fingernails. Anne feels as if she is playing out some scene, acting in a drama created by this young girl—someone's daughter.

"But Ben. He's so kind and gentle. He's quite virile, in case you were wondering."

"Is he very much older than you?"

"I'm twenty-six, and he's under sixty. It's one of those marriages I used to read about when I was a young girl. I never thought I'd be *in* one."

That was the right word. She is definitely in it, very far in it. Anne lights another cigarette.

"Well, I guess I should be going." She gets up and starts for the door.

"I'm glad you came by," Anne says.

"Can I come back sometime? When your son is here?"

Anne looks at her, not knowing what to say.

"There's not very many young people around here, and I thought it might be nice to talk to him. You know, about things. Music and all."

"Oh. Well, to tell you the truth—" Anne begins, and the word "truth" rings in her ears like a bell. The truth. Michael isn't right. How can she say this? "He's had a rough time—he's not feeling too well lately. I'm sure it will be all right in a few weeks, though."

"Well, maybe then. Bye." Lucy disappears out the door, letting it slam carelessly behind her. A little girl running out to play in summer.

Anne moves to the living room, still holding her cigarette, and looks for something to read. She doesn't want to sleep now. She sits on the couch and thinks about this morning, remembering that Michael still had on that tie when he came into the kitchen. She had helped him tie it right, and he went to bed with it. Then Dale got angry.

She listens to the noises of the house. Outside, engines and motors echo against the blue sky, and a radio is playing somewhere—its music filtering through everything like an odor. There are white lace curtains on the windows and the breeze moves them into the room; softly they rise and fall. It is hard to suffer when the air is so full of sound, and everything seems so fresh. But she feels something in the soft part of her, the part that trembles late at night, and it seems to be rising up in her, gaining strength; as if something has caught fire spontaneously deep inside her and it is burning outward toward sinew and flesh. There's nothing to do here.

She puts the cigarette out. Lights another. The blue smoke curls around her head. She thinks of Lucy, already in Florida, with a man retired; a girl who does not know what all of them are waiting for.

When she first found out her son had been killed in action, it was toward evening in the cold Illinois fall, and the sky was closing early. It lost its light in Illinois like a fainting spell, once the weather changed, and Anne was always vaguely depressed by the sudden darkness. Dale was in the den, reading. There was a football game on the television, or some sporting event, because she remembers hearing a crowd cheering wildly as she read the telegram. It said:

We are sorry to inform you that Michael R. Sumner, A13872520, corporal, USA, has been reported KILLED IN ACTION. STOP.

Date of death uncertain. STOP. You will be notified upon arrival of deceased's remains. STOP.

DEPARTMENT OF THE ARMY.

She remembers the walk down the carpeted corridor toward the den, toward the light there where Dale was reading, and where the crowd roared on the television. The light seemed to recede before her, and she came into the room soundlessly and put the telegram on Dale's lap as if it were something burning. She could not say the words; they did not go together. Dale did not say anything. He simply held the piece of paper in his hand and stared at it, as if he couldn't make out what it said. She cannot remember when he finally spoke, or what he said. They seemed to go from that room to several rooms full of crying people, and cigarette smoke and whiskey and even laughter. It was an endless funeral, everybody waiting for a body. All their friends milled about, in and out of the house, asking, "Any word yet?" Days passed. Then weeks. No word. Dale quit his job, and the two of them went weeping out of the city, headed for Florida and a new life.

It all happened so fast, the whole experience looms in her memory like an auto accident. She suddenly found herself in this house, someone else's house, and completely alone. Chicago, her whole life there, was like a scream she heard in her sleep. And Dale moved through the house as if he was afraid stillness might cause his death. But Michael's return, his coming back from death, was supposed to change all of that. She thought it would be home again, in Florida. She never thought his being alive would turn out to be such a useless miracle.

What are miracles for? She was going to be saved. Her life redeemed. She was glad for it, for the resurrection of her son, but now she cannot understand what the miracle was for. She must love him, and help him through whatever he will come to—but she can't help wondering what will finally happen to her. She cannot sit still in this house. Everything in it is odd and unattractive and faintly commercial. It is an unfamiliar motel—a place where she just sleeps. She does not believe she will be here until she dies—that this is her home, where she lives.

A car passes under the window.

She moves the curtain and views the road and the park—a grove of pine trees sticking up out of the sand. There is a bench standing in a cloud of light under the trees, near the road. Another car passes. A man on crutches, with one leg, hobbles over to the bench and sits down.

A bright green short-sleeved shirt, perhaps one or two sizes too big, ripples in the breeze, and seems to be held on him by the padded tops of the crutches.

Anne watches the man try to light a cigarette, and she sees his leg shift outward, as if he is trying to get the circulation going, and something about him strikes her. A feeling she doesn't recognize at first. She closes the curtain, and again the fire starts in the soft center of her body. Fear alights in her, descends like down in the breeze, the fragments of a leaf. A thing she dreamed, shortly after she heard Michael had been killed. They were all asleep in the house, the strange house that she had no idea she would actually move into before the year was over, and she heard a noise in the kitchen. It was the Chicago kitchen when she got to it, and she saw something there, something the dream would not give her, and she went back to her room afraid. When she got to her room she was told by a voice in the darkness to go back. "There is something for you on the floor in front of the refrigerator. Something there." She went for Dale, but when she tried to wake him she couldn't make herself talk; the words formed in her head but she could only moan when she tried to say them. She screamed but the sound of it stayed inside her, as if she were suffocating under a pillow. She went to find Michael. On her way she tripped over the wrought-iron railing in the hall and felt vaguely relieved that she was awake and going to see Michael—as if this knowledge was enough to prove he wasn't dead. She opened Michael's door and tried to turn on a light, but she couldn't find it. She stepped down and the floor was wet. Michael's bed was made. He was not in the room. His picture sat on the sill, on the windowsill, and there were flowers all around it. She screamed again, only she was inside the scream; she covered it, wouldn't let the air get to it. She went to the kitchen then, a sudden movement there which convinced her she was dreaming. Only dreaming. All she had to do was wake up. *This is only my bed,* she thought. But the kitchen floor was cold and there was something there. Something by the refrigerator. The door of the refrigerator opened and the light it made shone on something on the floor. It moved. She tried to get to the door to close it, but the thing on the floor moved. It would not let her near. She leaned down into the light to see what it was. She saw a limb, a leg with a boot on it. But when she got closer she saw that it wasn't a leg anymore, that it had insignia on it. It moved again. She tried to scream and the insignia became telegrams, neatly folded and stapled to the tattered sleeve. Each one said, "Michael is dead. Michael is dead." Dale came in laughing. He picked up the limb and told her to stop screaming. "This is Michael's," he said, and he took it with him upstairs to Michael's room.

VIII. THE TAPES

I don't know when I began to laugh. Someone put a field jacket over me. I was naked. I didn't have a scratch on me and I was lying on a stretcher in an open field, with high grass all around and so much smoke in the air you couldn't see the sun. Hueys went over us with so much noise the grass seemed to move. The field jacket only covered the top half of me. I sat up and put it on because I was shaking then. I don't think I heard any fire, everything seemed to roar—it was like everything in the world that could make noise was making it. Men were screaming, running back and forth in front of me. There may have been other stretchers around me. I laughed so hard I couldn't feel it anymore. Helmets bobbed up and down in the grass. A huey rose up over my head, carrying litters on either side. Two litters went up over me and disappeared over the trees beyond the field. I felt the wind, and I couldn't stop laughing. I ached. My stomach seized with convulsions and seemed to be coming apart, but I couldn't make the laughing stop. It was impossible to let it out, to let out any sound, and after a while, all I wanted to do was breathe in. I heard someone yelling above all the noise, and a grunt—a marine—came over to me and yanked my new fatigue jacket.

"You OK?" he said. He was very young, a face underneath the helmet you might see shooting baskets in front of a garage on Saturday mornings. Probably less than a year before that time, someone was yelling at him to cut the grass. I continued to laugh, although I was learning how to breathe with it.

"I'd feel pretty good too if I'd been through what you been through and made it back in one piece."

"Oh, but I'm not in one piece," I said. "No, sir."

Not in one piece. I was all over the place. I had lived like a mine for forty-one days. I couldn't wait to explode—send fragments of myself into the lovely hot blue green air. Make wounds. Mortal wounds.

The marine said, "The next bird will take you out."

I was laughing again. This time all the "ha's" were clear and distinct—each one equal in duration and volume. I hit the same note over and over again. The marine watched me, a suspicious glint in his eye. He couldn't decide if I was a real man or a machine placed there to test his understanding of everything he'd read was true about the world. It was the first time anyone ever looked at me as if I was a specimen, a bacterium in a petri dish, a rat trying to learn the maze. He put his hand on my arm without changing the expression on his face. Maybe he was looking for a switch to turn me off. He had only my flesh to tell him I was human.

I don't think I spoke to anyone. I ran *into* their fire to save myself. I can imagine what they thought, making an assault through that tall grass and here comes a naked man running at them through the smoke like an assassin at a birthday party. Maybe that's what made me laugh.

I heard another huey beating the air in the distance over the trees. The marine took his hand off me and crouched down next to me, his hand on his helmet, blinking into the rushing air. I stopped laughing then, I think. I can't remember when I stopped, or if I did—but I remember the wind from the helicopter moving the pubic hair which was my only armor, my only cover from the light and the air and the smoke—and that I started to laugh again, as if I hadn't really been laughing until then. The sky began to run over me and turn and I realized they were moving me. There was a black man at my feet, and all I could see were the white eyes under the helmet.

They strapped me in under the blades. The force was hot and terrific. It drew the air out of me. I was inside noise then. I stopped laughing. There was a plexiglass cover over my head, but I felt the wind of the blades as the huey lifted, felt the air rushing over me with the force of water, moving water. I was amazed to be inside the noise like that. I went up. I rose up over the field and trees, lying on my back watching the blades crack my view of the wet sky. I soared out with the noise, naked from the waist down. I vibrated with each pass of the blade, each explosion in the cylinders. I looked for peace. For sleep. I thought I might find peace up there once I got used to the noise and vibration, the wind and the smoke. I loved all the air, and the blue stretch of sky I was flying into. I thought I was going home.

IX. DALE

Eddie is sitting across from Dale, holding a beer in his gnarled hands, talking about the red tide, and the approaching end of fishing for a while. They are in a cool bar, and other people around them talk and laugh about fishing, the water, the heat, baseball, the war. Everyone drinks, makes some kind of noise. Men drift out; others come into the room, pull back chairs, take out their money, remove their hats. Cigarette smoke forms blue clouds in the sunlight which invades the room through a large picture window behind Eddie. Glasses rattle behind the bar, and there is a faint odor of fish and sweat in all the air.

"I know it's pollution kills them," Eddie says.

A group of men by the bar break out in a loud burst of screams and laughter.s his beer, lets out a long sigh. "What'er you gonna do?"

"About what?"

"When the tide comes."

"I guess I won't fish."

"What'd you do last year?"

"Last year was like a vacation. I didn't care about it. I went swimming."

Someone yells, "More beer."

Dale lifts his glass, studies the light in his beer, drinks a cold mouthful. He holds it in his mouth, lets the carbonation burn, then swallows it.

"Good, isn't it?" Eddie says.

"It's always good."

"Worried about your boy?"

"I'm not even thinking about him." This is a lie. Michael is everywhere in the room.

"Where do you think he was going?"

"I don't know."

"I thought he was going to jump out of the car."

"Maybe he just wanted to walk. He does a lot of walking."

"What's the matter with him?"

"Who knows? He came back that way."

Eddie finishes his beer and orders another. Dale holds his mug with both hands and stares at the beer left there, losing its head, the bubbles rising steadily and insanely to the smooth top where they dissipate in the air.

"You know, young people aren't suited for war anymore," Eddie says softly.

Dale raises his glass, drinks.

"Not that we've done anything wrong with them, or anything. We only wanted to make things beautiful for them, right? And we had plenty of money, and things were going so well. So this war comes and they don't know how to fight."

"Michael fought," Dale says.

"You know what I mean. Of course he fought. A lot of them did, and still are. But there's no—this isn't a criticism—there's no discipline anymore. You see what I mean? They're too affected by the whole thing."

Dale drinks the rest of his beer in a long gulp, feeling the cold liquid all the way to his stomach.

"You want another?" Eddie says.

"No."

"Go ahead. I'll buy."

"I don't want to go home. I guess so."

Eddie pays for another beer, and Dale sips it through the white head, staring at one of the glasses on the table behind Eddie. A hand is wrapped around it, moving slightly to the solid and measured tones of the conversation there.

"Nowadays, kids don't know about things like suffering and death and all that. They think death happens to old people like me. Or to Negroes in dark alleys," Eddie is saying. "So when they get over there and see somebody's brains strewn all over the place—stretched out like a goddamned dead rabbit—it does something to them."

"I don't know what Michael's seen. He hasn't talked about it."

"There's no manhood anymore," Eddie says, leaning forward over his glass. "That's the problem. I'm not saying Michael's not a man; I'm talking about all of them. I guess it'd be pretty hard to be a man when everybody else is acting like a sissy."

"Maybe Michael isn't a man. I don't know. I don't know what happened to him."

"Tell the truth," Eddie says. "Since you've mentioned it about Michael being a man and all—do you think anything could have happened to you over there to make you behave like he did today?"

"I don't know. I spent the war in Georgia."

"But you've seen some things. I have. I'll tell you, I have."

The group of men by the bar break out in laughter again. One of them howls, raising his arms. There are glasses all over the table, and hands, and cigarettes.

"I saw things I dream about today," Eddie says. "And you can't be a cop in Chicago without seeing some pretty horrible things, I'll bet. But you and I come from a different time, and we don't let things get to us. Kids today, they don't have any backbone. No inner strength; they've had it too easy."

"It's pretty hard on them now," Dale says. He remembers Michael the child, and camping trips in green forests, ball games in the summer, hikes in the snow when schools closed in winter. "I loved my son," he says with tightness in his throat. "What were we supposed to do?"

Eddie looks surprised. "No. I said it wasn't anything we've done wrong. We couldn't have done anything else. Although I taught my boys about things. I'm sure you did too. It's just what happened, I guess." He raises his glass, looks over the brim at Dale as he drinks.

"If it weren't for this fucking war, he'd still be my son," Dale says.

"We've got responsibility in the world. We can't beg off because we love our sons."

"Who are we protecting?"

"You know very well. We're protecting ourselves."

"I don't know anymore."

"Don't listen to those hippies, and those cracked congressmen," Eddie says. "We're in trouble, and we aren't going to get out of it easily. These crazy kids are acting just like Communists."

Communists. It's such a funny word. A sort of curse, and Eddie uses it the way most people do—to accuse. Dale knows his son is different, that perhaps all the sons and daughters are different. They are more conscious of how they feel, or perhaps they are better at showing it, and they value life as if it were a sacrament, an ecstasy full of noise and pleasure which older people cannot understand. They don't believe in or understand struggle. They don't build for anything. Life is a movie.

"We would've won the war a long time ago, if those damn kids weren't in the streets all the time. Fucking college kids."

Dale raises his glass and gulps the cold beer. He is cooler now, and not as worried about Michael. The hell with Michael. The hell with the war and all the rest. The hell with Eddie. This is supposed to be the best time of life and no one is going to ruin it.

"I want to enjoy myself and forget about all this shit," he says.

"I know just what you're talking about," Eddie says. "But we can't forget. Not really. We're all touched by it."

"That's an appropriate choice of words."

"What do you mean?"

"Touched."

"Your boy?"

"You saw him today."

"He was upset. I saw that. And I'll never understand what got him that way."

"The war."

"He was OK until we landed that blowfish."

"He hasn't been OK since he came home."

"What happened to him?"

"I don't know. That's the funny thing. He won't talk about it. I'm not sure he knows."

"Has he acted like that before?"

"I've never seen it like that. Not that bad." Another lie. Michael was worse, just before his first visit to the hospital. Dale cannot understand his own shame, his fear. Is Michael insane? How will the days lead them to admit their son's illness? Dale asks for deliverance in his sleep —the future talks with strangers about a son, a young man who is not anywhere: Will they lie about him—say he's in business in Denver? *My son lost his mind.*

"I was surprised you let him out of the car," Eddie says. "There's no telling what he might do."

Dale drinks some more beer, looks at Eddie as if something has just dropped from the old man's mouth.

"To himself, I mean," Eddie says.

"He's not that way. He's just—just afraid, I guess. He trembles and sometimes he cries. He's not violent."

Another group of men wanders in the door. They wear bright blue and orange shirts, like everyone else, and they are sweating heavily from the heat outside. The bar is dark, and they pause together, trying to get used to the light.

"Looks like some of that speedboat crowd," Eddie says.

"What am I supposed to do?" Dale says. "He's twenty-two years old. He's been to a war—something I've never seen, and I'm supposed to tell him he can't get out of the car?"

"I guess not."

"I can't be fathering him all the time. He has to grow up and be another person—a friend. Not a little boy, a stranger."

"He probably wouldn't have gotten out if you'd told him not to. I admire your courage, I guess."

"Buy me another beer, will you?"

"Sure. Don't worry about him so much. You're getting toward that age, you know."

"What age?"

"When you gotta start worrying about your ticker."

Eddie goes for more beer and Dale looks toward the men taking seats by the bar. He wonders if perhaps he shouldn't have insisted that Michael stay in the car. What might have happened if he had just said "no"?

Michael got out of the car without a word. He had stopped wailing by the time they came in with the boat, and all of them had lapsed into a sort of whispering conversation, as if a word too loud, or off-key, might touch him off again. They got to the car, and Michael sat in back and they started into the city, the road swirling ahead in the heat, and they were passing a stand of pine trees where the sun blinked like a strobe, racing behind each tree, and Michael had said, "Oh, the sun." Eddie turned in his seat, and asked him what was wrong and he said, "Look at the sun." Dale said something about how bright it was, and Michael asked him to stop the car.

"Why?" Dale asked.

"I want to get out."

"You can see it from here," Eddie said.

"I want to get out."

"Are you going to be sick?" Dale asked him.

"No. I just want to get out."

"What's wrong with you?" Dale almost screamed this. Eddie turned back to the road, lapsed into silence.

"I want to walk for a while. That's all. I'm all right, Dad."

And Dale thought, *By God I will; I will let him out.* He pulled off the road and Eddie opened the door, looking at Dale the whole time with a wry sort of smirk—as if he were saying, "Is this what you really want me to do?" Michael got out, crawling over the seat clumsily, dragging his foot against the seat belt.

"Good-bye," Dale said.

"See you," Michael answered him without looking. He crossed the road and headed toward the pines and the water behind them. Dale saw the back of his son, full grown, walking away from him, and he felt his throat tighten, his brow begin to burn. How could someone he held so close become so much a part of the world beyond his own flesh, so much a part of being someone else—a stranger.

Eddie comes back with two beers.

"Thanks," Dale says.

"Don't mention it." Eddie sits down with some effort, exhaling as he settles into his chair. "Yeah, you gotta watch the ticker from now on. That's what gets you these days."

"Or cancer."

"Oh, I hate that word," Eddie says.

"Me too. I'm scared to death of it. I know I'll get it too."

"Shouldn't talk like that." Eddie drinks, smacks his lips. Someone calls for more beer. "How come you never talked about Michael before?"

"I don't know. When I'm fishing, I just want to have fun."

"Me too. I'm sure glad we ran into each other. I was fishing alone for two, three years before you came along."

"What about your old friend—what's his name?"

"Bob?"

"Yeah."

"He's—isn't that funny, we were just talking about it—he's got cancer."

"Jesus."

"It's in his stomach. We think we got problems."

"He's only going to die. We've got to live."

"Nothing wrong with that, is there?"

"Maybe not. I don't feel like it's such a gift just now."

"The boy'll come out of it. You'll see. They can do wonders now with drugs and all. They'll bring him out of it."

"He'll never be the same. Never."

"You've got to go on living."

"I said that just this morning, to my wife."

"Right. And you meant it."

"This isn't what I thought my retirement would be like."

"It never is. I thought I'd go crazy at first. But I love it now. I'd love it even more if it weren't for the goddamned red tide."

"I'm tired of this place."

"Want to go somewhere else?"

"No. I'm tired of Florida, I think. And Michael. Believe it or not, it was easier when I thought he was dead."

Eddie looks down to his hands.

"I know that sounds horrible."

"You don't know what you're talking about." Eddie's voice is lower, and there is a tone in it almost savage, as if he is holding himself back.

"I guess I don't really mean that. But why does he have to be that way?"

"Who knows how the mind works? Maybe they tortured him or something."

"There's not a mark on his body. All the Army said was that he was maltreated. They didn't feed him."

"Well, they must have done something to him."

"He doesn't talk to us about it. He goes to this guy named Kessler, this—this—shrink, and talks into a tape recorder."

"What does he talk about?

"I don't know. Kessler won't let us hear the tapes. He says he barely gets a word out of Michael either, but at least he talks to the machine."

"They know best, I guess." Eddie finishes his beer, rises. "Can you give me a lift home?"

"I can't believe he'll talk to a recorder, and not me. I could help him."

Eddie stands by the table, watching Dale's beer. "I'll finish it, and we'll go," Dale says.

"I'm going to take a piss," Eddie says. Dale watches him move through the room, toward a hallway in back. His head lolls back and forth, and from behind, he looks younger. He is slim for his age and walks with all the assurance of a younger man. He is a veteran, and he fishes with Dale, and the war was ages ago, and he is healthy. Thinks about the world as if it were a book he has read. Why can't Michael be like that? What will happen to him when he is fifty, and the world tells him he may get cancer, or have a heart attack? He's got his whole life, all the years, and he can't even make it through the day. How does he sleep? Does he sleep? What goes on in his mind when he starts wailing like that?

Dale finishes his beer. Eddie comes back and picks up his gray hat.

"I guess I'll go home," Dale says.

X. THE TAPES

I went fishing with my father and a man named Eddie today—earlier today. On the way there we stopped at a Safeway store so my father could buy something—some lunch meat for the fishing trip, I think. I followed him around; I don't know what he wanted. I wasn't listening. While we waited in a line in front of one of the cash registers I noticed this blond woman, pretty young, wearing a tennis outfit, a white tennis outfit, and she was with another woman who seemed older. The other woman was wearing brown pajamas, and there was something wrong with her. She had kinky hair as brown as her pajamas, and her face was red, with eyes that seemed to bleed. They did not belong to her, the eyes. Somebody stuck them there and they were trapped. Her face was covered all over with a very fine down of blond hair.

My father twitched in the line in front of me, talking to Eddie, and I counted the varieties of chewing gum, Kodak film, and hard candy on the racks in front of the register, trying not to hear the two women behind me.

"Now you wait in line and pay the lady—here's the money," the blond woman in the tennis shorts said. The other only made a slight noise, a groan like a beam of wood about to crack. "Shush, now," the tennis shorts said. "It's easy. I'll be right outside." I heard paper crackling, an agitation of the air behind me. "Now stop it. Stop it." The voice of the woman in the tennis shorts was struggling. The groan grew louder, then subsided. I heard someone take in air, then the noise stopped. "Now, I'll go get the car, and you pay the lady. OK?" The tennis shorts walked past me, through the line and out the door. I watched her go, the quickness of her walk, her head erect, closed tight and determined. I felt something near my sleeve, and turned to see the other one standing next to me, staring at a fan of green money which was hooked to her hand as if it had been taped there. When I saw her hand I knew she was some other place, had always been there, and no one—not even the pretty, determined woman in the white tennis outfit—would ever bring her to this world. The money was foreign to her and seemed to cling to her palm like the wings of a stinging insect. She looked at it with eyes used to weeping, mindless weeping. Her mouth hung open, quivering. It seemed cut there in the leather of her face.

I looked away, tried not to see her. She was probably used to averted eyes, heads turned away from her. She touched my arm and I heard a voice like the voice of a man say, "Excuse me. Excuse me." I denied her. I didn't want anyone to see her, but I could not let those foreign eyes look into mine. She tugged on my sleeve, a ragged and faint plea from inside her hand. "Could you go out and get Martha?" she said. My father turned and looked at me, and I smiled, shrugged my shoulders. My father looked as if he were waiting for me to say something. I

shrugged again and he turned back to the cash register. "Please," the
voice said, and I knew that she was crying. I could not believe how
quietly she came apart. I turned and she looked right at me with thick
yellow eyes and said, "Could you go out and get my nurse? I need her
right now." She paused, weeping. She said, "OK?" I watched her eyes,
embarrassed for her because she was urinating through the brown pajamas. I didn't want my father to see that.

"Martha's coming right back," I said.

She dropped the small bag she was holding, whatever it was she was
supposed to buy, but she held to the money—or rather it clung to her.

"It's all right," I said. I bent down and picked up the bag, tried to
hand it to her. She raised her arms up under her neck, and cried. My
father said, "What's the matter with her?" The lady behind the cash
register called one of the clerks in the store, and he came to the front
looking harried and insulted. He walked like a ring of dangling keys.
"She wants her nurse," I said. I saw Eddie staring at her, his eyes fiercely
aligned. "She's all right," I said. "Just afraid."

"What do they leave somebody like that alone for?" Eddie said.

The clerk went looking for the nurse. I was still holding the small
paper bag, looking at the numbers blinking on the register. The woman
wailed. There was a puddle forming by her ankle and I thought about
how it might be tears, a way the body cries.

The tennis lady came back and took her out of there, scolding her
as she went. I heard her saying, "Looks like I can't leave you alone
anywhere. You can't be trusted. It will be a long time before you go out
again." They were mother and child, except the child was older, and not
of this world. She kept saying, "No no no." Just a child. Everybody and
everything will be too rough on her, and she must haul her alien soul
through life. I stood behind my father, watched the wrinkles in his shirt
near his waist and pretended, like everyone else, that I hadn't noticed
anything unusual. The whole store smelled of urine.

When we got outside, my father said, "You handled yourself pretty
well in there, son." He put his hand on my shoulder, and I walked next
to him, feeling almost glad it happened. It felt good to hear my father
say that. I remember everything he ever said to me, but especially the
praise.

When I was a little boy I used to catch lightning bugs and put them
in a glass jar. They were the only insects I could touch. I always hated
them, insects. But lightning bugs didn't seem so much like insects to
me. You could pet them, hold them in your hands, let them crawl up

your arm. I was always going to find out what made the tail light up on one of those things. Me and this kid who lived down the street used to catch whole jars of lightning bugs and take them into our tent late at night. They almost lit up the place. Larry and I used to spend the night in that tent during the summer, first in my backyard, then in his. The tent belonged to both of us. We cut lawns all of one summer to save the money to buy it. It was only a pup tent, but we saw it as a shelter, a home, a warm place in the dark. My father stayed with us on some nights. Larry's father was a policeman, too, but he worked the night shift, so he never spent the night out there with us, although occasionally, when he got home, he would come around and arrest all of us. He only did that when my father was there, so it never really scared me too much, although it was frightening to hear him rustling the tent, making loud noises out of his throat. He and my father would put on a mock battle, in which my father was invariably shot, falling to the ground with a groan. I guess they were good friends. I didn't mind Larry, but he was far different from me in the way he saw things, and in the objects he noticed in the world. He had a finely developed sense of tragedy, the maudlin kind, with crosses in all the wrong places, and death an expected outcome for the suffering hero. I was always the villain, the Indian, or the bank robber. He always died heroically, a look of smug satisfaction on his face, and I would have to walk away and suggest a new game with new heroes and new deaths. All of it planned in advance. He was also interested in chemistry sets and biology labs and other scientific things. I liked looking at things, at the green and yellow world, but I didn't know the names of everything the way he did. He knew what to call every bush and weed and berry that grew in the neighborhood. He knew all the animals, the insects, and even the rocks.

He told me lightning bugs have phosphorous in the tail, and that's why they light. I've always remembered that. Always believed it was true.

I was better at catching the bugs than he was. My hands were quick. Even my father commented on it. I've always remembered that he said I was good at catching lightning bugs. I thought about that when he made the remark that I handled myself well in the store where the woman in the brown pajamas came apart. I think I felt just as good.

I used to put the bugs in a jar and he'd poke holes in the lid for me so they could breathe. I'd fill the jar before it got too dark to see the bugs flying. That was the trick. Chasing the bug, not the light. Larry used to lose a good hour waiting for the sun to get far enough behind the trees and houses so he could see the light winking against the dark green bushes and trees.

My father held onto the jar for me, and one night when I was bringing him two bugs I'd just snatched out of the air he said, "You sure are good at that." I can hear his voice now, right now. Exactly the way it sounded then. And when we came out of the store, he said, "You handled yourself well in there." I swear it feels like a pronouncement from God. When he says things like that to me, it's not as if he thinks it, it's as if he is announcing some truth, and I believe it.

I remember those nights when he came out to the tent with us and how sometimes I wished Larry would go home so it would be just me and my father. He'd lie down between us, and the grass felt warm with him there. Larry talked about his father the whole time, about all the great things his father was doing, and my father would listen and say, "Is that so" every now and then. But when my father talked to us, when he told us about the things he did when he was a boy, there was nothing in the world I was afraid of. We'd rest in the dark under a cold sky and listen to the night sounds—the engines, far off, the roar of trains leaving and returning, an occasional siren, a horn. And the night bugs—the crickets, cicadas. Inside all the houses, televisions flickered like candles —Jackie Gleason screamed at his wife, and Norton, the surrogate child, waved his arms. And my father breathed next to me, talking about things I felt I would come to understand, come to know as he did. A world I would move freely in. . . .

Those times came to me when I was in the ground. My father's voice came to me. It kept me breathing. I heard planes, engines wavering like bending aluminum sheets, getting louder, louder. I listened for the other sounds—the sirens, the cicadas, the trains. No TVs. Laughing, voices crying out in a language I can't understand. I hear the voices whistling when the planes come. When the planes come. I hear the voices ringing like the cry of a taut wire. I hear the whine of the thin chords in each throat as the voices come for me. Each time they come for me. . . .

XI. MICHAEL

"Are you all right now?" Kessler says. The hair over his eyes seems fake.

"I guess so."

"You were screaming the last part of that."

"I'm sorry."

"Do you want to go on?"

"No."

"If you like, we—"

"No."

"Do you remember what you were talking about?"

"I don't want to."

"But you do."

"Yes."

"You don't need to tell me any more today."

"I'm scared," I say.

He glances over to the wall, his diploma. Behind his head I can see through the window to the black street, the pine trees in the grove.

"You want me to play the tape over again, so you can hear it?"

"No."

"Why not?"

"I know what's on it."

"What did you mean about the voices?"

"I'm afraid to think about it."

"Were you screaming like that before I came in?"

"I don't know."

"You didn't know you were screaming?" Kessler's face is a different shade of white now. He is watching my eyes, and his head seems large, molded from soft clay.

"I guess I felt it—I don't know." I never know when I'm scream-ing: it always comes as a complete surprise to me—like a soft moan in my sleep that wakes the whole house. It all seems like a shadow in a dream.

"When I came in you were saying something about 'when they came for you.' What did you mean by that?"

"Nothing."

"What did you mean?"

"I don't remember."

"You were screaming, Michael."

"I don't remember."

"Was it the Vietnamese?"

"I—" He is looking right into my skull now, peering through the hole in each eye, a frown on his face, as if he is studying a chessboard or an X-ray. I hear a phone ringing somewhere. Inside the clean walls, a mouse nibbles at wood, at plaster.

"Go on," Kessler says. His voice scares me: if I say anything to him I will fall over the edge of something into space.

"Well, Michael, was it them?"

His eyes are dull looking, seem to be covered with gauze. His hands lie on the table like dead fishes.

"I talk about lightning bugs, and sleeping in a tent with my father."

He moves his hands to another part of the desk and breathes out. "Is that it?"

"And a lady I saw in the store this morning."

"What about her?"

"She was—she lost control of herself."

"In what way?"

"She was retarded, and her nurse left her in the store and she wet her pants because she was afraid."

"What about the voices?"

"I felt sorry for her."

"The voices, Michael. Tell me about the voices. Who came for you?"

"I *hate* them," I say. "I *hate* them."

"You've told me that."

"I can't remember all of it. It scares me to think about it."

"But you do think about it."

"No, I don't. I don't think about it."

"Why are you so scared then?"

"Because I *might* think about it."

"It would be better for you if you did." He sits back in his chair. "Well, all right, tell me whatever you want. Tell me about the fishing trip." He folds his hands behind his head, his elbows splayed out. There are perspiration stains under his arms.

"I got scared on the boat, and I think my father is mad at me."

"What were you scared of?"

"Things happened, I don't know. Eddie—"

"Who's Eddie?"

"A friend of my father's. He talked about the war, and I got scared."

"And what makes you think your father's mad at you? What did you do?"

"I—I started shaking again."

"What did Eddie say about the war?"

"I don't want to talk about this now."

"What did he say?"

I try to think of something other than myself. I see his head moving and think about the air going in and out of it. What difference can it possibly make that he thinks, that he has thoughts, ideas which make him different from me, or anyone else? The air goes in and out and because of that he survives. All he's doing right now is surviving. He breathes.

"Isn't the session over?"

"We've got time. Go ahead. Answer me."

"I have to go."

He watches my face as if he is studying the detail in a minute flower.

"Your father gets mad when you—when you—"

"Not always. He doesn't understand it. I think he was mad today, though. He took me with him because my mother wanted him to. I guess he thought it would be just like old times. And I ruined it."

"I wish you would tell me what got you scared again."

"Just something Eddie said. That's all."

"You don't remember it?"

"Yes. I just don't want to talk about it. It wasn't anything. Nothing. But it made me think of—it made me think about it."

"The war."

"Yes."

"Are you thinking about it now?"

"No."

"What are you thinking about?"

"Have you ever watched people in a restaurant?"

"What do you mean?" He puts his hands down on the desk again. His brows crawl.

"Watch a crowd of people eating sometime."

"Why?"

"Have you ever done it?"

"Have you?" He's still looking at me, his hands moving up to grab the back of his head again.

"I have."

"Well, I guess I haven't," he says finally. I watch his face, the way it stares at me, the eyes scurrying beneath the brows. His tie is loosened at the neck, crumpled down the front of him, all broken. The sight of the tie sickens me—makes something inside, in my stomach, come loose for an instant.

"Do you want to tell me why you bring it up?" Kessler says.

"I think about what they're doing all the time."

"About eating?"

"Yeah."

He blinks his eyes, waiting.

"We all like to pretend we're doing something we enjoy," I say.

"You don't enjoy eating?"

"We pretend we're eating because we *want* to eat. We get hungry for something, and we think of that thing. Not just hungry. Not just hungry. No, we think we want chicken, or steak, or a salad. A cheeseburger, maybe. A certain kind of food and we go get it, or we cook it, and then we eat it."

"I don't understand what you mean."

"All people do that. All people who have food and prospects for food."

"So?"

"Watch people eat, Doc."

He puts his hands down and sits forward now. "Tell me what I'll see."

"It's survival. Eating a cheeseburger is an act of survival."

"OK."

"It doesn't look the same when you know that."

"What?"

"It isn't the same. When you see people eating now it won't be the same. It won't be like you're seeing them when they sunbathe, or walk the dog, or swim, or ski, or play cards, or anything else people do. Because you'll know. You'll know."

"As you do."

"Yes. Every one of them, every person you see, ceases to be a person when you take the food away. Take the food away for a little while and then watch what they eat. Then watch."

"Is that what happened to you?"

"I was hungry in the ground." I can't feel anything. I'm only a fragile membrane; there's nothing inside of me but ice-cold air.

"Michael?" Kessler says.

"What?"

"Are you all right?"

"I don't know." Air will get into my veins, will spread into my skin, and the fibers will evaporate.

"Maybe we shouldn't go on," he says. "But if you would tell me what you're thinking right now, right this minute, I think it would do you a lot of good."

"I'm waiting."

"For what?"

"I'm holding on here." I get up and start toward the window, but there's no place to walk in front of it. He has plants there, and a table with magazines on it. There's no place to walk.

"Are you scared?"

I can't figure out where I should go. I don't want to wait for it to happen. The icy air is still trapped. "It helps to pace," I tell him.

"You're thinking about it now, aren't you?"

"Yes." But I'm not thinking about it. I'm not thinking about it.

"Tell me."

I sit in the chair again, wait for the air to settle with me.

"Michael?"

"I don't want to be afraid anymore," I say.

"And you're afraid now?"

"Does this make any sense? I'm afraid I'm *going* to be afraid."

"It makes sense. You don't—"

"I'm afraid of it."

"You don't like the fear, what it does to you."

"Right."

"So you're afraid of it."

"Right."

"And that does things to you."

"Right. Right."

"But the original thing, the original thing you are afraid of—you have nothing to fear from that, Michael. That's over. Thinking about it won't bring it back."

"I'm shaking."

"No, you're not."

"I feel like I am."

"Try to relax. Thinking about what happened to you won't hurt you."

"I was so hungry after a while, I ate anything they gave me." I can't hear any sound in the room. Kessler's eyes don't move.

"Go on."

"I think I should go home," I say.

"I think we're getting somewhere. Why don't you finish it?"

"I have to go home."

I get up and turn for the door. Kessler gets up and comes around his desk carrying the tape recorder and some cassettes.

"Why don't you take the recorder with you, talk into it at home when you feel like it?"

He puts the recorder in my hands, a smile curling under his nose, as if he is welcoming me to some legion or club.

"Talk into this thing a lot," he says. "And bring the tapes to me, OK?"

He puts his hand on my shoulder, a gesture which seems forced, artificial. His day's work is done and I, one of his clients, am ushered out the door. He will go home to his family, and dinner, and television. I want to go home, too. I want to go back home. Instead, I go out the door and cross the street into the park and head for my father's house.

XII. ANNE

The breeze is tender and full of the salt mist of the sea. Anne feels her hair moving with the currents, and she squints her eyes just slightly to keep them moist, and to keep the hair out. She sits on the front porch steps of the house, waiting for Dale and Michael, happy that their trip has taken the whole day. She watches the cars pass, looking up the road now and then for Dale's Toyota. Just this moment she feels attractive, and she pictures the sight of her from the end of the road, what her husband and son will see when they come home. It must have been a good day for both of them. Perhaps they laughed, drank beer. They had been such friends before Michael left for the war. She had loved the banter, the loud and pretended criticisms they made of each other when they worked or played together. Her boy, a man.

When she held him at two, held him up in front of her, his knees on her breast, his hands holding her arms, he was the most beautiful and wondrous thing she had ever seen. She could not believe how it made her feel to stare into his eyes. She was him, and he was her, and they were both each other, all alive together at once in the world. She gained sustenance, protection, security, when she held him—all the things she thought she must have to offer him. She did not think she would ever be able to punish him.

But he gradually became Michael, the child. Another human being, someone other than Anne. She loved him as much, but she became conscious of things she did not like—his temper, the whining, the incredible selfishness. She should have had more children, so Michael could have learned to get along with people. She regretted that now, more than anything. But one was enough, as Dale used to say. And they had paid more attention to Michael than would have been possible with other children making demands, especially if the other children were as demanding as Michael had been. Michael really was another person when he grew out of infancy, and she had been able to adjust to it because he was her only child. But she noticed the differences between them as they went on with their lives. She liked people, had always enjoyed company and laughter. Michael never had more than one friend at a time, and somehow they always seemed more inquisitive and relaxed than her son. Michael loved books, but he never talked about them to anyone, and he didn't share her taste in reading. She liked romances and novels; Michael read police stories (a response, she was sure, to his father's work) and history books. He liked facts and statistics; she liked feelings and stories. Numbers weren't important to her.

She saw things in her son that reminded her of Dale, or even her own father. She saw things she didn't recognize at all, but this was her boy, her own. He lived with her, he and his father, and time passed and he grew secretly, through all the years. She took pictures of him on his first day at school—an event she had talked about for over a year before it happened, and which she received like news of a death in the family when the day arrived. She took pictures of him in high school. His graduation. It all went so fast. Then he was drafted and she was holding onto him, saying good-bye.

And he was someone else.

"I'll miss you," she said, and she was telling the truth. For the first few days she could not get over the terrible emptiness at the center of everything. Dale seemed to take up the change as if it were a hobby like tennis or handball. He wanted to go out every night, and he talked about it as if it were something he had looked forward to for several years.

That was the beginning of a long period of small talk and long silences between them. They weren't festive anymore—not even when Michael's letters came.

And when Michael was reported dead, she dreamt of his death, of the event. The precise moment in time. It bothered her that she could never know it, never experience her son's death. Then he was alive again. Not dead. Her mind would not accept the world for a while. It took the Army over a year to return her son to her.

Now a blue car passes, gleaming in the last rays of the sun. Up the road she sees a man walking across the street toward the park. The street is empty. It occurs to her that perhaps there has been a tragedy, and she is only waiting for it to fall on her. The boat sank, and everybody drowned. She sees herself receiving the news, her face turned slightly upward, trying not to see the lips of the man with the message. A boating accident. Such are the awful ironies of life. She knew a woman in Chicago who feared for her husband's life, developed an ulcer worrying about it. The woman talked incessantly about his job—her husband was a street cop, who worked with Dale—and all the possibilities for death, the impending loss, the loss. One day, on the way to the doctor's, the woman was stopped on the street by three young boys who took her purse and then shot her in the stomach. She nearly died, leaving her blood on the concrete sidewalk. Anne could not believe the mythological irony of it, could not believe there wasn't some design after all, some logic in events. As if time had personality, and events were a culmination of some inexplicable game.

Although she considers some of the possibilities, Anne is not worried. She wishes they would get home. She does not want to think of any more incredible scenes. A chill leaks into the breezes, and she feels the skin on her shoulders forming bumps. The sun is visibly weaker, so she looks directly at it, a yellow wafer burning the edge of the horizon behind the trees. *Where are they?* She stares back toward the end of the road, looking for another car. When there are cars, the possibility of their arrival seems greater. When there is nothing, she cannot believe they will ever come.

If only Lucy wasn't married. Michael could use a girl, a young girl who thinks like he does, who would calm him, make him forget his fear. There must be other young women around Englewood who could be interested in him, care for him. If only he would get a job or go to school —that's the way you meet people.

She sees a man coming down the street, walking with his head down, way in the distance—but she knows him. It is Michael. *Where's Dale?* She gets up, smooths her dress behind her, and moves down the steps toward the advancing shadow in the distance. He doesn't see her, and she wonders if he will look up before he gets to her. She stops walking and waits for him in front of the next-door driveway. He comes steadily, staring at the ground in front of him, his hands barely swinging by his sides. When he is only a few feet away, he stops and raises his head.

"Hello," he says.

"What are you doing? Where's your father?"

"He dropped me off along the beach. I wanted to see the water."

She moves toward him. "Have you been to see Kessler?"

"This afternoon."

"Is your father with Eddie?"

"I guess."

"What happened, son?"

"Nothing."

"What's wrong?"

"Kessler gave me a tape recorder, to use at home, and I lost it."

She takes his arm, and begins walking with him toward the black driveway in front of the house.

"Where did you leave it?"

"I set it down next to me—I was down by the sea wall—and I guess somebody took it."

They start up the rise of the driveway.

"Why did your father drop you off?"

"What?"

"I thought he—I thought he would—"

"I got scared on the boat."

"So he dropped you off—that's, that's—" She sees him looking at her so she stops. "I thought you two would stay together and we would go out to eat tonight."

"I'm not very hungry."

Inside the house she watches Michael rise up the stairs toward his room, as if he is leaving the earth. *Dale left him by the road and went on with his day.* She goes into the kitchen, looking for something to do. She cannot bear another night in this house, waiting for the sun to disappear out of the sky, waiting for the windows to go dark. *How could he do that, leave his own son next to the water, and go off to fill his day with events?*

She hears Michael stirring upstairs, hears his voice. She goes to the stairway and listens. *Is he crying?*

"Michael?"

She doesn't hear anything. The phone rings.

"Michael?" she calls, louder.

The phone rings again.

"Michael."

He comes to the top of the stairs, his face reddish in the last light peering around the corner of the world.

"Are you all right?"

"I lost the tape recorder."

"We can get you another one. All right?"

The phone continues to ring, seems to get louder and more insistent.

"Shouldn't you get that?" he says.

She walks to the phone, which hangs on the kitchen wall.

"Hello?" She hopes it is Dale.

"This is Lucy. What are you all doing for dinner?"

"I don't know, Dale's not home yet," she says, trying to sound polite.

"Why don't you come over here—my husband wants to meet you."

"Not tonight," Anne says. But she thinks of the quiet house and the darkening windows, and adds, "I'd love to, but I don't know when Dale will get home."

"You can come any time—Ben is a fabulous cook, and he can whip something up in a moment's notice."

"Let me call you—all right?"

"OK. 291-2125. Got that?"

"Maybe you better call me, I haven't got a pencil." Anne wonders how Lucy knew her number, but she is sure the question would be embarrassing.

"I'll call you back in one hour—and don't say no. OK?"

"All right," she says, but Lucy is already gone.

She hangs the phone up and goes back to the living room. Michael is sitting on the top step of the stairway, his hands under his chin.

"Want to go out to dinner?" she asks him.

"I'm not hungry."

She walks up the stairs, stands in front of him.

"I don't mean right now. A little later."

Michael raises his head, looks into her eyes.

"Please?" she says.

"I wish I hadn't lost that tape recorder. He just gave it to me."

"Michael, please don't worry about that."

"What will I tell him?"

"What difference does it make? We'll buy another new one to replace it."

She hears a car pulling up in the driveway outside.

"That's your father."

"Yes."

"Michael, will you go with me? Please?"

"I guess so." He lowers his head. She hears the kitchen door open.

"I'll let you know when we're leaving—I want to talk to your father for a little while first."

She leaves Michael still crouched on the steps and goes to the dining room quietly, listening to Dale singing in the kitchen.

When she enters the room, he stops and turns toward her unsteadily—a methodical gesture which tells her he has been drinking.

"What happened to you today?" She holds herself erect, her arms folded in front of her.

"Went fishing." He leans on the counter behind him, and raises his hand in a sloppy military salute. "Didn't catch a fucking thing."

"Michael is upstairs," she says. "He made it home, in case you were wondering."

"You got your arms folded, uh-oh. Bad news."

"Why did you leave him like that?"

Dale moves to the kitchen table and sits down, heavily, exhaling loudly as he settles. "Fish weren't biting today. Too much noise." He rubs his face with both hands.

"Why did you leave him?" Anne still stands by the door, and she sees Dale's head in front of the white windows as if it is a shadow reflected on a screen.

"He wanted me to."

"Tell me what happened." She moves to the table, stands next to him where he sits.

"He went loony again, in the boat. We had to quit and come in."

"And then?"

"On the way back, in the car, he said something about how bright the sun was and I had to let him out. He asked and I let him." Dale looks up at her now with watered eyes. "I'm drunk, but you'll have to understand, today was a defeat, and I'm not a good loser."

"You want me to feel sorry for you?"

"That'd be asking too much. Why don't you leave me alone?"

They know each other too well. She sees in his face that he will not listen to any words she can possibly say—that he knows she is angry, and that he doesn't care.

"I haven't got enough for you too," she says.

"Enough what? I don't want anything from you," he says, his eyes covered again with his hands. "But—" He takes his hands away, looks into her eyes, then turns away.

"But what?"

"Something's going to happen."

"What do you mean?"

"I've been thinking about him all day. Drinking with Eddie, then by myself in half a dozen bars, trying to avoid coming here—trying to avoid seeing Michael. He's a loner, Anne. One of those. He's been that way all his life. And he's going—"

"He's right upstairs. Not so loud."

"He's going to do one of those things loners do."

"I don't know what you're talking about."

"Assassinate a president. Axe-murder somebody—maybe a family or an old man on social security, or—"

"Stop it."

"Now who's loud?"

"Stop it. You're not making any sense."

Dale shrugs, raises his brows, and stares blankly at the opposite wall. As he talks his eyes don't seem to be alive—they are brilliant stones caught fast in a gray mold, and Anne can see he really means what he is saying. "He's not a mannequin—something's going on in his head. All the time. It probably reels with things. How long can he do that before he explodes?"

Anne sits across from him, tries to get in front of his eyes. "Do you really believe that?"

"Think about it. Today, we caught a fish and he was sitting there, wailing into the air like a trapped animal, a monkey, an ape in captivity crying for its babies. Eddie was staring at him—oh, Christ. It was horrible."

"What made him start that?"

"Eddie said something about the war—then Mike, he—" Dale puts hands up to his eyes again, and Anne sees the tears coming there, as if he brought them with his fingers. "What're we going to do, Anne? Huh?"

She reaches out, touches his arm.

"He's going to do something," Dale says. "I know it. I don't know how to stop it. What do we do?"

"Honey, you're being silly," Anne says. "Stop it now. You've been drinking, and it's got you thinking crazy."

"Michael's crazy."

"He's not right. He's had a terrible experience."

"What'd they do?"

"They hurt him."

"What'd they do, Anne? There's not a mark on him."

"You've got to stop it now. What if he comes in here?"

"They took advantage of his weaknesses, his—they took advantage of his weaknesses. That's how they do it—that's how, they get your head and twist it till you don't know who you are."

"Honey, please."

"It's like they knew us. Our family. Our lives. And—and they knew they could play on—they could take advantage of—"

"Now stop it." Anne reaches up, takes his hand away from his face.

"They could do a job on him, knowing us. Knowing by looking at him that we hadn't done something right—that we'd somehow, some-way messed him up, made him vulnerable."

"This is nothing but self-pity," Anne says. "You're feeling sorry for yourself."

"That's right, jump right in and make me feel better."

"It's not you that I'm worried about."

"Don't you understand?" he says, his voice rising. "I feel sorry for all of us!"

Anne takes her hand away, looks out the window. *He puts on this display, and what happened today—leaving Michael off on the road as if he were a hitchhiker, drinking all day—these things are naturally forgotten.* She can hear Dale breathing across from her, his hands in front of him now lying limp and pink on the blue tablecloth. She doesn't know what she should say, so she watches the sun lift the clouds on the horizon, turn them into a blue gray mountain landscape over the white sea. In the distance, gulls climb into the foothills and all the near pine trees have turned black.

"We're supposed to go out to eat," she says finally, not really wanting to go, but hating the idea of staying in the house with Dale while he slowly sobers up.

"What?" he says, his voice cracking.

"Lucy—a young girl who lives behind us—came to see me today, and she's invited us back there for dinner." Anne is conscious of Dale's head moving back and forth, slowly, but she still watches out the window. "You don't have to go if you don't want to but Michael said he would go, and I'm going."

"Michael said he'd go?"

"Yes. Do you want to go?"

"I don't want to go if you're going to be mad at me. I don't need that."

"I'm not mad at you anymore."

"Just bored and disappointed, right? No, thanks."

"You really don't give me much of a chance, you know that?" She is looking at him now. "Am I supposed to apologize to you?"

"Nobody has to apologize to anybody."

"If you say so."

"Shit."

"Are you going or not?"

"Why don't you go ahead and tell me what a bad boy I've been today? Isn't that what you want?"

"You shouldn't have left him there."

"He wanted to get out. What do you want me to do? Force him to stay with me? He's a man. A grown man."

"You could have stopped with him."

"He didn't want that."

"How do you know?"

"Ah, Anne—I was there today, you weren't."

"You shouldn't have done it. And you shouldn't have gotten drunk feeling sorry for yourself either." She gets up from the table and starts for the door. "I'm going to get Michael, and then we're leaving. If you want to go, fine. If not, there's crackers up there, and bologna and mayonnaise in the refrigerator."

"Is there any beer?"

She goes out without answering. When she gets to the bottom of the stairs she is almost afraid that Michael will be there, at the top, and that she will know by looking at him that he has heard them arguing. But the stairway is empty and dark. She goes up quietly to his room and knocks. Michael opens the door and she sees that he has been sitting in the dark.

"Ready to go?" she says.

"Is Dad mad at me?"

"No. Why do you ask?"

"He was mad at me today, I think."

"He thought you were mad at him."

"Is he here?"

"He's in the kitchen. Come on, let's go eat."

"I'm scared, Mom."

She puts her arm around his shoulders, feels the warmth of his living body, a body she had pictured lying in tall grass turning black in the sun, and she tries to hold him close to her, against her as she has done so many times in the circles of memory.

"Don't be afraid. Remember what I said to you last night? We're together, and as long as I'm with you it will be OK."

"I don't know what I should do."

"Just listen, talk if you want to, and have a nice time. These people are kind, and the girl is very young and pretty." They move down the stairs. Michael leans into her, and they step down each holding the other, as if they are descending into cold water. When they get to the kitchen Dale is still seated at the table, his head in his hands. He looks up and says hello to Michael. Anne stops, takes her arm from around her son and says, "Are you going?"

"Who are these people again?"

"Our neighbors, in the house behind us."

"You going over the fence?"

"Why not?"

"You going too, Michael?" Dale says, his voice cheerful and slightly dry.

Anne watches Michael's head turn toward Dale, a slow movement which betrays his fear.

"I guess so."

"Feeling better?" Dale says.

"He feels fine," Anne says. "Come on if you're going." She pulls Michael toward the door.

"I feel OK, Dad," he says as they go out.

XIII. DALE

Dale sits at the kitchen table, thinking, *The only thing worse than drinking alone in a bar is drinking alone at home.* It has been a curious day. One he will long remember. He cashed a check as soon as he left Eddie and went purposely to get himself good and drunk, a thing he rarely enjoyed. He was by himself, in a place called The Foxes and Hounds, drinking beer and thinking about his son, when a tall red-haired man, not much older than Michael, with one arm missing, and a tattoo of a seal with a ball on its nose on the other arm, walked up to him and said, "Hey, man, I need some money."

"Everybody needs money," Dale said. He didn't think he would have to talk to anyone, and it unnerved him to have to look at a man with one arm.

"Come on, buy me a drink and I'll tell you a joke. Make you laugh."

"I don't feel like laughing."

"It's good for you—makes you forget your problems."

"So does this." Dale held up his beer.

"Come on, man. Do me a favor, I'm a veteran."

The bartender came over and said, "This guy bothering you?"

"I guess not," Dale said. "Go ahead, tell the man what you want."

"A beer," the red-haired man said. He sat down on the stool next to Dale. "Thanks, man. I really got a thirst."

"You're a veteran of Viet Nam?"

"Where I lost this," he said, holding up the shortened and pinned sleeve.

"Must have been pretty bad." Dale wanted him to tell the story. He had been trying to dream Michael's experience since the first day of the boy's return, and here was someone with physical evidence of the war's possible wounds.

"I saw it fly up in the air. We got hit with mortar and I swear I thought that red arm flying up there in all that smoke was somebody else's. I didn't feel a thing."

The bartender brought the beer and the man took it in his hand, stared at it as if it might be the last cold drink of the condemned.

"Man, I'm thirsty." He raised the glass and drank the beer slowly.

"You like that stuff, don't you?"

"It's one of those times, man. You know what I mean?"

"You say it didn't hurt?"

"You know when you're real thirsty, and your mouth is so dry you could pull feathers out of it? A beer is real sweet then, man, and you got to drink it slow. This is one of those times." He raised the glass again.

"My son was in Viet Nam."

"You don't say—was he killed?"

"No, he's home."

"Good. That's where he belongs. It's where all the boys belong."

Dale looked at his watch about then, wondering about Anne and Michael. He left Eddie at least an hour before he came to The Foxes and Hounds and he had been drinking for some time before the red-haired man interrupted him. But he had no sense of the day, of where the sun was, or what the working world might be preparing for.

"Ready for the joke?" the red-haired man said.

"Tell me about Viet Nam. What do they do to prisoners?"

"It's not as bad as some of these guys now are trying to make it. We beat a few of them, but not very often. Just the ones that deserved it.

"No, not us—them. What do they do to our prisoners?"

"Your boy a prisoner?"

"Yes."

"How long?"

"Forty or fifty days. Not very long. He escaped."

"Brave kid."

"You don't know him. He's not brave at all."

"Got to be brave to get out of there alive—especially if he was captured."

Dale finished his drink and ordered another one. The red-haired veteran looked at him with pleading eyes, like a dog standing by a dinner table, and Dale thought it must have been a stare the man worked on in front of a mirror.

"You want another one?"

"Thanks, man—ask me anything you want."

When the beers came, Dale said, "So what do they do to captured soldiers?"

"I've heard lots of stories, man."

"Like what?"

"Like roasting guys on a spit—shoving a bamboo pole up your ass, and out your mouth and roasting you over a fire."

"What else? What do they do to men they don't kill?"

"Torture, you know. Beatings. Starving them. I don't know any more than you do—just rumors and all."

"Were any of your friends captured?"

"Shit, man. Everything happened to my friends."

"I wish I knew what happened to my son." Dale looked at the short sleeve, the pin. "He won't tell anybody."

"That's too bad. Maybe he doesn't want to think about it."

"But he does think about it—all the time. It's got him paralyzed."

"I had a friend who got that way about it."

"You did?"

"Yeah—real bad. He came home, you know, not really the same person. Real moody. He was in Na Trang and they got hit pretty hard, and a lot of his buddies got divided right next to him and he didn't even get a scratch. They sent him out again, into the bush and all, but he was ready for home, and they finally shipped him back and when he got here nobody knew him."

"Michael's a stranger." Dale felt a cold draft in his stomach, and he didn't want the man to go on.

"He moped around, in and out of jobs, dating one girl after another, then one day he went into a supermarket and grabbed a can of grapefruit juice and a bag of pistachios and walked up to his hotel room and started firing a pistol down on the street. Nobody knew where he got the gun, but he killed four people, and wounded a few others and then he—"

"Don't, I don't want to hear this."

The man took a sip of his beer, and stared at Dale apologetically. "I'm sorry, man. I guess you *don't* need to hear this."

"It's just that I don't know what's going to happen."

"Nobody ever does. It'll probably be all right. It takes time to get over something like that."

"If only I knew what 'that' was."

"You know, for months, after I lost this arm, it itched."

"Yeah, I've heard that happens."

"You talk about torture. There's nothing you can do. Nothing. There ain't nothing to scratch."

Dale finished his beer and pushed his glass down the bar.

"It still itches every now and then," the man said. He drank the last of his.

"Want another?"

"Sure. I ain't thirsty anymore, but I sure love the beverage."

Dale put a dollar on the bar and said, "I've got to be going, but go ahead and have another on me."

He went out into the street, his hands in his pockets, wondering if he should go home. The sun was hot, although it was beginning to sink, and people were leaving the shops along the street, heading for home before the traffic jams, all of them carrying packages, scurrying along the street as if they were trying to avoid being snatched by something hanging above them in the air.

He knew he could not go home, so he went to his car and locked it, then he went down the street toward the Holiday Inn thinking he would try the beer there. He could not get the words of the red-haired man out of his mind. Michael would explode, and kill someone. He read the articles about it as he walked along, the headlines bold and black, and Michael's picture suspended under them—a high-school picture, kind of blurry, with the eyes focused on something beyond the camera, something horrible. His father was a policeman, people will say. *That's the way it always is, the old man is a cop and the kid's a murderer. Cops are too mean with their kids.* And was he mean? What can a man expect of his son?

A car full of young girls passed, the laughter echoing along the street like the screams on an amusement-park ride. Dale walked past an old woman carrying a shopping bag, a man walking with a little boy, leaning down to hold his hand. The boy tried to keep up, his tiny feet stretching to match the steps of his father. "I can't keep up, Daddy." Dale watched the little boy, and remembered Michael's hand—how it felt when he was only three years old and he tried to keep up as they walked. It was so small that Dale couldn't tell it had fingers unless he held it up and looked at it.

He came to a corner and waited for the light to say "WALK," while Michael walked on up the street with his father. Dale watched them go, remembering all the cold mornings in Chicago, and the days with his son when there were expectations, and dreams, and they did not know war.

The light changed and Dale crossed the street with a crowd of people who had collected around him on the corner. He did not notice them until he was in the middle of the crossing, and he began looking around for another child. No one had children with them. He stopped and looked back over his shoulder for the little boy with his father, but he couldn't see them. He went on to the Holiday Inn, thinking about Michael's victims as he went.

And Anne.

When she thought Michael was dead she was no longer his wife. He meant nothing to her. He tried to help her bear it, thought they would bear it together. But she couldn't share anything with him, couldn't bring herself to go on with their private life—the exchanges they had perfected over the years which had brought relief and laughter and even joy. She would not talk about anything else but her son and where his body might be. And when Dale mentioned his work, or the weather, or the arrangements for Florida and a new life, he felt as if he had snatched a strange woman's purse and then tried to introduce himself.

When he got inside the bar he sat in a booth in the corner where it was dark. The waitress came over and he ordered a martini—deciding a beer was a beer, but he needed something stronger now. He had to figure out what to say to Anne. How to tell her about today, and about what he was afraid they were all headed for. The booth was comfortable, soft black leather, and there was a red candle on the table. He lit the candle and leaned back, waiting for his drink. Across the room was a group of men in shirt sleeves throwing darts at a small multicolored board, laughing and talking quietly, as if they were playing the game in church.

The waitress brought his martini, and asked if there would be anything else. "I wish I knew," he said.

"Pardon?"

"Nothing. That's all."

She left the check and went back to the bar, to sit and watch the game, no doubt. She was someone's daughter, untouched by anybody's war. Michael should have been a girl. This thought made him think of the woman in the store that morning, who pissed herself. She was Michael. She wailed in the same way, her eyes without life. Michael seemed to understand her, to comprehend a language which only puzzled everybody else. What a strange thing insanity is. The mind can convince you of anything, make you believe things only a comedy writer would think of. It is slapstick—dancing on water, hanging on a flagpole, suspended above the world no matter where the body positions itself. Fuzzy-haired victims shuffling around wearing white pajamas in a gleaming hospital corridor, wailing about shipwrecks, football games, weddings. Gray-skinned people talking to themselves, or to something in the air only they recognize—and nothing anyone can do to stop the drama going on inside, the theater of the skull where the audience is victim and actor all in one.

When he had finished his drink, he got up and went into the men's room. It gleamed in bright lights, like a hospital, and Dale stood in front of the mirror, staring into his eyes. He was beginning to feel the effects of his drinking so it was hard to look directly into his own eyes. He knew that eventually he would have to go home. But what would he say to Anne?

Two of the men who had been shooting darts came in, talking about skill and scoring, and one of them said, "I'd like to kill that son of a bitch."

The other laughed. "You just can't stand to lose."

"I'd like to kill him. The way he grins when he makes a shot. He's a bastard."

They each stood in front of a urinal.

"Fucking cock. That's what he is."

"We'll beat him sometime—then we can laugh."

"Houston. I wish he'd never come in here."

"He's got nothing better to do. He's one of those retired fools."

Retired fools. Dale finished and went to the blow dryer.

"I hear he's married to a young one. A good-looking chick."

"Well, one of these days, I'm going to kill that bastard."

Dale went out and back to his table. He put some money under the check, and went out into the street thinking about murder, and what makes it happen. Michael would explode and assassinate somebody, he was sure, but he didn't know what he or anyone else could do about it. How to make him come back to the world, before he took someone out of it.

When he got to his car he realized that he had come to know two things on this day: that Michael would kill someone before this was over, and that it had been a mistake to retire.

Yes, he thinks now, sitting in the quiet kitchen, *it's been a curious day.* The sky outside is white now, and against the black trees it reminds him of Illinois, and winter. His mouth is dry, and he wonders if he should go over the back fence and ask for a drink. Say hello to everybody and be there to explain Michael's behavior for Anne. He feels a vague ache in his stomach, a tremor of white fear, and he gets up, stands in front of the window watching the pine branches sway in the breeze. Outside, the world is going into its night paralysis, all the noises hushed by distance, and darkness, and closed windows. The refrigerator snicks on behind him, its motor whirring like water running in a drain. He thinks about all the automatic things in the world, the engines and motors which click on because of some change in the environment, or air pressure, or temperature. Like a brain, some elemental thing changes and it clicks on, or off: That's how a motor works. We learned the word "automatic" from nature and the seasons. Now everything works that way—half the time you don't even notice it. *And what can a man who has been a policeman for twenty years do?*

The phone rings, pricking the sense of fear in his stomach. He rushes to the wall, as if he has been waiting here all this time for the ringing to start.

"Dale, are you coming?" It's Anne, her voice toneless, almost disinterested.

"They force you to call me?"

"Sort of—yes."

"You want me to come?"

"If you want to."

"Do you *want* me to?"

"Are you coming or not?"

"How's Michael?"

"Well, he's not saying much, but he's doing all right."

"What do you mean? Is he relaxed, or scared?"

"He's just listening to us talk, that's all. He's fine."

"I don't know—should I come?"

After a pause, Anne says, "Let's not be silly, OK? I'm not mad at you anymore, and these people are very nice."

"I'm sorry, honey." Dale's throat begins to burn. "I guess I shouldn't have let him get to me today."

"Let's not talk about it. I've got to get back out there, Michael's all by himself with them, and you know how he likes to talk."

"Are you in the house?"

"No, I'm down the street in a phone booth. Of course, I'm in the house. Are you too drunk, dear?"

"No. I'm fine. I'm getting a headache, and I'm hungry."

"Come on over then."

"We've got to talk about Mike tonight. All right?"

"We'll see. Just come on. I'll meet you at the fence."

"I've got to take a shower first."

"Well, make it quick. They're holding dinner for you."

"What are they having?" he says, but Anne has hung the phone up. He stands there by the wall, listening to static in the line, and waits until the dial tone clicks in his ear.

XIV. MICHAEL

"I think that's the strangest thing," Lucy says. She sits across from me, in a lawn chair, her legs crossed. She holds a drink in her hand, and waves it at me. "I'm left-handed, but I can only dial the phone with my right hand."

"You can't dial a phone with your left hand?" Ben says.

"I can, but not as well."

"Well, you hold the phone with your left hand, so you're used to dialing with the right." Ben is next to her, in a lounger.

"I guess so."

They look at each other. Then back to me.

"Do you dial with the opposite hand?" She says.

"I don't know," I say.

Ben sips his drink, his eyes peering over the top of the glass at me.

"I like strange things like that," Lucy says. "Did you know that you always fold your arms the same way? I read it in a book about body language."

I wonder where my mother is. My hands are cold, and I feel the breezes circling around my head. I stare at my hands, then at my knees, so I won't have to look at Lucy and her husband.

"Do you like books?" she says.

"I used to. I haven't read one in a while."

She straightens in her chair, leans toward me. "I have lots of books if you want to borrow some."

Ben shifts in his lounger, crosses his legs in front of him, never taking his eyes off me. When he sees me looking at him, he says, "Sure you won't have a drink, old buddy?"

"I'm not much of a drinker anymore," I say.

"What sort of books do you like?"

I hate all her questions. She stares at me, her eyes so wide I don't know how they stay in her head. I see them drop into her lap, like eggs from a torn carton, and only the sockets there, facing me—and her husband embarrassedly picks them up, puts them back, saying, "Sorry, old buddy, this happens once in a while."

They look at each other. She says, "What sort of books do you like?"

"Where's my mother?"

"She went to call your old man," Ben says.

Just then my mother comes out of the house, quietly, as if she has stolen something. "He'll be over soon. He wants to take a shower."

"Good," Lucy says.

"I'll start the dinner then," Ben says, getting up out of the lounger. "Sit here."

"Want another drink?" Lucy says.

"Yes, I think I will. I need to catch up to that husband of mine."

Lucy stops in front of her; they look at each other as if one of them has stopped in mid-sentence. My mother says, "He had a few before he came home."

"Oh," Lucy says. "I heard that wrong. I thought you were running off somewhere after him."

I wonder how she could have thought that. My mother settles in the lounger, her eyes following Lucy as she crosses the patio toward the house. I don't know where to put my hands. My neck begins to ache, tired of holding my head up.

"Everything all right?" Mother says.

"Yes."

"Want to talk?"

"OK."

"Your father is coming after a while."

"I know." It's almost completely dark. My mother is a gray shadow lying across from me. If I look up I will discover if there is a moon.

"He's not mad at you, son."

"I ruined his fishing."

Ben comes out, the door slamming behind him. He crosses to the corner of the patio behind me and lights a Tiki light which rests on a pole there. "This'll give us some light, and keep the bugs away." He lights another at the other end of the patio, then goes back into the house.

"You sure you're OK, son?" My mother's face is a yellow mask with holes in it now, black holes, and nothing shining anywhere. "I wish we were back in Chicago, and it was 1968, and I didn't have to—" She stops, hearing Lucy coming out with her drink.

"There you go," Lucy says. She wears shorts, and I see a bruise on her upper thigh. In the light it looks like a hole in her leg. She sits in the chair, holding another drink for herself. Holding up her glass, she says, "My one and only vice."

"It's got impurities in it," Mother says. I can't tell if she is smiling or gritting her teeth. I hate the yellow light.

"You're not going to let me forget that, are you?" Lucy says, laughing. She looks at me. "I told your mother this morning that I didn't smoke because I like to keep my body pure." She laughs again. I look for the moon. The sky is dark blue, and there are clouds shifting in it like gray seaweed. Lucy talks to my mother now about what she has discovered about dialing the phone, and I search for the place where the moon hides. I cannot see a star anywhere. The horizon is still washed in weak light from the sun, but the moon hides.

"Michael?" Mother says.

"What?"

"Lucy asked you a question."

"Oh," I say. Lucy stares at me in the shadows of the yellow light.

"What kind of music do you like?"

"He always liked the Beatles," mother says.

"Oh, they're great," Lucy says, turning to Mother. I watch the tendon in her neck bulge. "I have all their albums. Ben hates for me to play them while he's home—he's not much for modern music—but I love to listen to their music while I'm cleaning house."

"I bet you play it very loud too," Mother says.

"As loud as I can." Lucy turns back to me. "What's your favorite album?"

A moth circles the Tiki light at the far end of the patio. It dives toward the flame, pulls up, banks around behind the bowl which holds the kerosene, and disappears somewhere in the night.

"Michael?" Mother says.

"What's your favorite album?" Lucy says again.

"I don't know. I don't think about that anymore."

"What do you think about?"

Mother sits up in the lounger. Lucy turns to her, a queer look on her face. "I'm sorry," she says. "I forgot." Mother nods her head, looks at me, as if she is waiting for something to happen.

"I'm all right, Mother."

"You don't like the Beatles anymore?" Lucy says.

"I haven't heard their last album. I liked the 'White Album.' "

"Me too. That's a great album."

"I don't listen to music anymore," I say.

"That's too bad. I don't listen as much as I'd like to."

Mother sits back in the lounger, looks over to the back door of the house. Ben comes out, holding a plate, and a long fork.

"How do you like your steaks?" he says.

"Medium rare," Mother says. "For all of us."

"Me too," Lucy says.

"I know how you like them," he says. He walks to an electric grill, and plugs it in to a socket on the outside of the house. He leans down and turns it on, adjusting the dial as if he is tuning a television. Above him is the Florida sky, turned nearly black, pestered slightly on its tattered edges by the Tiki lights. I can't see the clouds anymore, and the moon rises stealthily behind one of the houses. I will see it soon.

Ben comes over, pulling up another lawn chair.

"Everybody happy?" he says, sitting down. He struggles with the arms of the chair, as if they have volition and are trying to keep him from sitting. "Getting old," he says, looking at me with a smile on his face. His hair is gray and thin. He is lean, dressed in loose clothing. He reminds me of Eddie. He moves his arms as if they are an irritant, something he needs to shake off.

I watch the moth return to the Tiki light, drawn to it by something irresistible which resides in the tiny fibers of its brain. It does not recognize the shape of its own death.

"Don't you want something to drink?" Ben says.

"I'll have something with dinner," I say.

He looks beyond me and says, "There comes your father."

I hear the fence rattle. Mother gets up, goes past me, touching me on the arm. Lucy stares at me, her drink raised partway to her mouth.

"Just in time," Ben says.

"Really," Lucy answers.

Mother returns, holding to the arm of my father. He is shaved and clean, his hair shining in the Tiki lights.

"Ben Houston, this is my husband, Dale Sumner," Mother says. My father takes the old man's hand.

"Glad to meet you, what's for dinner?" He laughs, a signal that he is not serious. Ben chuckles, says, "Steak, and assorted vegetables." The moth rises up into the darkness, then dives for the flame, in a series of spiraling motions, as if it is tied to a string and buffeted by the wind. Each time it gets closer to the flame. I smell the charcoal in the grill heating up.

"Let me get you a chair," Ben says. He moves off the patio and into the dark on the other side of the lights. My father turns to me and smiles.

"How are you, son?"

"Fine. I'm fine."

"Hungry?"

"A little."

"I'm starving," he says.

"I'm Lucy." She rises out of the chair.

"Oh, I'm sorry," Mother says. "I forgot. I know you, and I didn't think."

"I'm Dale," my father says. They touch hands in front of me.

Ben comes back with another chair. "Sit here," he says. "What'll you have?"

"Whatever everybody else is having."

"Gin and tonic?"

"Fine."

Mother sits across from me again. Lucy settles into her chair, but my father stands in front of me, leans down, and says, "Everything's OK?"

"Yes," I say. But everything is not OK. It's not OK. There's no moon yet, only streetlights, and the neon shops in the distance. I want to see the moon. The Tiki lights waver in the breeze, seem to move the darkness up and down. My father sits in the chair next to me, touches my arm.

"Let's have a talk tomorrow, OK?"

"Sure."

"Are you retired too?" Lucy asks. Her drink is almost gone. A wisp of black hair falls over her brow.

"Yes. A long time ago, it seems."

"That's what Ben says. All he does anymore is ride around town and shoot darts with the boys."

"Darts?"

Ben comes out with two drinks, hands one to my father, and says, "Darts. It's one of my habits."

"Do you gamble?" Father says.

"Inveterately." Ben sits, struggling with the chair again.

"Were you at the Holiday Inn today?"

"He goes there all the time," Lucy says.

"I was there today," Father says. "Heard some men talking about you in the bathroom. Houston, right?"

"Right."

"Boy, were they mad at you." My father sips his drink, the ice cubes rattle. Beyond him, I see the moth tightening the circles around the flame.

"Sore losers."

"Ben takes their money."

"One of them said he wanted to kill you."

"They were pretty mad," Ben says. "They don't like an old man, who's supposed to be blind, beating them at a game like that. I've been shooting darts ever since I was ten years old. A long time. My father used to own a saloon, and he was pretty good at it too. We played a lot, after hours, and sometimes in the morning." A smile crosses the old man's face. "He was a good man."

"Where did you grow up?" Mother asks.

"A place that probably doesn't exist anymore."

"I hate it when you talk that way," Lucy says. Her drink is gone, but she holds the glass in her hand, twirling it, staring at it.

"It's true, love. I'm older than most of the buildings around here."

"Did you grow up in Florida?" Mother says.

"New York. Upstate. A little place called Albanact."

My father reaches up and touches the inside of his ear. "I lived in a city all my life. That's why I wanted to come here. We're from Chicago. And they got pretty cold winters up there." He lowers his arm, sips his drink. His face is yellow in the light, and the skin seems stretched and ruined—like leather that has gotten wet, then dried in the sun.

Lucy begins talking to my mother, a conversation I can't hear clearly. My father crosses his legs, says he is hungry. Ben puts his drink on the table, goes over to the grill, and puts the steaks on. The smell is moving with the smoke high over our heads, into the sky where there is no moon.

"Probably rain tomorrow," my father says. I don't know if he is talking to me or not. When I look at him, he is sipping his drink, staring across the patio at the smoke rising from the grill. Ben comes over and sits again.

"Better get the vegetables going," he says.

Lucy gets up and starts in front of me, looking at my mother. The bruise on Lucy's thigh seems darker, almost black, in the light. I can't take my eyes off it.

"Want some help?" Mother says.

They both move off into the house, and my father and Ben stare into the darkness beyond the lights. The steaks begin to sizzle. I think of the fire on my legs, the run to the beach, and the water. I feel my head beginning to move, as if there are hands on either side, pushing it back and forth, back and forth.

"You ever go fishing?" my father says.

"Occasionally. I prefer golf, if I can't find any victims on the dart board."

"You really make money at that?"

"Lots of it sometimes."

"Must be fun."

"It keeps me interested. I was a lawyer for forty years, and I was bored most of that time. All I wanted to do was goof off, take naps in the afternoon, and play darts whenever I wanted to."

"You don't mind not having anything to do?"

"But I do have something to do. Just what I want, whenever I want. This is the life."

"I thought it would be that way for me. But so far, it hasn't been."

"Want another drink?" Ben reaches for my father's glass.

When he is gone, my father says, "I've made a decision concerning you and me, Michael."

I hold my head still, look into his yellow face.

"I'm tired of sitting around and doing nothing," he says. "I'm tired of fishing because I think I'm supposed to have fun at it, instead of because I want to."

"You don't like to fish?" I say.

"It's all right once in a while. But not every day."

"What about Eddie?"

"We'll still fish now and then. I want to try to get a part-time job or something."

"You do?"

"And I'd like it if you'd go with me, try to find something too."

I hear laughter in the house, my mother's voice. "A job?" I say.

"Something to keep you busy. Keep your mind off—" He looks back to his hands, as if he expects to find his drink there.

When he raises his head to see what I will do, I look for the moth.

"You know what I mean," he says.

I don't see the moth, just the wavering flame, the black smoke. I smell the steaks burning over the hot coals, hear them crackling, and I feel the hands on my head again—cold hands, softly covering the top of my skull.

"Where'd you go today?"

"I went walking along the beach."

"Where else?"

"To Kessler's."

"Did you talk?"

"Where's the moon, Dad?"

"What?"

"Where's the moon? I don't see it."

"Maybe there isn't one."

"I know there is."

"What's so important about the moon?"

"I want to see it."

"Why?"

"I don't know. It seems important."

"What did you talk to Kessler about?"

"He gave me a tape recorder to talk into at home."

"Are you going to?"

"I lost it." A breeze rises up behind me, pushes the smoke up over the house.

"How?"

"I don't know."

"Try to remember." He leans toward me, his head tilted as if he is holding a phone on his shoulder.

"I sat down in the grove for a while. Then I went up to the end of the street, out to the highway." Another burst of laughter inside the house; Ben pushes open the back door, starts to come out, then changes his mind. The door slams. "I walked along the interstate a few miles, then back toward the ocean. I like the water. I didn't think about the tape recorder until I was on the way home."

My father leans back in his chair. "I don't know, Michael," he sighs. "I swear I just don't know."

"I didn't mean to lose it."

Ben comes back out, gives my father his drink. Standing in the light he seems to lean like a tombstone.

"Dinner is almost ready. Want to eat out here or in the house?"

"Whatever," my father says.

"What about you?" Ben says to me.

"I don't care. I wanted to see the moon, but it's not up there."

"Sure it is. Look behind you. It's hiding behind those pine trees in your side yard." It is there, a white circle with a thousand black fingers crossing through it.

"There it is, Dad. There's the moon."

"I see it."

"So you want to eat out here then?" Ben says.

"I don't care," I say. "I just wanted to see it. That's all."

"Shall we go inside then?" Ben moves toward the door.

"We'll be right in," my father says.

I get up, my legs feeling like electric wires, and my father rises next to me, putting his hand on my shoulder.

"Son, don't do anything foolish in there."

"I'm all right," I say. "I'm not thinking about anything."

We walk together into the bright house.

XV. DALE

"I've been drunk before," he says, leaning back on the bed. He supports himself with his elbows, and Anne pulls his shoes and socks off.

"Where's Michael?"

Anne pulls at his pants. "He went to bed. And so are you."

"They're nice people." His head feels weak and constrained by air —as if he is trapped in a tire, all rolled up and forced to breathe.

"You had fun."

"Nice people."

Anne unbuttons his shirt, pulls the sleeves down his arms. "Sit up now," she says. He leans forward, against her breast. He hears the air going in and out of her, while she removes his shirt.

"Going to get a job."

"You are?" She lays him down on the bed, reaches for the lamp.

"Michael too."

"What?"

"Mike and I are going to look for a job." Anne still holds the lamp, her hand relaxed and seeming to rest there on the neck, as if it is a body she touches.

"When was this decided?"

"Tonight at dinner. Gonna get a job."

"Michael said he was going to get a—he's going with you?"

"Maybe we'll work together. Sumner and Son."

"You *are* drunk." She turns off the lamp. "Go to sleep." She leans down, a shadow, and kisses him on the forehead.

"Where're you going?"

"I'm going to read for a while." She is still leaning over him.

He feels the bed beginning to rise up, and whirl.

"Come to bed." He reaches for her, takes her arms.

"Don't."

"What's the matter?"

"Let go. You're drunk."

"Aren't you?"

"I'm not that drunk." She pulls away.

"Gotta be real drunk to roll in the sack with old man Sumner." He tries to sit up, falls back on the pillow.

"I didn't mean it that way." She moves toward the long shaft of yellow light at the door.

"You look like a painting," he says.

"Were you serious? About Michael?"

"And me. I'm going to get one, too."

"He said he would go with you?" She stands in the light, only a black figurine.

"Come here."

She moves back to the side of the bed, but she stands too far away. He can't reach her. "What?"

"Come here."

"I don't trust you."

He takes a deep breath, lets it out slowly.

"Well?" she says.

"When was the last time we made love?"

"When you were drunk? Or sober?"

"That's not fair. I almost never get drunk, and you know it."

"But whenever you do, you always reach for me."

"I'm an affectionate drunk," he says, rolling his head back and forth on the pillow. "And you're a cold bitch."

"Good night," she says, turning for the door.

"Wait." He sits up, with some effort, as if his arms won't stiffen enough to hold him.

"Go to sleep."

"I want to talk."

"I'm listening."

"Come over here where I can see you."

"Let's talk tomorrow."

"I can't tomorrow."

"Why?"

"I'm going fishing with Eddie."

"I thought you were going to look for a job with Mike." She leans now on one leg, her hands on her hips, a dark lovely shadow.

"I am. I really am."

"And fishing too." Her head moves to the side, and he can see in his memory the expression on her face.

"I told Eddie I would go with him. Don't worry. I'll take Michael."

"Not on the boat."

"No. We'll go down to the sea wall."

"Are you going to leave him there?"

He falls back to the bed. "It's no use," he says. "You've booked today in your catalogue of Sumner crimes, and I'll be hearing references to it until you find one you can file in front of it."

"Good night." She walks into the light, drawing it out of the room with her. The bed moves slowly around the room, in tight circles. The sound of his breathing keeps him awake, although he is not conscious of anything but the bed.

"I said I was sorry, goddamn it." He hears the voice, and knows what he said almost minutes after the sound of it passes him. He thinks of the dinner, the drinks and talk afterward, Michael sitting in one of the wooden chairs off to the side, staring at the books which lined the walls. Lucy talking about body language and premarital sex. Ben and his darts. Money. The price of everything. Television commercials, the moon landing. The miracle of Ben Houston, who saved Lucy from the clutches of mean divorce. Anne watching Michael, as if she thought he might suddenly begin to bleed there on the Oriental rug. *Excuse me, I've got to stop this blood flow. Go on, I'm listening. Stand back. Don't do that, honey.*

Steak's just right. The forks click on plates, everybody chewing. Michael's mouth opening and closing, moving to chew as if he is afraid his teeth will break. *Aren't you hungry, son? Steak's just right. I love charcoal-broiled steaks. There's the moon, Dad. I just wanted to see it. He's a shy one, isn't he? Not right. Not right.* He thinks he's a prisoner of war. *One day he went into a supermarket and grabbed a can of grapefruit juice and a bag of pistachios and walked up to his hotel room and started firing a pistol down on the street. Nobody knew where he got the gun. It's not his fault.* Torture. *They did something to him. An Oriental rug under Michael's feet. No No No. Where's the moon? I just want to see it. Your steak too done, Michael? Don't force him to eat. If he doesn't want it. Let's go into the den and have a few drinks. He killed four people, and wounded a few others. Excuse me, he's bleeding again. That's an expensive rug, try not to get any blood on it. He's going to do something. He's going to do something. He's going to do something.*

PART
TWO

I. MICHAEL

I have to get rid of the beads of water on the window. I see a gray pane when I open the one eye not buried in my pillow, and beads of water moving like stealthy insects close me in. Cars sizzle on the black streets outside, and the window is covered with water, beads of water. It is quiet except for the cars.

I hate the water, the rain. The incessant falling of it. The color gone from the universe, and puddles everywhere. I can't see out the window, I can't see the pine trees, and the roofs of the houses.

I close my eyes, try to remember the sun, the heat. My father walks past my door and goes into the bathroom. I heard him talking this morning before I opened my eyes. He's out there, waiting for me.

I get out of bed and raise the window, then I search the room for a rag, something to wipe the beads of water away. I hear my father come out of the bathroom, the water running in there, and I take the pillowcase off one of the pillows on the bed. I reach out and wipe the water away, stretching to reach the top pane. The pillowcase won't absorb the beads —it only makes them smaller and forms them into thin lines. I go to the bureau and take out one of my undershirts. It works better, the glass begins to squeak with each rub. The rain is thin and cold on my hand. When I take the undershirt away I notice tiny beads beginning to grow back. I sit there, holding the shirt, watching the water build up on the window, and I know I won't be able to get it clear and keep it that way. It feels good to have the water gone for even a little while, so I start wiping it again. The second time I clear it the shirt begins to feel cold. There are thousands of water beads in it, and if I wipe long enough, they will begin to escape. I hate this sort of problem. There's nothing I can do but get another shirt and keep at it, but I know it's no use.

"Michael?" my father says through the door.

"I'm up," I say.

"Can I come in?" He opens the door with this. I'm still sitting on the sill.

"What are you doing?" A smile leaves his face.

"Just sitting here."

"Why is the window open?"

"I'm trying to wipe the water off the windows." His mouth opens, slightly. "I don't like the water," I say.

"Well, get dressed, we're going job hunting."

"I don't want to go out today."

"Get dressed." He says this in a quiet flat voice. He leans toward me, wearing a burgundy robe which hangs open in front of him.

"I'd rather stay here, Dad."

He turns toward the door, talks to the frame, the walls. "Well, we're going out to find work. For both of us. I won't listen to any lazy tales about how you want to lay around here."

"I don't like the rain."

"You're sitting there with the window open, getting soaking wet." He raises his head to the ceiling, tilts it to the side. I wonder where his eyes are. "Get dressed and come downstairs." He walks out, leaves the door open.

I start to get dressed. I have a pair of Levi's on when he comes back into the room.

"You going to try to find a job dressed like that?"

"I guess not."

He comes toward me, holding a handful of ties. "Pick one." He smiles, holding his arm out for me.

"I have the one you gave me the other day."

"Pick one. That other is too old and frayed. Pick a good one." His stomach bulges through the robe. He smiles at his arm, his mouth open so I can see his bottom teeth, his tongue. "How about this one?" he says, holding it up to the gray light.

"OK."

"Sure?"

"Yes."

He looks around the room. "Let's see what you're going to wear."

"I don't know yet."

"Well, how can you pick a tie? Come on, son."

"I'll wear something to match the tie."

He goes over to the closet, roots in among the clothing in there. Pulls out a brown suit.

"How long since you've worn this?"

"I was just out of high school." I wish he would leave the room, go away. Water builds up on the windows, I hear the rain hitting hard now.

"We'll brush it off and it'll be fine." He comes toward me.

"OK," I say to his hand as it rises to my shoulder.

"Now put this on, and come on down to breakfast."

"I will."

He turns to leave. "Eggs?"

"Yes."

"Don't be too long."

I pull off the Levi's, take the suit off its hanger, and place it neatly on the bed. I put on a white shirt, with little buttons on the collar, and then the suit, its cold wrinkles touching the hair on my legs.

My mother comes to the door. Her hair falls dully into her eyes, and she holds her white satin robe closed in front of her with a small fist.

"Why is the window open?"

"I'll close it."

"Where's your father?"

"He went downstairs."

"You look nice." She smiles. "Where are you going?"

"Dad wants me to go with him."

"Oh," she says. Her voice is a different note of music.

I pick up the tie, put it around my neck.

"Want help with that?" she says.

"I can do it."

"Do you really want to go?"

"He wants me to."

She comes into the room, stands in front of me; the satin wrinkles in the robe make gray arrows which seem to emanate from her small hand.

"Michael, if you don't want to go, tell him."

"I can't. He wants me to go."

"Why can't you tell him?" I can see the window in her eyes, and I remember the water, the beads of water.

"I don't want to hurt him."

"Really?"

"I'm afraid to tell him."

"You want me to tell him?"

"No. I'll go. It doesn't make any difference. The water can't hurt me."

"What?"

"Nothing. I'll go."

She puts her hand on my arm. "Are you all right?"

"I'm fine." I watch her eyes, a slight twitch in them when she starts to turn away, then focuses on me again.

"Sure?"

"I'm getting dressed."

My father calls from the bottom of the stairs, "Michael, I've got the newspaper. Come on down." The hand squeezes my arm, and my mother leans over and kisses me.

"Be careful today," she says.

"OK."

"I love you." She backs away, still looking into my eyes.

"You too," I say.

She closes the door, and I get another undershirt out of the drawer, go to the window and clean it one more time. But the rain is hard now, and I only get my hand wet. I throw the undershirt on the bed and close the window. Across the hall in the bathroom I watch my eyes while I brush my teeth. The water in the sink glistens, and the toothpaste drips out of the corners of my mouth. I look like a wild dog.

"Michael?" my father calls again. "Hurry up. We don't want to get a late start."

I look at my teeth. They're getting harder and harder. In the jungle they felt like rubber in my mouth.

"Michael?"

"I'm coming."

I dry my face and go downstairs. The living room is brighter because of the picture window. I feel clean, and the water on the big window in the living room keeps running down, washing in streaks toward the sill. When I get to the kitchen my father turns around, spreads his arms. "Behold the young executive." He stands in front of the stove, the eggs bubbling in grease behind him.

"I'd rather have poached eggs."

"Ah, you can eat them this way." He drops his hands, smiles apologetically.

"I don't like them in grease."

"They won't be in grease. I'll put them in a napkin first. Don't be so picky." His voice is playful, the way it was when I was a boy and he wanted to tell me he was sorry for something.

"OK."

He turns to the stove. "Picky picky picky."

I go to the table and sit down, stare at the tablecloth.

"Your mother up yet?"

"Yes." I put my hand up to my face, feel the whiskers there. "I should shave."

"After breakfast, while I'm dressing." He takes a limp white piece of plastic out of the pan and puts it on a paper plate. "Now, where's a napkin?" He comes to the cabinet next to my head. "Watch out."

"I already brushed my teeth."

"Good." He moves back to the counter by the stove, his feet shuffling on the tile floor—a sound like short bursts of air escaping from a rubber ball.

"I can't eat breakfast."

"Sure you can," he says picking up the plate. He comes over to the table bearing the egg covered by the napkin, as if it is a dead bird he has found in the yard and wants to show to me. Near the table, he staggers slightly. "I drank too much last night."

He shuffles around the kitchen collecting toast, a knife and fork, another napkin.

"I've made up my mind about something, Michael," he says after he has arranged everything in front of me. "We're going to be friends again."

"I can't eat breakfast, Dad," I say without looking at him. He stands next to me, breathing quietly, his hands on his hips. The smell of the egg frightens me, makes me feel the air again in my veins.

"How about poached?" he says finally. "I'll poach a couple of eggs for you. I should have known better than to—"

"Let's just go." I'll do anything to get away from that egg, even rush the time when we'll have to go out into the rain. I'll have to go out in rain again.

"You want to go, then?"

"Yes. I'll go up and shave and you get dressed. We'll go now."

"OK. Whatever you say. Whatever you say." He turns and walks out of the kitchen. He stops in the dining room, I see the shadow of his body on the wall. "You glance at the newspaper when you finish shaving. I shouldn't be long."

I follow him upstairs and watch him slip quietly into his room. He seems excited, so of course I have to go. I want to hide in my room, crawl into some quiet space there and be invisible for a while. The window in my room is running with water now. I sit on the bed and try to remember why I came up here. To float into the air and coil up in one of the corners like a cobweb. The room is gray, and there are shadows on the walls. It's not my room. I dreamt of my room for so long, any other room is still foreign. But this is my bed, the one I always had. I lie back, rest my head on the pillow, the bare pillow. I stare at the ceiling and try to think of something other than the water on the windows, and suddenly I remember the tape recorder, and Kessler's face when he gave it to me. I want to talk to the tape recorder now. I wish I hadn't lost it. I wish it was here now so I could talk into it. I feel peculiar today. I feel like someone else. I want to stand back and look at myself. The rain keeps hitting the window. Really, what is there to be afraid of? This is my father's house. House. Florida. I couldn't believe I had to come here, that they'd moved here while I was. . . .

. . . I'm so afraid even underwater I can feel the sweat on my white hands. I can't see anything. Everything is green and moving. I feel grass, and sand. I want to hide under some reeds which brush my face. My lungs are shrinking inside, shrinking, shrinking. I can't breathe. I'm in the water, in the water, and it's ice-cold. I feel something on my collar. It gets tight around my throat and suddenly the water is gone, I'm in the air. The ground comes up at me, water runs down my face, drips into the white dirt. Shadows are all around me. I crawl along the ground, try to get out of there, back to the water. I am a little boy trying to get away from my father. I crawl toward blindness and one of the high shadows kicks me. The noise I make surprises me. I fall forward on my stomach. I'm going to be shot. Something hits—on the back of my head, so hard I don't feel anything. "Dad!" I say. They move around and hit again. The world withdraws all of its light, and then I don't feel anything. I hear the sound I make echoing down into the center of something long and black. I'm inside a cold throat of some kind. The thing keeps drinking water. I'm going to drown. The water washes over me, I feel myself falling, being thrown down away from air and light. I can't hold onto anything. I scream but there is no sound. I hit something, at the bottom of a long fall, and then I'm on sand again, lying in front of a great fish. It has a human face, especially its mouth, and long sharp fins attached almost at the jaws. I feel as if he has vomited me out on the sand. He leers at me. His eyes flash like strobe lights, blue strobe lights. I lie on hard sand, where grass pokes through in weak little clumps. The face stares at me as if I am some rotting dead thing. My hands and feet begin to bleed. I leak out all over the sand. I hear my father calling me. I know I have to go home. I am beginning to cry. He calls me. He comes for me. I want to find him. He comes over a dune, behind the fish. He is on all fours, sniffing along the ground like a dog. I scream. He comes down to me, puts his hands on my face. I am crying. He tries to pry open my mouth. He has hold of my jaws, his hands wet and cold. He pulls the skin away from my teeth, screaming at me in a language I can't understand. He grunts and snorts and I beg him to save me. Save me. Then something comes down from above us—a blanket of some kind, a cover, and it blots out sound. It is totally dark. I feel my father's breathing. He whispers something to me. "Don't move now. We've got them. Don't move now." He has hold of me and I feel his heart beating and I know he will take me home. I hear voices, and my father begins to evaporate in front of me. I scream for him. The world lights up, and I am hanging upside down from a bamboo pole. My head drags in the tall grass. . . .

"What are you doing?" My father stands over the bed.

"Nothing."

"What's the matter, son?"

"Nothing. I'm all right. I was just remembering something."

"You were thinking about it again, weren't you?" He smells of Old Spice cologne, his face neat and smooth. There is a tie around his throat, pulled tight.

"I guess I was."

"Want to tell me about it?"

"I was remembering what it was like when they captured me."

"And?"

"They hit me with something and I dreamed about you."

He smiles, comes to the edge of the bed. "About me? You thought about your old man in that horrible situation?"

"I dreamed that you tried to save me."

"I would have, too, if I could."

"I wish you had."

"Take it easy." He puts his arm around me, his coat rustling like leaves on a tree.

"I gotta shave now."

"You didn't shave yet?"

"I forgot. I came up here and I couldn't remember what for. So I started thinking." My hands fumble together in my lap.

"Well, go shave, and let's be on our way." He rises up next to me, his head tilting to the side. "OK?"

"All right."

"I'll go find out where we should start." He goes out of the room, but the Old Spice remains. I go to the window. The rain has let up a bit, and I can see the house next door, the black driveway. A cat scurries along by the fence between the houses, trying to dodge the rain. His coat sticks out like white fishbones.

"What do you see?" My mother comes up behind me. She has dressed, and her hair is pushed back in neat swirls.

"A cat."

"Where?" She leans toward the window, peeking over my shoulder.

"He's gone now," I say.

II. ANNE

"Where were you?" Lucy says. "I let it ring ten times."

"I was asleep," Anne says. She holds the phone on her shoulders, trying to light a cigarette.

"I almost gave up."

"It's a habit I've gotten into. Since we moved here. I stay up very late at night, usually."

Lucy makes a sound in the phone, a clicking of the tongue perhaps. "Well, let's do something today."

"I don't know. I'm not really in the mood for rain."

"It'll be fun. Come on."

"What do you want to do?"

"Let's go shopping."

Anne thinks of a tape recorder for Michael, and says, "All right, give me a few minutes."

"Half an hour. I'll pick you up." The phone clicks. No one says good-bye anymore, the sudden break in the connection like losing consciousness.

She goes to her room and puts on a blue print dress and a pair of black low-cut shoes. She stands in front of the mirror, examining her figure. She is still very slim and she derives a sense of pride from the smooth fit of her clothes, the line of shoulders and hips. The light from the gray windows behind her seems to wash through the dress so she can see the outline of her legs. In a year she will be fifty, and she is already in Florida waiting for the end, the way her parents did, and Dale's parents, and everybody's parents she has ever known. Why do people come here? There is nothing to do in the sun but pretend to be free; and when it rains? What do the old people do when it rains? So they are going to look for a job—Dale wants to work, and he thinks that is what Michael needs. But he doesn't need work, he needs people—his own people, and friends, and something to look forward to. Through everything, he must be loved.

Dale went out the door this morning, smiling, balancing two cups of coffee in the rain, and Anne went back to bed. She thought about Michael the boy, the child—the numberless days of life in Chicago, all the early mornings, the play, the laughter. Michael running through their apartment screaming, Dale growling behind him, a monster, pretending to give chase, almost catching up. The calm moments of holding, explaining the world, holding the boy's small hands. The nightmares—his crying out loud in the night—then quiet, sniffling in her arms, his small head on her breast, his voice young and afraid, so new in the dark, so completely new in the world, saying, "The bird was chasing me." She whispering, "You OK now?" And Michael's thin voice, "I'm OK."

She remembers a dream she had when Michael was nearing his fifth birthday. She was fighting in the dream, against the building of some highway. She was the leader of a group that seemed to want to get in the road, stop traffic. There was no logic in the dream. Traffic crowded the road and yet she whirled her arms there to stop the burly construction workers from building it. One of them said, "What do you want to stop the road for, lady? There's already traffic on it." She saw the cars, saw them rolling by without drivers. One of them screeched, a loud scream of tires, just as she told the man, "Well, I'm going to stop it." She turned and saw a crowd of people standing around the front of a stopped car. It was quiet suddenly, and she thought about being the leader of all those people, not letting the cars pass, and Michael came into her mind. He was at her side in the beginning of the dream, although she didn't remember it. It was one of those tricks dreams play on you: a shift in plot near the end which imposes a condition or event which did not exist in the beginning—except when the shift occurs the event is real and does exist. She thought about Michael. "Where is he?" Then she knew a child had been stricken by the car, had fallen under the wheels. The crowd shuffled around in front of the car, talking quietly. One of them said, "You'll be all right, honey," and there was Michael, under the front of the car, his legs flat and surrounded by yellow fluid. Someone propped him up, holding his head off the asphalt, and he had a faint smile on his face: a smile she knew in the valves of her heart. She screamed. She let out words she could not remember, seeing him there before her helpless eyes, smiling for her. She ran to him, tried to touch him, and then she woke up with his smile in her eyes. She did not move for a moment, out of breath and frightened in the terrific darkness. Dale slept next to her. She heard the whirring of the fans, the cars moving outside her window. She got up, crept into Michael's room. She stared at him all curled up in the sheets. "Alive," she said. Then she reached down and picked him up. He came awake slowly, his head resting in the crook of her shoulder. "Wake up," she said, crying. "I've had a bad dream, a bad dream." Gradually he became aware of her, hugged her with his miniature hands. She listened to his breathing, saw the smile of the trapped child in the dream, and sobbing quietly, she said, "See? I have bad dreams too. I have bad dreams too." She rocked him. Then she sat down on his bed, tried to look into his blinking eyes.

"Son?" she said, tears filling her throat. "Don't ever go out into the street unless you're holding my hand. OK?"

"OK," he said.

"Promise?"

"I promise."

She held him against her, held the time with him in her memory, forever. That time, that quiet time, and he was holding on, alive in her arms, holding on, holding on.

"Ready to go?" Lucy says.

"You want some coffee first?" Anne holds the door half open, peering at Lucy who stands on the front porch dressed in a white raincoat, Levi's, and a pair of blue tennis shoes.

"Let's have coffee in the mall," Lucy says.

They rush to the car in the light rain. The air is blue with water, as if the sun leaked all the moisture, and the rain makes circles on the hard surfaces of the earth.

"You look nice," Lucy says, when they are in the car.

"What is this?"

"It's a Buick."

"This is like a throne."

"Ben likes big cars." Lucy turns the key, the engine whines like a blender.

"Can you control this thing?"

"I can barely see over the steering wheel, but I'll manage."

The car moves along the main road toward the highway. Anne studies the black pine trees along the street, thinks of all the green needles, needles like frozen grass on each branch. They never fall, completely—the trees are never bare. Yet all the yards fill with white needles every year, and no one seems to do anything but complain about these terrible pine trees. They write articles in the newspapers about it, as if the needles are one of the curses, one of the enemies.

When they reach the highway, Lucy slows the car and turns to look for traffic on her left. "How's Michael?" she asks, weaving her head back and forth in front of the window.

"He's better."

"He *is* a quiet one."

"He was always that way. But since—well, he's been hard to know, lately. Since the war."

Lucy eases the car onto the highway, cars roaring by them in the next lane. The windshield wipers slap back and forth in front of them. "I wonder if we will ever get out of that business over there," she says. She studies the road in front of her with head held high, her chin turned up, a serious look on her face—the kind of look young people get when playing their music, or pinball machines, or any of the other devices which create noise, confusion.

"*We're* out of it—we've got Michael home. That's all I care about right now," Anne says.

"There are people just like you who still have sons over there. Don't you feel sorry for them?"

"There isn't anything I can do about that."

"You could carry a sign."

"I have enough to carry, worrying about Michael."

"I felt so sorry for him last night."

Anne straightens her dress, settles back in the seat to watch the windshield wipers. "He was all right. He enjoyed himself."

"I could see he wasn't very happy."

"No. I guess he's not."

"Ben didn't like him very much at all."

This must be part of being pure—honesty, even if it creates awkwardness, even if it hurts. "Did you tell him what happened to him?" Anne says.

"Ben's not—he's not really very sympathetic toward other people," Lucy says, her voice taking on the tone of a nurse, or librarian. "He thinks Mike is silly. He said what happened to him happened to a lot of other boys too."

Anne stares out at the passing road signs, the way they grow from tiny shadows in the distance into great metal squares announcing the green miles to other places, pointing with thick white arrows the way to Tampa, or Pensacola, or some street named for one of the other war veterans in the story of the earth.

"What would we have done without the Indians?"

Lucy turns her head, looks into Anne's eyes, then back to the road. "What?"

"What would we have done? I mean how would we know the way to Tampa if we couldn't put arrows on all our signs?"

Lucy laughs. "You know, that's interesting. I wonder what we would use?"

"Rifles?"

"Oh, but the English used arrows—didn't you ever see *Robin Hood?*"

"Everybody used arrows, I guess. Read the *Iliad.*"

"What's that?"

"A book. About war."

"I don't like war stories. I don't like war."

"War. It's such a peaceful sounding word. It ought to describe ripples in water or something."

"I like talking to older people like you," Lucy says, smiling at the windshield wipers and the road beyond.

Anne wishes for a cigarette, but she doesn't want to smoke up the car, steam the windows. She thinks of the words "older person" and watches the way the water forms on the windows, swept away by the wipers before the completion of any design.

After a long silence, Lucy says, "Have you ever been to this place?"

"Once, and it should have been spelled m-a-*u*-l. I've never seen such a crowd."

"Not even in Chicago?"

"Not anywhere."

"Maybe it was the opening or something. It hasn't been there too long."

"I didn't pay much attention. I went shortly after we moved in. I wasn't looking for anything. I was just spending some time."

"Well," Lucy says, looking at her again, "it probably won't be too bad now. We're lucky, and we're early."

"You feel lucky?"

"Sure. Don't you?"

"I don't know. Sometimes I do."

"I feel lucky all the time."

And pure. Lucky and pure, such a perfect combination for a young body. "I want to look at tape recorders," Anne says, after a pause.

"What do you want a tape recorder for?"

"It's for my son."

"A gift?"

"Sort of."

"Is Michael all right?"

Anne turns to see Lucy staring at her. "What do you mean?"

Lucy moves her eyes back to the road, holding the steering wheel in her delicate, pure hands. "I mean, is he—you know, safe?"

"Safe?"

"Well, Ben says sometimes men who are unstable do crazy things."

"You mean hurt somebody."

"Yes."

"You don't have to worry about him," Anne says, slowly and evenly.

"Oh, I'm not worried."

"I'm sorry, but Ben doesn't know what he's talking about."

"I've made you angry."

Anne turns her body, faces Lucy. "You have a way of saying things you shouldn't. You talk about people in their presence, as if you needed to make some commentary about personal relationships to some sort of listening audience. You can't distinguish between the things people talk about and the things they're only allowed to think, or say to someone else when the party in question isn't present."

"I'm sorry."

"You can tell anyone else that your husband didn't like Michael, or that he's worried Michael will brain somebody—but you can't say that to me without hurting me, without causing—"

"Shouldn't I be honest?" Lucy holds the wheel in two hands, frowning at the road as if holding the wheel causes her pain.

"There's a difference between honesty and simple rudeness."

"I didn't mean to offend you. I'm sorry, really."

"Really," Anne says in the same tone of voice Lucy uses when she says that word.

"I *am* sorry, Anne. Please forgive me."

"I know you don't mean it. I know."

"I've just always tried to be as honest as I can with people. Especially people I like."

"Those are the people you probably should never be completely honest with," Anne says, thinking of the times she has wished that Michael had remained dead, the times she has recognized that thought as if it were an insect in her food.

"What's wrong with your son, Anne?"

"He's just afraid of—he's afraid of things. I'm not quite sure."

"He doesn't talk to you about it?"

"Sometimes. I don't understand it fully. He's told me things that don't make any sense. He hates the rain, but he wants to—he likes being in the water, the ocean."

"He does? Does he swim very often?"

"No. I'm not talking about swimming. He told me that once when he had an episode of fear, he ran into the water, that he felt peaceful there. This morning, he was afraid of the rain."

"God," Lucy says. A truck passes, throwing water onto the windshield.

"Where is this place anyway? I don't remember it being so far."

"The exit's right up here."

Anne smoothes her dress. "I could sure use that coffee," she says.

"Maybe I could help him," Lucy says.

"He's got plenty of help."

"Sometimes it helps to have a younger person to talk to," Lucy says, a wide smile on her small white face. She steers the car up the ramp, and to the left where the mall entrance looms in the blue rain like a primitive shrine. "Ben says I should stay away from Michael," she says, turning the car into a parking space; the power steering screams like a trapped child. "But I'm not going to. I can help."

"I'm not sure anyone can help him," Anne says, getting out of the car.

The rain is thin. Anne puts her hand up to her forehead and walks toward the entrance to the mall, leaning forward in the steady breezes as if the rain has force, resistance. Lucy moves next to her, a gray shadow in the whiteness of the air.

When they are inside, Lucy brushes the water off her coat, shakes her head to throw the rain out. Anne takes off her scarf, a red bandanna she collected years ago and found in a drawer this morning.

"Is he getting professional help?" Lucy asks.

"Yes. Where's the coffee?"

"Tandy's. It's right around the corner."

They walk out of the wet footprints near the entrance, and move into dry cool air, artificial lights in front of the shops. The mall is bright and clean, and there are not many people. It is oddly quiet, and there is no music.

"You were right," Anne says. "Hardly anybody here."

"It's early." Lucy walks with her hands in her pockets, her head bowed as if she needs to watch her feet, put them on the right squares. "Is his doctor doing any good with him?" she says.

"I don't know. We don't talk very often."

"You don't talk to the doctor?"

"I don't talk to the doctor at all. And Mike doesn't talk about it when he's home. Except to tell me things he's told the doctor in the sessions."

Lucy takes her hand out of the coat and puts it on Anne's arm. "This way," she says, pulling gently toward a giant floor-level sign which reads "TANDY'S." The entrance is under the letter "A." The room is small, with little round tables and a counter to the rear. Above the counter is a lighted board with a list of the coffees available, and pastries, and pies. A waitress in a black dress stands in front of the counter, smiling a welcome.

"We seat ourselves," Lucy says.

They take a table near the counter. The smell of coffee is strong in the room, and Anne thinks of the number of times she has ordered more than she could possibly drink because of that odor. There is soft music in the ceiling, and ashtrays on all the shiny tables. She is glad she has come here, glad she is not spending the morning waiting for Dale and Michael to return, as she did all the years in Chicago. Glad she is not asleep in bed, dreaming the soft, mechanical dreams which haunt her mornings. Dreams she does not ever remember, but which create

108

moods and fears that color the walls, the furniture, the air.

The waitress brings two menus, offers another smile, and returns to the place she occupies by the counter.

"They've got great coffee in this place," Lucy says.

Anne studies her menu.

"You going to have something to eat?" Lucy says.

"If you do."

They each order a Danish, and an exotic South American coffee. While they wait, Anne lights a cigarette, plays with the place mat in front of her. Lucy sits across from her with her hands below the table, rocking back and forth staring distractedly at the other tables.

"How can you help?" Anne says.

"I don't know. I just want to. I feel sorry for him."

"Don't."

"Don't help him?" Lucy looks into Anne's eyes now, her head tilted slightly to the side, as if she is trying to read something upside down.

"Don't feel sorry for him."

Lucy leans forward. "Anne, do you realize that the war is going on right now?" She sits back again, waves her arm in a short semicircle around the room. "Look at all of this. I don't know very much, but it seems to me that there's something wrong here."

"What do you mean?"

"Look at it. Everything goes on—this mall is new, it's *new*—people come here to shop, buy thousands of dollars worth of stuff—everybody eats what they want, nobody suffers. The war isn't there. It's like traffic. People die in it, that's all. All anybody does about the war is go to funerals or watch the news. They go to the funerals in brand-new cars, and they watch the war on new color television sets. Doesn't that seem odd to you?"

The waitress brings the coffee and sets it in front of them, carefully, as if she is afraid one of the cups might explode. She places the pastries in front of them, then puts the check facedown on the edge of the table and disappears without a word.

Anne sips the hot coffee. She holds the cup in front of her, stares at Lucy stirring cream and sugar into her cup. "I don't think about it," Anne says. "It's the government—they decide, and they're in a position to decide. They know what this is all about. I don't."

Lucy places her spoon on the saucer in front of her. "It just doesn't seem right," she says. "My parents talked to me a lot about what they went through in World War Two. Ben remembers too—that's all he talks about. He can't believe this shit."

"What does Ben think we should do?"

"He thinks we should go in there and finish it."

"That would bring the war home," Anne says. She takes a bite of the pastry. It is sticky and full of raisins.

"Well, I want to do something. Helping Michael will make me feel better."

"You can't do anything," Anne says. She reaches over and puts out her cigarette.

"Thanks," Lucy says. "It was getting in my eyes."

"Sorry."

"If I just talked to him? Made him feel welcome?"

"What would Ben say about that?"

"He doesn't have to know."

Anne takes another bite of her pastry, thinking about Ben, his age, and what might happen with Lucy and Michael.

"Are you attracted to my son?" she asks, when she is finished.

"Should I be honest?" Lucy has a half-smile on her face, but her eyes are serious, almost severe.

"Yes, this time."

"I won't hurt you?"

"I take it you're not attracted to him."

"I don't know him. But—now you said to be honest—I think he's —well, he's—"

"Ugly."

"That's too strong a word. He just doesn't have a very handsome face."

"Ugly."

"Personality is the most important thing. I don't know him yet."

"He was so beautiful before the war. I guess because he was himself, and he moved differently." Anne feels something rising in her throat, and a burning in the eyes. Her son, her boy.

"Maybe if he let his hair grow out." A smile returns to Lucy's face. She drinks her coffee, staring at Anne over the rim of the cup.

"You don't know what it's like," Anne says. "To raise a son, a child —to know another person you brought into the world—" She breaks off, lowers her head toward the coffee.

"Hey," Lucy says, reaching out her hand. "He'll be all right. I promise."

110

"If he had a girl friend, a woman." Anne is crying. She raises her head and looks at Lucy. "Not you. But somebody like you."

"He'll meet somebody. Everybody does. It takes time." Lucy strokes Anne's hand, pats it against the table. "Come on now. Let's go have some fun."

Anne takes a handkerchief out of her purse, wipes her eyes.

"Ready?" Lucy says.

"Yes. I'm sorry."

"Feel better?"

"Yes."

"See?" Lucy says, a smile on her face like that of the waitress. "It does help to talk to somebody."

III. MICHAEL

The car carries us along the highway which stretches out beside the ocean. We are in a warm, dry shell, knifing through the blue mist toward home, toward my room and rest. The ocean is white and gray, tumbling in the breezes, moving its ragged designs toward the tattered edges of land. I close my eyes and listen to the whirring of the engine, the slapping of the wind and rain. My father drives quietly, his head fixed at a slight angle, as if he is waiting for a phone to stop ringing somewhere. A few minutes ago, he said, "I told you I knew what I was doing." Next to me, on the console between my seat and his, is a newspaper folded in half, and circled on the page of ads is a listing which says: "WANTED: BRIGHT YOUNG MAN TO JOIN OUR FULL- AND PART-TIME SALES FORCE; we sell the best line of appliances in western Florida. Apply at DILL'S. 1342 DELANEY ST., ENGLE-WOOD. Mr. Baldwin."

"Aren't you excited?" my father says.

"Yes."

"It's the beginning, son."

He falls quiet again, moving his hand on the steering wheel slightly back and forth, as if the wheel is hot and he can't keep his hands on it. I study the rain. I don't feel anything. I have a job, now—and I don't want it. I am afraid of what will happen to me there. I cannot believe Mr. Baldwin wanted to hire me.

He gave me an application to fill out and left the room. It was an office no larger than a bedroom closet, and he was busy with people outside among the shelves. He left me there for almost an hour. I wondered where my father had gone, what I should do. I sat there, trying not to think of anything. I held the application in my hand, stared at it, remembered the girl in the brown pajamas in the store yesterday, and the way the money seemed to cling to her hand. I wanted to put the paper somewhere, so I laid it on the desk. Then I stared at my hands, at the knuckles and the hair which only shows up when there is light. My stomach burned, felt cold inside.

When Mr. Baldwin came back, he went behind his desk and said, "Finished now?" He was tall, red-haired, with whiskers like a cat. While he talked he reached up and pulled on the long thin hairs under his nose, as if he needed help to form the words with some physical action. I could not listen to him. He talked about himself, the store, me. I couldn't make any sense out of it. Then he said, "Well, let's see that application."

"It's right there," I said.

He leaned forward and picked up the blank paper.

"This?"

"Yes."

He searched among the other papers on the desk. "There's nothing on this one. Have I lost it?"

"No, that's it. I didn't fill it out."

"Why not?" He leaned back in his chair again.

"I don't want the job."

"I don't understand. What are you here for?" He pulled the hair.

"My father wants me to get a job."

"Is he the fellow came in here with you?"

"Yes."

"But you don't want to work?"

"I don't think I can work."

"Why not?"

I looked away, toward the door. I wanted to leave.

"Look," he said. "It's none of my business, but you look healthy, young, intelligent. I just wonder why you don't want to work."

I didn't want to answer him. I thought of the woman in the store again, the manager with his keys, walking as if he didn't have time for anything but stamping prices on produce, taking money out of clips.

"Well, I'm sorry," Mr. Baldwin said. He started to get up.

"I'm afraid I *can't* work."

"Why?"

"I'm a veteran. I was a prisoner of war."

He put both hands on the desk, leaned over and shook his head.

"I'm sorry," he said. He did not look at me. "I think I know what you're going through. My brother-in-law was a prisoner."

"He got out?" I said.

"They left his body in the jungle. You wouldn't believe what they did to it."

"Yes, I would," I said. Then I felt something cold, with a sound to it, a tone, moving up the back of my head.

"They found my brother-in-law's body on a spit, in the jungle—"

I put my hands up over my ears. "OK." I said. "OK."

He put his hand out. "I'm sorry. I won't talk about it."

"I have to go," I said.

"No, wait." He got up, came around the desk. "Let's try something."

"What?"

"You come to work for me, only a few hours a day. You name them." He sat on the desk, leaned over me. "What do you say? We'll see if you can work."

"What do I have to do?"

"I'll train you, a little at a time. You can sell small appliances."

"I don't know."

"I can't pay you. Not very much. But it's better than nothing." He smiled, the hair over his nose moving.

I looked at the hand on his knee, the way the veins seemed to rumple the skin like a blanket on an unmade bed.

"My father wants me to work."

"Well, get him off your back. Maybe I can help you."

"Why do you want to do that?"

He smiled. "Do I have to have a reason?"

"OK," I said. Anything was better than another interview. At that moment I thought I liked Mr. Baldwin. When I left his office he put his hand on my back the way Kessler does, and he shook my hand, said he'd see me in the morning.

"If you could work on Saturdays it would be a help for me," he said. "But you don't have to. That would be the best time for me, though, because all my help is here then. We could spend more time together, learning the ropes."

"OK," I said. When I got outside, my father was waiting for me.

"Well?"

"I got the job."

He grabbed me, hugged me against him. I didn't know what to do. I started to put my arms around him, but he pulled away. "That's just great, son," he said. I couldn't tell if he was happy or nervous. He couldn't stand still, and I followed him around while he talked about it. Then he said, "Got to call Eddie. Maybe he can meet us for lunch. It's a cinch he didn't go fishing today."

We went to a phone: I stood outside while my father talked to Eddie. I realized then that Mr. Baldwin didn't even know my name.

We met Eddie at a place called Brodie's. I didn't want to look at him, or talk to him. I followed my father into the bar, glad to be out of the rain again. We sat at the bar, me to the left of my father, and Eddie on the other side. They talked, and I watched in the mirror behind the glasses of the bar, watched my face in the clear glass, my face. It wasn't me. I thought about the first time I saw myself in a mirror after I was rescued. I didn't see anything behind the eyes. No one could convince me that the figure in the glass was alive, was Michael Sumner.

"Michael's got a job," my father said, putting his hand on my shoulder.

"Think he can handle it?" Eddie said.

My father turned to him. "Sure he can. This is just what he needs."

They went on talking about me. Eddie said he hoped I would be all right, hoped I wouldn't lose it again. That's what he called it. "Hope he doesn't lose it again," he said. What have I lost that Eddie can possibly know? I tried to eat a hamburger but I couldn't. I watched my father putting wads of bread into his mouth, thought about his throat, his teeth, the quiet chemicals and devices going to work, so he could go on into tomorrow, and the next day, and the day after.

"Son, you've got to eat more than that," my father said. He pointed to my plate, to the hamburger and potato chips lying there in light brown perfection.

"I ate some," I said.

"I don't know how he lives," Eddie said.

I ate some more, watching my father's face in the mirror. He talked to Eddie, smiling, chewing, turning to his food between sentences. Eddie leaned into his food. He is an old man, trying to go on. I hate him.

When we were finished, Eddie talked about fishing again, maybe tomorrow. "You come too, Michael," he said.

"Michael's got to work," my father said.

"Well, come if you can," Eddie said. He put his hand out to me, and I touched it, felt the bones. "Take it easy," he said.

"Where are you going now?" my father asked.

"I don't know. Want to shoot some pool?"

"Let me take Michael home." My father looked at me, smiled. "No, I don't think so. I'm going to spend the afternoon congratulating my son. See you tomorrow."

Eddie waved and disappeared like a man going under water. My father turned to me and said, "Let's run to the car."

Now the car turns off the highway onto the main road into town. My eyes are tired, and I feel as if I have been crying. My father whistles, carelessly. I don't know where I should go, but I can't stay too much longer. *I am not home.* Everything is foreign, including this man who sits next to me pretending that he is not thinking. I don't know what has happened to all of us.

"Now, we've got to find me some work," he says.

"I've got to see Kessler this afternoon," I say. He watches the road, turns the wheel, a mortal man.

"Whatever you say."

In front of us the clouds are dispersing, and through the rain I can see the white sky turning blue.

"Looks like the sun is coming back," my father says.

"Yes."

"Never gone for long in Florida."

"Is that why you came here?" I watch my hands, feel my father move in his seat.

"We thought you were dead, Michael."

"I know."

"We didn't want to be in that place in Chicago. Everything reminded us." His voice is soft, weak.

"I used to love that house."

"You did?"

"It was all I thought of."

"Well, it was your home." He clicks his teeth, turns his head to watch a passing car. "But you live here now. This is your home," he says, turning back to the road.

The rain thins out, begins to withdraw. The opening in the sky floods wide yellow rays of late sun. I want to be home again, in that house. "I wish I was back there now," I say.

"Chicago?"

"Yes."

"You can go back there if you want." I know he doesn't mean this.

"I guess."

"You've got a job here now. Why don't you try that out?"

I listen to the tires on the road, try to think of every detail in the house I left for the war. My father looks at me, then back to the road.

"What happened to you, son?"

"What?"

"What happened to you over there?"

I can't look at him. I stare out the window at the black driveways, the green lawns. We pass a young child on a three-wheeled bicycle. His head turns as we pass, he smiles, waves.

"Well, we'll be home soon. I want you to tell your mother about the job."

"I don't really have a job," I say.

"What?"

"He just wanted to do me a favor. He doesn't even know my name."

"Did he tell you to come to work or not?"

I see my father's house at the end of the street, a big brown car parked in front. "He said I should try it."

"Well?" My father notices the car. "Who's that?"

He slows the Toyota, pulls into the driveway and up the hill. "You might know it. Just when we have good news, company shows up."

"I didn't even fill out an application, Dad."

He turns off the engine, pulls the keys out, lets his hands fall to his lap. The noise is gone out of the air, and outside a great blue hole opens in the gray sky. "The guy hired you. Didn't he?"

"He said I could work whenever I want."

My father pulls open the door, slides out of the seat. "Then you're hired," he says over the top of the car. I watch his head disappear toward the back door of the house. I stand in front of the car, listen to the water dripping off the bumper. The driveway shines like a black mirror, and I can see my body rising up out of it, clouds shifting and separating over my head. I know how perfect it is to be a tree, to stand for decades in the same place, never having to move at all. I hear the back door slam, turn to see my father standing on the porch watching me.

"You coming in?"

"Who is it?"

He walks toward me, whispers loudly, "It's just Lucy." Then he frowns, waves his arm, beckons, "Come on."

When I get to him he puts his arm around me. "I've already told your mother we have news," he says.

IV. DALE

Anne stands at the sink rinsing the breakfast dishes. Dale sits at the table, the bright morning sun gleaming off the last of his coffee.

"Maybe I'll stay home today," he says.

"What for?"

He makes a gesture with his left hand, a movement like a soft caress. "Maybe we could—?"

"Dance?" she says.

"It may look like dancing, but that's not what I was thinking."

Anne turns from the sink, opens her arms. "Come here."

He rises from the table, goes to her. She puts her arms up around his neck, leans into him. "Have I told you that you were wonderful yesterday?" she says.

"No."

She kisses him, leans back in his arms.

"You're getting my neck all wet," he says.

She laughs, pulls away, and grabs a dish towel off the counter. "Sorry. That's the price you pay when you attack the dishwasher." She wipes her hands, and as she finishes, Dale takes both her hands while they are still wrapped in the towel, and holds them up to his chin. "Everything's going to be all right," he says.

"That's the first time you've ever said that," she says, smiling.

"I believe it. He's going to work. He talked this morning."

"And he ate a full breakfast."

"He's coming back, Anne. He's finally coming back." These words feel as if they have been framed in his heart. He wants to laugh with them, throw them out into the room and play with them.

"And all because of you," Anne says. She kisses him again, on the mouth. He closes his eyes and holds her against him.

She pulls away, kisses him on the chin. "Let go. I have to finish."

"Let it go. Let's celebrate."

"When I'm done." She turns back to the sink, her hands disappear in the water. "Can you find out how long Mike's going to work today?"

"Anne," he says, coming up behind her, putting his hands around her waist. "Let's go upstairs."

"As soon as Michael leaves."

"I've got to take him."

"Why?" She tries to turn, puts her head back on his shoulder. He feels the texture of her hair on his face.

"He hasn't driven since he got out of the hospital."

"So?"

"Well, I think he wants me to."

She turns back to the dishes. "Let him drive. It'll show him we trust him."

"You talked me into it," he says, lowering his hands down the front of her robe, and inside. She leans back, purrs softly, quietly—as if someone is watching them.

"That's nice," she says.

"I want you."

She reaches down, takes his hands away, getting water on his shirt. "Not now. Don't start something until the offspring is gone." He puts his hands on her shoulders, leans forward, and kisses her on the back of the neck.

"Come on."

"Michael is right upstairs. You want him to catch us sprawled on the counter?"

"That makes it more exciting. We might get caught."

"You *want* to get caught—why don't we go to the mall and do it on one of the benches?" Her hands stir the water again.

"That's an idea," he says.

"You're impossible."

"*You're* impossible. I'm so possible, I'm considering the mall."

She laughs again, high and fine. All his life with her he has delighted in the sound of her laughter. She takes her hands out of the water, dries them, then turns her body so she is against him, her arms around his waist.

"Thank you," she says. "Thank you for being patient with Mike, and for taking time with him."

He smiles down at her, squeezes her. "You too. He was happier with that damn recorder you bought him than the job."

"He's going to make it back," she says.

"With you and me."

"I thought we lost him, and when he came back—"

"Hey, don't get all misty-eyed now."

"Dale. Let's move back to Chicago."

He pulls away, looks into her eyes. "Are you kidding?"

She moves her head down. "No." He stares at the crown of her head, the fine thin gray hairs which swirl out from the center like white clouds in a whirlwind.

"And Michael's job?"

"He knows he can get one now. He can find another one there."

"You *are* serious, aren't you?"

She looks up to him again. Her eyes move across his face, and back, as if she is reading something there.

"I like it here," he says.

"Will you think about it?"

"Why?"

"You said you were going back to work. What difference does it make if you work here or Chicago?"

He puts her arms down, walks to the table and stares out the window. "Come here," he says.

He feels her body next to him. Without looking at her he puts his arm around her and points with the other at the whitening sky, the small black gulls in the distance. "You don't have that sort of thing in Chicago. Ever."

"I'm tired of this heat," she says.

"You don't remember how you hated the winters there." He squeezes her shoulder. "We've made a good life here. The land warms us. I like that."

"You don't know what to do with yourself."

He looks into her eyes. "I've been bored, sure. But I was bored in Chicago too. Plenty of times."

"I'm scared," she says, lowering her head.

"Of what? The house is paid for. I'm getting six hundred dollars a month for doing nothing."

"We're not the same."

"Because of Michael. Not Florida."

"Time. I'm afraid of time. This is like a dream."

"A good dream," he says.

"Not for me."

He leaves her and walks toward the dining room. He stops by the door, leans against the white frame. "I can't believe this."

"I'm sorry," she whispers.

"What?"

"I'm sorry. I didn't mean to hit you with this right now."

"Have you been talking to Michael about it?"

"No, why?" She stands in the light from the window, her hair almost translucent.

"He talked yesterday about how much he missed it."

"He did?" She moves to him. He turns into the dining room, looks at the stairway.

"He'll be coming down," he says.

"Will you think about it?" She stands behind him, but he can remember the expression on her face, in her eyes. He never felt she was happy, but he thought it would come, and now he can't believe she has had the nerve to tell him about it. He feels betrayed. As if she has done this to hurt him; as if she has just told him she wants to go back to an old boyfriend, return to some other lover.

"OK?" she says.

He cannot face her. "Leave me alone about it, will you?" he says, moving toward the stairs.

"Don't be hurt," she says.

He stands at the bottom of the stairs, looks up to the empty hallway, the ceiling. "Michael? You ready to go?"

"Dale," Anne says. "Please don't be mad."

"I'm not going to think about going back," he says. "So why don't you think about staying?"

She turns and walks into the kitchen, a quick exit which sticks in his mind like a film going too fast. He goes to the couch, sits down, and unfolds the day's newspaper. This morning, he went out in his bare feet to get it—could have leaned on the box and read it there in the hot Florida sun. He waited for twenty years to move here—paid off a seventeen-thousand-dollar mortgage, then sold the house for over fifty thousand. He already had land in Florida, but in the rush after the report of Michael's death, the long wait for a body, he sold that land and bought this house, this perfect house in which he is only now beginning to feel comfortable. Perhaps his life would take the turns he wanted it to: his son would finally return, become Michael again, and Dale would end up where he always dreamed he might end up—still young, retired with a reasonable income, his son returned from the war, and his wife in a comfortable home out of the snow and wind. He should never have mentioned a job to her—that's what got her thinking, got her wondering. And he realizes now that it was Michael he wanted the job for, Michael whose helplessness and paralysis made retirement seem like an endless vacation turned sour in the heat.

Michael comes down the stairs, dressed in the same brown suit he wore yesterday. His hair is combed to the side, but it is so short that bits of it stand up, so it looks as if there are thorns there.

"You want to drive?" Dale asks him.

Michael stops in front of him. "I don't know."

"You can if you want. Or I'll take you."

"Well, yesterday—" He stops, puts his hands in his pockets, looks at the floor. "Yesterday, Lucy said she would drive me."

"OK," Dale says. "I don't see why she should have to do that when we have a car, but—"

"I don't have to go with her," Michael says, removing his hands, patting the back of his head.

"No. Go ahead."

"OK."

"How are you going to get to Kessler's?"

"I don't know. Maybe I'll call."

"I may not be here."

"That reminds me, I've got to get the tape recorder." Michael turns to the stairs. Anne comes in from the kitchen, drying her hands.

"Ready to go, Michael?" she says.

"I've got to get something," he says, moving up the stairs. Anne watches him through the railing.

"You know Lucy is taking him?" Dale says, after Michael is in his room.

"No," she says, quietly. Then, "Lucy?"

"What's going on there?"

"How did that get arranged?"

"He said she offered to do it yesterday."

Anne bites her lower lip, looks up the stairs. "She says she wants to help."

"How's she going to do that?" Dale folds the paper in front of him, thinks about Lucy and Michael together, riding toward a job which might be a short step toward sanity. "I don't like it," he says.

"I don't know if I do or not."

Michael comes down the stairs carrying the tape recorder. He seems to bounce down the stairs, the way he did when he was a boy and he was heading out the door to play basketball.

"See you," he says, opening the front door.

"Is she here?" Dale says, his voice weakly incredulous.

"I'm going around to meet her." Michael smiles, closes the door.

Dale watches him out the window, walking up the street, his head cocked to the side. "Maybe she will be good for him," he says.

"She's very nice. I like her," Anne says. "But—" She stops, puts the towel over her shoulder.

"But what?"

"But I don't like her help. I don't want her help."

Dale leans back into the cushions of the couch. "You thinking what I'm thinking?" he says.

"I don't know what I'm thinking."

The phone rings. "That's probably her," Anne says as she goes to answer. Dale watches her body move across the room and wonders if he will love her after all. It excites him to think about it, but he doesn't want to make the first move. Not after the talk about Chicago, her swift anger because he wouldn't consider giving up what he'd worked a lifetime to earn. She comes back into the room, heads for the stairs. "It's for you," she says.

He goes to the phone, draws it up from where it hangs by its cord, like a fish twirling out of water.

"Let's go catch a few," Eddie says.

"Oh, Eddie, hello," Dale answers, stalling for time. He has to think of something to say, some way to get out of it.

"It's beautiful out there," Eddie says. "We'll take the boat."

"We're getting a late start, aren't we?"

"Won't matter. Fish eat lunch too."

"What about the speedboats?"

"We got them no matter when we go."

Dale thinks of Anne, upstairs getting dressed, preparing for a long siege until he tells her he will think about moving back to Chicago, and suddenly he wants to be out of there—out the door before she can come downstairs and say no to him, before she can ask him where he's going. Let her wonder. Let her think about how she has hurt him, wounded him.

"You want me to pick you up, or meet you there?" he says.

"We'll save some time if you meet me."

"At the marina?"

"Right," Eddie says. "See you in half an hour."

Dale hangs the phone up quietly, goes to the back door, turns and looks back into the dining room, back to the end of the stairway, his hand quietly opening the door. *Let her wonder,* he thinks. *Let her wonder.*

"My wife gave me the same shit," Eddie says. He sits in the boat, putting bait on his line. Dale already has his line in the water.

"You're right, it's beautiful out here," Dale says.

"Nothing better." Eddie casts his line. The sky is white at the edges, but a deep shade of blue at the top of the dome, and there isn't a cloud anywhere. A slight breeze makes white-tipped waves in the distance, and the shoreline, with its tall trees and houses and piers and parked boats, looks like a mirage in the heat.

"What'd you do?" Dale says, after a while.

"About my wife?"

"Yeah."

"I took her fishing with me a few times, kept her busy. Then she met some people—you know, made some friends." Eddie looks into Dale's eyes, a serious frown on his face. "Women are screwed up," he says, slowly. "They don't ever know what they want."

"My wife wants to go back to Chicago."

"No, she doesn't. She wants to go back to being young." Eddie smiles back out at the water. "If you could take her back, she'd only be there for a month before she wanted to come back to Florida."

"I can't take that chance."

"I'll tell you a story about women," Eddie says. "They don't like men. They hate men."

"Seems like it sometimes."

"They don't like being what they have to be, so they convince themselves that they are trying to make a man happy, that they are doing for him, and all the time they're making him miserable." Eddie spits into the water. "It's got something to do with what Freud said about them. They don't have a prick and it kills them."

"I just wish she wanted to stay here." Dale leans back, stretches. "I love this air."

Eddie leans over the side of the boat, takes water in the palm of his hand and washes it over his forehead. "Getting hot out here." Dale watches Eddie's hand shake as he puts his cap on, tends his line. He really is an old man, staring out at the vast blue gulf waiting for something. A man is old for a long time, a very long time. Long enough for other men to grow old, to grow from youth to middle age.

"How's your boy?" Eddie says.

"Went on his first day of work."

"I remember my first job."

"How long ago was that?"

"Nineteen twenty. I worked in a mill."

Dale looks at the side of Eddie's face, at the lines by his eyes, the gray hair sticking like wire out of his forehead.

"A long time ago," Eddie says.

"Do you ever get really bored?" Dale asks him.

"Like I told you before, at first I thought I'd go crazy. But not anymore. I'm used to this place. I love it."

"If it wasn't such a problem with Michael, I'd—"

"Why don't you go back to Chicago?" Eddie says. His voice is severe, a sort of savage tone building behind the syllables. "You don't really like it here, either."

"No. I like it. I love it. I just don't like not working."

"Why don't you quit worrying about it?" Eddie pulls back on his rod. "Thought I had something."

"Now that Michael has a job, maybe things will settle down."

"You worry about him too much, you know that?"

"I feel like I have less to worry about now."

"You always had less to worry about." Again, the savage tone creeps into Eddie's voice.

"What's wrong with you today?"

"Let's just fish, OK?" He spits into the water again. Dale watches the white pearl floating on the green swells, dissipating with the wash of the water toward the sides of the boat.

A plane crosses the blue dome above them, leaving a thin white trail in the air which divides the sky. The sounds of the water against the boat, the call of the birds overhead, and Eddie's breathing mix in the breezes with the soft drone of the airplane.

"I'm getting thirsty," Dale says.

Eddie reaches under the seat, pulls out a bottle. "Here."

"I want something cold."

"Should have put something in the cooler."

"We'll get a beer when we go in."

Eddie moves his head back, stretching, looking for the plane.

"Are you all right?" Dale says.

Eddie looks at him. "I'm fine. I want to fish. I don't want to talk."

"What's got into you?"

"Nothing. Forget it." Eddie stares at the water.

A woman's trick, Dale thinks. *So there won't be any talk, just fishing.* But he needs to talk. Just when he was thinking that he might find a little order, might discover the first tender rays of peaceful light, she has to hit him with her secret wish to return to Chicago. It occurs to him that it might all be a complex plan, a sort of psychological conspiracy on the part of Anne and Michael. Disturb him, first one, then the other. *Make him miserable so he will take us home.*

Yesterday, after they got home, and they told Anne about the job, Michael went up to his room, changed into a pair of Levi's and an undershirt, then came right back down. They sat in the kitchen and talked. Michael never did go to Kessler's. Lucy stayed most of the afternoon, listening to everybody, watching Michael. Dale talked about the jobs he held in his life—funny stories about the times he was fired, the times he gave unbelievable excuses for not being able to work. "I told the boss in a gas station once that I was allergic to gasoline," he said. Lucy laughed. Michael looked at her, a smile on his face. It all seemed so natural, so completely normal. After Lucy was gone, they settled into a quiet evening—Dale reading the newspaper, Michael in his room talking into his tape recorder, Anne in the kitchen cooking a big dinner—baked chicken and potatoes, tossed salad. The smell of the food warmed him, made him feel like a father again, the head of a family. He did not want it to end, this first peaceful evening since Michael's return—a time without tension, without fear. And Michael came down to dinner without being asked—even ate nearly a full meal, his mouth actually chewing the food without seeming to count the strokes. It had been a good evening, and this morning Anne ruins the importance of it by springing the idea of going back to Chicago.

"Got something," Eddie says. He reels it in, studying the line intently as it moves in the water.

"It's about time," Dale says.

"I had to hook it twice. It's a sheepshead, I think."

Dale takes a pole with a net on it and moves over next to Eddie. "Bring it up here," he says.

Out of the water the fish spins on the line. Dale lowers the net under it, lets it fall into it, then pulls it into the boat.

"It's a grunt," Eddie says. "Not very big."

"He's a fighter." Dale reaches into the net, pulls out the fish. It squirms in his hand.

"Give it to me," Eddie says. "I'll get the hook out."

Dale hands it to him, smiles.

"Maybe we'll be lucky today," Eddie says. His eyes seem on the edge of a smile.

"I'm sorry I'm such a complainer," Dale says.

"Everybody needs to bitch. Let's do it over a beer, later. I want to fish."

"So do I."

Eddie does smile now, his eyes blinking. "I'm one ahead of you."

"I'll catch up," Dale says. "We've got a lot of time yet."

Eddie picks up the fish in his trembling hands and puts it into the cooler.

V. MICHAEL

"You sure you don't have to be at work now?" Lucy says. She sits next to me on a senior citizens' bench in front of a supermarket. Dill's is down the street to our left, on the corner. I don't want to go in there yet. I'm afraid of what will happen. I didn't fill out any forms, and it occurred to me on the way over here that Mr. Baldwin may not be there. What would I do then? I thought at first that it might be just what I need to happen, to get me out of it. But then I got scared, and I asked Lucy to stop with me for a while. She talks a lot, but she is nice, and she doesn't study me so much. She hasn't asked me yet how I feel, if I'm all right. I guess I want Mr. Baldwin to be there. I'm afraid to find out.

"I can go in any time," I tell Lucy.

She looks out at the passing cars, the gleaming cars. "Anyway," she says, "I didn't want to go to school. I think school is so boring, don't you?"

"I didn't like it."

"So I got married to my first husband, Robert."

"I never really had a girl friend," I say.

"Really?"

"No. I went to a junior prom once—but my dad drove us there, and it wasn't like a real date. It was sort of embarrassing."

"I'll bet it was. Really. Didn't you have a license yet?"

"I didn't get my license till I got out of high school."

"Good grief."

"I didn't mind. I never went in for that social stuff anyway."

"Why?"

"I don't know. I was never very popular."

Lucy smiles at me, as if she understands more than I am telling her. I like her eyes, the way the light shines in them, the way the color lifts them.

"My first husband was so good to me, in the beginning."

I look at her hand, resting on the bench between us. She wears shorts and a white halter top. Her skin is brown, almost another race.

"I still miss him sometimes."

"What happened to him?"

"You don't need to hear about that. He just—changed. He became a different man." She turns away from me, stares down the street where cars seem to drive out of the sun. It is warm on this bench, and I don't want to move. I feel rested, calm. I cannot take my eyes off the skin by the top of her shorts. "So we got divorced," she says, turning back to me. "That's how I met Ben." She smiles, recalling something.

"I feel good," I say.

"You do?"

"I feel better than I've felt for a long time. Since the war." I don't really feel that way, but I think I can. I think with her I will be all right.

"I'm glad," she says. Then she frowns, bites her lower lip. "You know, even though I'm married, and I do love my husband—there's no reason you and I can't be friends."

"I would like that." I picture myself putting my hand on hers. I smile at her, caress her hand. I am breathing new air.

"Sometimes, you need someone to talk to." Her hand is still there, next to me. I could put my hand on it if I would only move, but I can't make it happen.

"Nothing in the world is ever as bad as we think it is," she says.

"You don't know," I say. I forget about the hand. I hear laughter behind us. Down the street a car honks its horn, swerves to miss another.

"I guess I don't," she says. "I don't have the kind of experience you have."

"I don't think anybody does."

"I shouldn't have brought this up."

"Why?"

She puts her hand on my knee, smiles into my eyes. "I don't want to talk about negative things. Let's talk about something nice."

A black man walks across the street in front of us, carrying a brown bag in his hand. Across the street a fat woman waits by the corner, holding a basket full of fruit in front of her like a shield.

"What's your favorite food?" Lucy says.

"I don't have any right now."

"What?"

"I don't like to eat."

"Why?"

"I used to. Before the war I weighed almost two hundred pounds. My father said I was getting fat."

"And you don't like to eat at all?"

"I eat a little bit. To stop my stomach from aching." A slight breeze moves her hair into me. I feel it on my face. She is very close to me.

"Will you ever like to eat again?"

"I don't know. I ate last night."

"Do you get sick or something?"

"A lot of things happen. I think of some things, and I get a bad feeling in my stomach, so I don't want to eat."

"We're talking about negative things again," she says.

"I guess."

"Isn't there something we can laugh about?"

"I don't know." She smiles at me, her mouth slightly open. The fat woman across the street begins to cross, holding the basket tight against her. Her head moves back and forth like a turret as she walks. A tiny thing inside views the world.

"What's the funniest thing you know?"

"Something happened to me on the holiday that might be funny."

"Tell me."

"I thought I wanted to be a fish."

She makes a sound, but I can't tell if it is laughter. She stares down at her hands, a painful look on her face.

"I went into the water," I say.

She raises her head, looks at me. "I really should let you get to work."

The fat woman gets to our side of the street, and walks along behind us. Her feet slide on the concrete, as if she hasn't the strength to lift them. An old pickup truck rattles past in front of us, and a dark-skinned man sitting in the back waves his arms, yells at the fat woman.

"What did he say?" Lucy asks.

"I didn't hear him."

"Was he yelling at us?"

"No."

Lucy turns, looks at the woman moving on down the street. "God," she says. "Wouldn't you hate to look like that?"

"She must eat a lot."

Lucy puts her hand up over her mouth, her eyes get narrow, seeming to give off light. "That's something to laugh at."

"There's somebody inside there," I say.

Lucy laughs behind her hand. "Don't," she says.

"I wouldn't want to be in there."

"There's probably enough room for both of us." Lucy takes her hand away, rolls her head to the side, a quiet laugh which dies as her head moves. She takes a deep breath.

"I'm serious," I tell her. I don't want her to laugh.

She folds her hands in her lap, lets out a breath of air, then looks into my eyes. There is still laughter quivering at the corners of her mouth. "I'm sorry," she says.

"It's terrible."

"I'm sorry. Don't be so serious."

"I wonder if fish laugh at each other," I say.

"It's human to laugh," Lucy says.

"I know."

She gets up, smooths her shorts, pulls at the edges of them on the inside of her legs. "I'm starting to sweat."

"It's a nice day."

"You better go."

"I don't want to yet."

"Well, I have to go," she says, pushing her hair back with her hand. "Want me to pick you up?"

"OK."

"What time?"

"Can I call you?"

She shrugs. "I don't know if I'll be home."

"If I don't get you I'll walk."

"You sure?"

"I like to walk."

"So do I. Why don't we go together some time?"

"I'd like that."

"Let me know next time you go," she says, moving away. "And call me this afternoon if you want a ride."

"I will." I watch her walking toward her car, the way her body moves. She stops by the door of the car, looks at me, frowns.

"You better get to work," she says.

"I'm going." I get up, walk toward Dill's. Lucy gets in her car, watches me as I pass. I hear the engine start and look for her as she passes in traffic. She doesn't look at me, and I notice that there is something comic about her tiny silhouette perched inside such a large gleaming machine.

I walk along the street, feeling clean and new. I feel the sun on the shoulders of my brown suit, and I watch my shoes crunch on the sandy sidewalk, and I feel good that I have somewhere to go. I don't think I will be afraid. The street is almost white in the heat, and bright colorful Florida shirts pass by—people smiling or walking purposefully somewhere. I feel like one of them, all of them. A man with a camera around his neck smiles at me as he passes. I wave, a slight movement of my hand, and he nods. It's as if we all know something about each other, and we acknowledge it silently when our eyes meet.

I get to the front of the store, and realize I can't see inside unless I get against the window. I'm not sure who will see me if I do that. I stand there on the sidewalk, looking at my reflection in the glass, the people walking past, behind, and in front of me. I am a character in a movie; the camera focuses on me in the crowd. I rub my face, think about the inside of the store and Mr. Baldwin, the theater audience, watching the figure in the glass trying to decide what to do. I walk out of the picture and down to the corner. Cars wait at the light there, parked in the crosswalk, and more people walk around them toward me. Their feet shuffle and scuff on the street, a sort of quiet rhythm for the soft drone of the engines. I look up the black road for Lucy's car, but there are so many I can't distinguish one from the other. Wires crisscross above my head and on down the street. There are signs everywhere. The light changes and the cars in front of me move slowly through the last people filtering across the street. Smoke rises into the air around their feet as the cars lurch forward, stop, start forward again. To my left other cars wait now, and more people begin to cross, and I know I am a forgotten piece in a chess game. No one will move me. I wait by the corner and watch the light change again and all the pieces being shuffled back and forth in front of me. I walk back to the window in

130

front of Dill's, stand there with my hands in my pockets watching, watching my head and all the other heads going by it and wonder where Mr. Baldwin is, whether he can see me. I want him to come out and get me. I don't know if I will ever go in unless he does. A little girl skips in front of me, stops as she passes, stares up toward the sky over my head.

"Look, Mommy," she says.

A woman walks into view in the glass, takes her hand. "Come on," she says crossly.

"Look at that," the girl says, pointing.

The woman looks. "What is it?"

"A plane."

"Yes, I see it."

"Is Daddy in that one?"

"No. Now come on." The woman pulls her out of the picture.

I watch them walking toward the corner, the woman leaning down, holding the little girl's hand.

The door next to the glass swings open and a young man in a burgundy shirt comes out pushing two lawn mowers in front of him. He stops when he gets outside and latches the door open, then he pushes the mowers to the side, along the front of the store by the window. He goes back into the store and comes out with two more.

"Moving out?" I say.

He stops, looks at me, a frown on his face. "What?"

"I just wondered what you were doing."

"We're having a sale."

"Oh."

He sets the other two mowers in place and goes back into the store. I walk over, look at the price tag which dangles off the handle of one of the lawn mowers, and he comes out with two more, pushes them up behind the one I'm looking at.

"Want to buy one?" he says. Now he is smiling.

"No. I came to—" I don't know what to say to him. He stands there, watching me, waiting for me to finish. "I work here," I say.

"What?"

"Is Mr. Baldwin in?"

"Yeah, he's inside."

"He hired me yesterday."

"Oh, really?" He comes toward me, offers me his hand. "I'm sort of new here too. My name is John Kendal." He takes my hand, shakes it in front of him, looking at it as if he thinks there's something in it. Then he looks up at me. "What's your name?"

"Mike."

"Mike?"

"Mike Sumner."

"Glad to meet you," he says, letting go my hand. He starts back toward the door. "Well? You coming in?"

"I guess so," I say.

He stops, waits for me. "Look," he says. "Don't be nervous— Baldwin is a great guy."

"I know."

"There isn't anybody better in the whole world to work for." He smiles. "You'll see. There's no pressure. No harassment." He puts his arm around my shoulder. His face is round and smooth. His hair is thick, black, and it crosses his white forehead in a straight line, covers his ears.

"I've never sold anything before," I say.

"Neither have I. You'll learn." He moves me toward the door. "Come on."

Inside the store is cold. Color televisions squat in rows on the floor and the walls are lined with shelves. There are toasters, blenders, type-writers, electric knives, popcorn makers—I've never seen so many little machines—crowded onto all the shelves, and along the back wall behind a glass counter, refrigerators and freezers reflect the sun shining through the windows. Everything gleams, carries light. Some of the televisions are on, the voices mixing with laughter and organ music. I don't remember seeing any of this yesterday.

"Baldwin's in his office," John says.

"I know how to get there," I say, moving away from him.

I walk back behind the refrigerators to the little office where Mr. Baldwin sits at his desk drinking coffee. When he sees me he says, "Michael, come in." He gets up, offers me his hand.

"You remember my name," I say.

"Of course." He gestures for me to sit. "Ready to start?"

"I guess so."

"How are you?"

"Fine."

He takes two great black books from a shelf behind him and hands them to me. "This is the line," he says. "Read through these, get familiar with as much as you can."

"OK." I hold the books in my lap. They're heavy and solid, full of little reference tabs.

"For now you'll be selling the small stuff—what we call 'small appliances.' The big stuff—televisions, dishwashers, freezers, and so forth—we call that sort of stuff 'major appliances.'" He looks into my eyes, seems to be waiting for something.

"Major appliances."

"Right. Get to know the difference." He points to the books. "Everything in those books is a major appliance."

"OK."

"You don't know the difference right now, but you will."

"Should I read these here?"

"Sure. I won't be in here much." He moves to the door, holds the frame in his hands, leans down toward me. "If I need you out here I'll let you know."

"I won't know what to do."

"You don't have to. Not to sell the small stuff."

"OK."

"Everything on the shelves, except for the stereos, is a small appliance. So if I need you, you should hang around the shelves. All right?"

"All right."

He starts out, then leans back in. "I've got some books on selling I'll let you have later."

"OK," I say, but he is already gone. I hold my breath for a minute, trying to gauge the quality of the air, of the blood in my veins. I'm OK. I feel almost excited. I did it. I came in here and got started, and I don't feel anything going on that I can't control. I want to read these books, get into them so I won't have time to think. This is what my father was talking about. My father. The thought of him, in the car yesterday after we'd left Eddie, gives me a soft ache in the back of my throat. I think of the sound of his bare feet on the kitchen floor yesterday morning, the way his teeth looked when he asked me to pick a tie from his arm, and suddenly, I begin to cry. I cry for my father and for me. We've gone to our places in this world, no longer becoming anything—and he shuffled across the floor with those eggs, trying to be friends, trying to get to know me. I know he wants to save me. My father. My father.

VI. THE TAPES

They dropped us in a field and told us to link up with Rizzolo and his squad, which was to our left. We crawled along a concrete culvert, looking for green uniforms in the tall grass. Brinkman was next to me, breathing through his nose, his eyes bulging. I could see the dirt under the grass, the white grass, and could smell the rotting insect-filled air. Water was thick and green in the bottom of the culvert. The sky was full of smoke and helicopters, the noise like thousands of independent explosions above us. Brinkman's face ran with sweat, but he kept his mouth closed, his nostrils open wide, drawing in air. I was so tired, I could feel the oxygen in my blood filling my fingers.

"Where the hell are they?" Brinkman said.

I saw a green uniform sticking out of the grass ahead of us. "There," I yelled. Then I coughed. I thought it was funny that in the middle of that, I did something so natural as cough. Brinkman looked at me. His face was white as a cigarette. We crawled on toward the uniform, listening to the helicopters withdraw. I don't know if anyone was firing at us then. One of the men behind me kept yelling, "Oh fuck! Oh fuck!" I had never been so scared.

"Where's Rizzolo?" Brinkman yelled. I heard a crackling noise to our left, on the other side of the culvert, and suddenly the concrete started screaming, coming apart above us. The air filled with white dust. Brinkman speeded up, his boots kicking up dirt and grass in front of me. I felt the man behind me crawling over my legs. "Move it—they're firing at us." I tried to run on my belly. I kept screaming "Who? Who?" Brinkman stopped, turned the top of his body so his head was back toward me. "Who the fuck do you think?" He laughed, then started on, his boots kicking at me again. It really was sort of funny. I didn't laugh, but I felt somehow I would live to do it later. I loved Brinkman then. I tried to stay with him, keep his sprawling boots right in front of me.

He stopped again when he got to the green uniform in the grass, and I heard him scream, "FUCK!" He ducked his head, shook it back and forth, then raised it up to look back at me. He was crying, his face red, his mouth drawn wide. "They're all *dead!*" he screamed. "They're all dead, for Christ's sake!"

Hall came up next to me. "Return fire," he said. It seemed as if he was whispering only to me, a secret we shared. "We're in deep shit, now."

I faced the culvert, dust and pieces of stone chipping into the air like gravel thrown by a speeding car. I didn't know what to shoot at. I couldn't see anything. I held my weapon against the top of the culvert and fired it in the direction of the crackling and the smoke. I felt my heart beating against the ground. In front of me, on the cement, I saw a red ant crawling toward one of the cracks, its tiny legs moving so fast I couldn't see them. When it got to a place where stone rose out of the concrete, it stopped, raised up as if to climb. I wasn't firing anymore. I watched the ant, amazed that it went about its business in the middle of that.

Hall screamed into a radio, trying to get the choppers back. The man next to me, a black named Sears, stopped firing and put his head down. I thought he was hit. I touched his arm. He jumped, looked at me with yellow eyes. "We're fucked, man," he said. I wanted to run. I turned and looked at Hall, who was lying on the ground behind us, holding the radio with both hands and screaming into it for help. Brinkman pulled another clip off his belt, looked at me. "What's wrong?"

"We gotta get out of here," Sears said.

Someone screamed further down the line. I pulled my weapon back and crawled back to Hall.

"What are we going to do?" I yelled.

"Keep firing, goddamn it."

"We're trapped," Sears said.

Hall looked at him, his eyes fierce and alone. "Get back up there."

I crawled back up next to Brinkman, put my weapon on the concrete again, tried to see something through the grass, the dust and smoke. Sears was firing next to me, crying. I heard a sound like a horn in the distance. Then the ground shook in front of us, a cloud of black smoke full of sparks erupting there.

"Mortar!" Brinkman yelled.

Another one hit, behind us. Another. Another. No one was firing anymore. I looked at Brinkman, who held his weapon in front of him, moving his head around as if he were looking for the next one. Hall came up next to me.

"All right, we're going to move down toward the end of this thing." He tapped the culvert with his pistol. "Keep low and go fast." He pulled back and went behind us, and we rolled out and followed. Hall was hitting everybody's legs as he passed, pulling them along. Another shell hit behind us. Then another. I couldn't hear them coming. Just the funny sound, like someone trying to play a horn, and stopping on the first note, then the explosion. As we moved along, I saw Wilan in the grass by the culvert. He was lying close to the ground, as if he had sunk into the dirt there. I didn't see any blood, but he wasn't moving. Then I started to move, started to move without being conscious of anything except the ground in front of me and my breathing.

Brinkman stopped near the end of the culvert. Hall was there waving his arms, screaming for us to spread out. The culvert emptied out into a long ditch, and we were collected at the corner of it where the concrete rose a little higher out of the grass. Everyone tried to get behind that small place at the end of the culvert—a piece of ground no bigger than a child's swimming pool—and we started pushing each other. Everybody squirmed. A shell hit in the ditch a few feet away and sprayed us with water and hot sparks. I had my head down, trying to crawl under my helmet. Hall was screaming, his voice losing its force with each explosion. I don't think anyone was firing. We were all waiting there.

"Spread out along the wall," Hall screamed. It sounded as if he was crying. "Come on, for Christ's sake! *Move!*"

I started moving on my belly toward the thinner part of the wall, but I couldn't make myself go out there. I felt someone crawl over my legs. I turned and saw Sears, his face clenched like a fist. "Goddamn it," he said. He threw himself forward, started firing, firing in all directions. He was screaming, "Fucking bastards! Fucking bastards!" I started firing over the culvert again. A shell hit in the culvert to my right, a flash of light so sudden I lost my vision. The sound of it exploded in my head, a scream that shook my skull. It was like an animal scream in the center of my ear. I was stunned by it. So much so that I swear I thought I was home listening to my stereo and someone had screamed over the loud music. I looked at Sears, wondered who he was, and what he was doing there. He was still screaming, firing his weapon. I looked at his ear, the perfect design of it. Someone screamed behind me. I thought it was Brinkman, but when I looked over my shoulder I saw, behind my boots, Caswell writhing on the ground, holding something against his abdomen. He was fighting with something, struggling fiercely with some tiny thing which doubled him up. I crawled back to him, tried to pull his knees down. I saw the roof of his mouth, his teeth, in a scream so close to the ground it raised dust and chips of grass. He coughed, his mouth open wide. I thought he was going to vomit. I looked at Hall. At Hall. Hall. Caswell made another sound. His mouth opened wider, then closed. I touched his knee, moved his leg down away from his body. He stopped moving. I put my hand on his ankle, looked into his face. It was me, my face. I screamed, crawled into the grass toward the ditch. I heard Hall yelling at me. I wanted to crawl until it was quiet. I thought I'd find a park somewhere, women with children in strollers, old men on park benches, birds on the ground and brown bags everywhere. I heard the grass moving, cracking in the distance to my left. I stopped. I don't know how far I crawled. I looked up and saw black heads moving toward me in the grass. I moved faster, got up and ran in a crouch, ran until the ground came up to meet me. I lost my weapon, my helmet. I crawled down an embankment and into water. I tried to become a fish, hiding in the reeds.

VII. ANNE

"I can't believe I got you out of bed again," Lucy says. She stands in the kitchen with a feeble smile on her face.

"I wasn't sleeping," Anne says. She closes the back door. "How'd it go?"

Lucy moves to the table, sits there as if she has just entered a new restaurant. "I think we're going to be friends."

"What do you mean?"

"We had a nice talk."

"He talked to you?"

Lucy smiles, offering a gift. "He said he was feeling good. Better than he has felt—are you ready for this? Better than since the war."

Anne goes to the table and sits across from Lucy. The top of the table is warm from the sun.

"Well?" Lucy says.

Anne doesn't know how she should feel. She has tried so hard in the past few weeks to make Michael comfortable, and now this girl, this young pure-bodied daughter of someone else, says she has made him feel good in less than an hour.

"What should I do?"

The smile leaves Lucy's face. "Aren't you happy?"

"I guess so. I wonder what will happen, though."

"He's going to be my friend."

"Lucy—" Anne looks at her own hands, the clumps of skin at the knuckles.

"What's the matter?"

"I don't know."

"He's going to get better, really."

"What if—" Anne doesn't know what this girl is after, and that is what she wants to ask. "What if he—you know—gets serious?"

"Forgive me," Lucy says. "I'm going to be honest again."

"I know you're not attracted to him."

"No. Listen." She frowns, looks out the window. Anne watches the side of her face, the way the sun glances off her black hair. Lucy puts her hands together on the table in front of her, turns back and looks into Anne's eyes. "Your generation is hung up on things," she says. "You worry all the time about sex, and what it means, and why it exists."

"*My* generation," Anne says.

"Really." Lucy smiles again, trying to apologize without saying anything. This thought strikes Anne as if it has form and substance, as if Lucy has thrown something at her.

"Your generation," Anne says slowly, "your generation ignores sex too often."

"We don't ignore it. We enjoy it."

"So do I."

"Good."

"So does Michael."

"OK."

"I'm not talking about sex, anyway. I'm talking about—"

"Love?"

"Yes, OK. That's what I'm talking about."

"You wouldn't like it if Mike loved me?"

"Ben wouldn't like it!"

Lucy blinks. Anne realizes she has gotten loud.

"I think you're back to sex again," Lucy says quietly.

"Lucy, you're not listening to me."

"I know what you're saying."

"I wonder if you do."

Lucy studies her hands again, the lids of her eyes beginning to tremble. "I've been honest with him. I told him I wanted to be his friend. He understands."

"You're sure."

"Yes."

"And what about Ben?"

Lucy looks up, a half-smile forming. "Ben knows how I feel. He doesn't worry about things like that."

"All men worry about things like that."

Lucy puts both hands up to her cheeks and leans on them, frowning. "I just want to help."

"I'm afraid, Lucy."

"Don't be."

"I told Dale I wanted to move back to Chicago."

"You don't really."

"I told him this morning. And I do."

"Why?"

"I can't stand it here. I hate the heat, the sun. I don't have any friends."

Lucy bows her head. Anne reaches across the table, touches her hand.

"You know what I mean. In Chicago I had life-long friends—so did Dale. And it was home. Michael needs to go home."

"What did Dale say?"

"He won't consider it."

"Well, I hope you don't go back." Lucy smiles.

"Michael's alone here, he has too much time to think."

The sun retreats behind a cloud and the room suddenly darkens. Lucy looks out the window. "He's got a job, now," she says. "He'll make friends there."

"Michael doesn't make friends easily. He never did. Now—"

"Has he always been shy like that?" Lucy is facing her again.

"Ever since—ever since he was a boy."

"I wonder why?"

"It's just the way he is."

"He talked a lot today. But you know, I couldn't get him to laugh." Lucy leans on her hand, plays with the air on the table with her other hand as if there is a pencil there, or a toy. The sun returns to the room, seems brighter than before. "You know what he said to me in the car?"

Anne watches the black hair, the eyes.

"He said he always feels as if he's on the way somewhere. He doesn't know where. Just that he's on the way somewhere and doesn't know where."

"That's why I want to take him back to Chicago," Anne says. "He needs to be home, and this isn't it."

"It probably won't be in Chicago either. Too much has gone in between."

"I know that," Anne says. "I know that. But what if there's even a flicker of hope?" She pulls her robe tight around her neck, starts to slide out of the seat. "I've got to get dressed."

"But he—" Lucy stops, moves her eyes back and forth as if she is watching something move in Anne's eyes. "Anne, I saw another man come back from that place, and I panicked." Her mouth begins to tremble. "I think I did wrong. But *he* was home—and it didn't do him any good. In fact, it might have been worse because he came back to the world as it was before he left it. That's what he called it too. The world."

"Your first husband?"

Lucy nods her head, looks out the window again. "I gave up on him too soon. I was afraid of him."

"You're not afraid of Michael?"

"No. He's gentle, almost meek."

"Dale thinks he's going to explode."

"So does Ben."

"Maybe he will." Anne sees her son, a shadow looming in the feeble light of the world, holding a knife, slashing through soft, white-draped victims. Michael bringing the war home.

"I don't think Michael is capable of anything violent. I think it's the violence he's trying to forget," Lucy says.

"Did he say something to you about it?"

"No. I just know he's sensitive, that he notices other people."

"What do you mean?"

"This morning, I laughed at a fat woman." Lucy smiles, puts her arms out in a wide circle. "She was really fat. She could barely walk. And Michael was sorry for her. He told me that there was somebody inside all that fat."

Anne feels a brooding laugh stir within her. "That sounds like Michael."

"That's what I mean," Lucy says. "He's too sensitive to do any violence to anyone."

"I wish Dale believed that."

"Michael will convince him."

Anne thinks of an event early in Michael's childhood, an event she remembers frequently now, because it reveals something to her which she cannot put into words. Michael had found a one-eyed turtle, a freak of nature that interested everybody who saw it. The tiny eye, like a bead of water, rested in the center of the hard beak-like head. Michael kept the turtle in the garage in a box with sand and grass, and made a pet of it. He'd come home from school and sit by the box, watching it, touching the hard shell, and talking to it about the things he learned in school. Anne stood by the garage door and listened to him, to the tiny child's voice explaining the world, and she wished more than anything that he would share such things with her. When she went in to be with him, it was always an intrusion. She felt it, felt the change in his voice, his words. And one day, he put the turtle out at the end of the driveway, made a sign which read "SEE THE CYCLOPS TURTLE 10 CENTS." She went out, stood next to the box.

"What are you doing, son?"

He sat on the concrete in a pair of blue overalls which were too big for him, the cuffs rolled clumsily around his ankles. "Nothing," he said. He looked at the turtle, then back to her. "Nobody believes me about him."

She knelt down next to him. "Who won't believe you?"

"Nobody."

"Well, why are you charging money to see him?"

"Nobody believes me because they want me to let them see him." Michael smiled then, a smile full of satisfaction. "So if they want to see him, they can pay me."

She went back into the house, vaguely disconcerted. She watched from the kitchen window as gradually the neighborhood children began to gather around the box. She saw Michael stand up and try to push one of the boys away from the box, and while he was turned away, one of the other boys reached into the box and took the turtle into his hands, raised it up over his head. She ran to the door, called, "Michael!" hoping the sound of her voice would scare the other children. Michael went to the boy with the turtle, reached for it, but the boy was taller and he held the turtle up, sneering at Michael.

"Stop it!" she screamed. She moved down the steps, went across the grass almost in a trot, trying to get there before the boy could run with the turtle. But he didn't run. He turned, looked at her with defiance she could not fathom in a young boy, and then he threw the turtle down hard on the concrete driveway. It cracked, made a sound when it hit like a flowerpot full of dirt. Michael screamed, lunged at the boy, grabbed his arm and whirled him around, clutching with his small hands as if they were talons. She went to him, tried to get him away. Michael screamed, pulled the taller boy, who laughed and sneered. She took her son's arms, moved him away. The other boy stood there, laughing. She saw his mouth open, his eyes gleaming at her son in triumph, and she let herself go. "You little son of a bitch!" she said. Then she swung her arm and hit him with the back of her hand. He went down in front of her, crying almost before the fall was complete. She was instantly sorry, knelt down next to the boy. "You go home," she said. "You go home." Michael ran into the house, without a sound. For hours after that he was silent, brooding. She could not console him. Then, when he was climbing into bed that night, he said, "You shouldn't have hit him, Mama." He smiled, put his hands under the covers.

"I know."

"It was only a turtle."

"That boy deserved what he got," she said, pushing his hair back off his forehead.

"I wish I could have stopped him," Michael said, then he began to cry. She hugged him, felt the heat of his breathing against her breast. "I wish I could have stopped him."

"You should see where he works," Lucy is saying. "I think he'll do all right there. It's a busy corner."

"Where is it?"

"In Englewood. It's within walking distance."

"I don't remember ever seeing it."

"It's on the corner, across the street from the Emporium."

"And it's called Dill's?"

"Yes."

Anne stands up, moves toward the door. "I've got to get dressed."

"Want to go over and see him?"

"Oh, no. We shouldn't do that."

"Don't you want to see him?"

"I don't know."

"He doesn't have to see us. We can stand across the street. Maybe we'll catch a glimpse of him selling something."

"I want to be here when Dale comes home," Anne says, leaning on the door frame.

"Where'd he go?"

"Probably fishing. His friend Eddie called him this morning."

"We've got time," Lucy says, pouting.

"I'll see where Michael works. I don't want to be following him around."

"What are you going to do?"

"I don't know. Right now I'm going to get dressed." Anne waits by the door, watching Lucy slowly move out of the seat. "You can stick around if you want, help me with the dishes."

"No, I guess I'll go." Lucy moves toward the door, her hands clasped in front of her. She stops, touches the doorknob, seems to study it for a moment. "I told Michael to call me when he gets off. If he wants a ride home."

"OK," Anne says.

"Want to go if he calls?"

"Yes. I'd like that."

Lucy turns, looks into Anne's eyes. "You shouldn't let yourself be so bored."

"What should I do? Hitchike across the country? Go dancing in the evening?" Anne tries to smile, but there is a taste in her mouth that she does not like—something bitter, and full of salt.

"You could do lots," Lucy says, numbly. Then she opens the door and goes out into the sunlight.

VIII. MICHAEL

Mr. Baldwin puts his head around the corner and says, "You want some lunch?"

"I'm not hungry."

"I'm sending John out for food. Want to come on out and help me until he gets back?"

"Will I have to sell something?"

"Maybe. Come on. You got to get your feet wet sometime."

I put the books down on his desk.

"Bring those. You can study them out here." His head disappears around the corner. I hold the books against my breast and walk out to the counter which runs in front of the refrigerators. Baldwin stands there at the end of the counter, his hands leaning on the glass. The store is empty.

"I turned off the TVs and stereos, so there won't be any distractions." Baldwin stares at me, as if he is waiting for me to say something. Then he says, "How're you holding up?"

I am afraid he heard me crying. "I'm OK," I say.

"Think you can do this?"

"I don't know."

"All you have to do is try to help each person who comes in. Answer their questions, that sort of stuff."

I nod, think of all the possible questions.

"And don't forget to ask for the sale."

"What?"

"Ask them to buy whatever they are looking at—you know, say, 'Can I get that for you, sir?' That sort of thing." He rubs his cheek, smiles out at the windows. "It's easy," he says.

"I don't know anything yet."

"You will. Read those books."

I page through the books for a while, look at the shiny pictures of devices I never dreamed existed. There are beautiful women, with white teeth, smiling next to all the gleaming metal, the bright-colored plastic. Mr. Baldwin whistles down at the other end of the counter, the sound echoing in the empty store. I stare at the pages, try to make sense out of the confusion of color I see there.

"You know, John's a veteran too," Baldwin says.

I nod, go back to the book.

"He spent fourteen months over there."

My hand rests next to a picture of a refrigerator which dispenses ice water, crushed ice, and orange juice through a small compartment in the door. Underneath my hand is the word "CONVENIENCE" in large script.

"He liked it, I think."

"What?"

"I think he liked it."

I turn the page. There is a freezer full of meat.

"It probably made a man out of him."

I see the word "dimensions," read the small numbers there.

"I'm against the war. I'd march if I didn't have to work."

Built tough, with a door lock and a light to let you know it's doing the job, night and day. . . .

"It's a civil war. We got no business fighting in that mess."

And there's an interior light. . . .

"I hope Nixon gets us out of there soon. There's been enough killing."

Tough porcelain enamel. . . .

"What do you think of all the demonstrations?"

No defrosting ever. . . .

"Michael?"

"What?"

"What do you think of the demonstrations?"

"I've never seen one."

"Are you against the war?"

"I'm afraid of it. I hate it." I try to go back to the book, but Baldwin comes down the counter toward me.

"You must have had a terrible time," he says.

No defrosting ever No defrosting ever No defrosting ever. . . .

"Hey," he says. He puts his hand on my shoulder. "Take it easy."

"I'm all right." I feel it coming down, falling like rain in my head. I try to look into Mr. Baldwin's eyes, try to find him there.

"Don't think about it," he says. His mouth moves, a rubber opening.

"I'm all right."

"I shouldn't have brought it up."

"Do we have this freezer?"

He looks at the picture in the book. "Not on display. But we can get it."

"It doesn't need defrosting." I look at the picture, then back to Baldwin. "It doesn't need defrosting, ever."

"I know," he says, almost whispering. Then, he looks at my hands. "Maybe you should knock off for a while."

"What?"

"Take the rest of the day. Come back next Saturday."

"I'm fine," I say.

"We shouldn't overload you the first day."

"I'm all right. Let me stay another hour." I think of my father, the way he hugged me.

"You're upset."

"No. No, I'm not. Honest." I try to put my hands away.

"It's all right, you don't have to prove anything to me."

"Please. My father—" I look out the front windows at all the bright heads in the sun. It's like a silent movie, the way everything moves in the glass without the slightest sound.

"What about your father?"

"I want to study the books a while longer."

"You sure you're all right?"

"Yes. I'm fine."

"All right, stay until John gets back. But then I think you should go home, rest." He puts his hand on my back, smiles at me the way Kessler does. "Come back next Saturday."

"I can work every day," I tell him. I feel my hands beginning to sweat.

"I don't want you to do that. Not yet." He moves away, toward the back office.

"You wouldn't have to pay me."

He smiles, folds his arms. "I know. But I don't need you until Saturday."

I look at the floor by his feet, see a cigarette butt crushed there.

"We don't want to overdo it right away," he says. "Trust me."

"OK," I say. He disappears into the office. I study the cigarette butt, think about the smoker who put it there, and wonder who in this random existence might have stepped on it.

After a while he comes back out, wanders out to the front of the store, his arms folded again. He stands in front of the windows, leaning on a washing machine, watching the people pass outside. He is only a shadow in the glass. Only a shadow. . . .

. . . The jeep swerves in the darkness.

"We going to make it?" I say.

Rizzolo is driving. Brinkman sits next to him, and Wilan is next to me in back. Behind us is the compound, and beyond that the green hills which turn black at night.

"Got to keep this thing moving," Rizzolo yells.

The jeep coughs. "Are we running out of gas?" Wilan says.

"No," Rizzolo says. "The jeep needs some R and R too."

Brinkman laughs. He draws on his cigarette, holds the smoke in.

"Is Caswell going to meet us in town?" I say.

"If he can get Hall to let him go," Wilan says. He snaps his fingers. "Hall can't stand that dude."

"Caswell's crazy," Rizzolo says over his shoulder. The air is hot and full of water. The jeep hits a bump, and I feel the bottom of the seat.

"Stay on the road," Brinkman says.

"Got to. Nowhere else to go." Rizzolo laughs, then whistles.

"I want to keep my feet dry for a while," Wilan says.

"They got infrared?" I ask. Brinkman takes a long pull on his dope, holds it high in his chest. As he lets the smoke out he says, "Hope not."

"No," Rizzolo says.

"How do you know?" I watch the back of his neck in the darkness. The moon makes shadows there from the moving trees.

"I know. Don't worry."

Brinkman turns in his seat, points toward the hills behind us. "The enemy is that way," he says. "We been rooting in the grass looking for the bastards for the last three weeks."

"Didn't find them either," Wilan says.

"A Company found them," Rizzolo yells into the wind.

Wilan lets out a high laugh, his head rolling back. "They don't want to go looking anymore either."

"I'm not sure this is a good idea," I say. I have to tell someone how I feel. I want to know if any of them feels the same way.

The jeep hits another bump, all the heads bounce.

"Lousy shocks."

Brinkman offers me some dope. "Make you feel better."

"I don't want any," I say. He turns back to the road, his head tilted to the side. He has such confidence. Even Niles's death didn't bother him for long. "We're all going to make it," he says.

"This is like a spaceflight," I say.

"How's that?" Brinkman turns in his seat again. The wind blows his hair out, whips it back against his head.

"We're out here. Out here away from earth, going to the moon."

"People go to town all the time," Rizzolo says. "Hall's got you scared of the place."

Wilan touches my arm. "Everybody goes there. If Hall wasn't such a prick we'd spend every weekend in that place."

"There's women there," Rizzolo says.

"I know guys that swim in the ocean, every weekend," Wilan says.

"Hall's against fun." Rizzolo leans back in the seat, moves the steering wheel as if he is dancing with it. The jeep lurches back and forth. "He's afraid we'll get soft and won't be any good when we go into the bush."

"He's been here before," I say. "He knows this place. He knows what he's talking about."

Wilan hits my arm. "Will you quit it? This place is crawling with MPs. You'd be in more danger if you were in Chicago."

"I wish I *was* in Chicago."

"What do you come with us for, Sumner?" Wilan is staring at me, his eyes reflecting the moon.

"What?"

"All you do is gripe."

"Leave him alone," Brinkman says.

"He's such a pussy."

Brinkman leans back, puts his head upside down in front of me. "Punch the son of a bitch, I can't reach him."

I watch the black trees by the road, think of the enemy in there with the insects, watching us. "I wish this thing had a top," I say.

"Gripe gripe gripe."

"I see the lights from the town," Rizzolo says.

Wilan is next to me, watching the side of my face. I try to keep my eyes on the road, on the lights in front of us.

"I wish Caswell was here," Wilan says. "He's crazy."

"He'll come next time."

"We'll leave Sumner back at the compound. He and Hall can rub each other."

Brinkman turns and looks at me. "You going to take that?"

"What am I supposed to do?"

"Tell him to go fuck himself."

"Go ahead," Wilan says. I believe he is serious, and I don't want to fight him. I don't want to fight anyone. Brinkman settles back in his seat. I wish I had not done this. I wish I had not come to this place. . . .

"Slow day," Mr. Baldwin says.

"What?"

"I didn't mean to scare you. I know you were concentrating."

I didn't see him come back to the counter. "That's OK."

"You learning anything?"

"Yes."

"Good." He nods his head, smiles. "John ought to be back pretty soon." He sighs, leans back with his hands on his stomach. "I'm hungry."

I smile at him, look back to the book. I watch my hands turn the pages, as if they had volition, moved without any signal from me.

"I guess I'll go back and do some work. Give me a holler if somebody comes in."

"OK."

He stops next to me, touches my arm again. "Don't try to handle it by yourself, OK?"

"OK."

"Call me."

"OK."

He squeezes my arm and walks into the back office. . . .

. . . The room is yellow with high walls and long bare windows down both sides and along the back wall. Each window is nearly as wide as the double doors of the entrance. The walls seem thin and weak.

"Let's have some recreation before we go to one of the clubs," Rizzolo says.

"I want to go someplace where it's dark and there's women."

"Brinkman, that's all you think about," Rizzolo says.

There is a bar along the left and some random tables, each with four straight-backed bamboo chairs. On the right, a huge pillar rises up through the ceiling. The paint is chipping away and metal shines through. Pool tables line the wall opposite the bar, and pinball machines clutter the corner by the door.

"I want women," Brinkman says.

"This is like a USO," Wilan says. "Shit."

Men lounge around the room, drinking. Music blares from a juke-box by the bar. The pinball machines blink and ring.

"Some club," Brinkman says.

"Let's get a drink, at least." Rizzolo goes to the bar. The rest of us follow. No one notices us. Everyone is in uniform.

Rizzolo orders a beer for all of us. I put the glass against my forehead before drinking any of it. I hear the Rolling Stones singing "Let's Spend the Night Together." I take a long sip of beer. I watch the long black windows.

One of the men at the bar, an NCO, moves down next to me. "You from the base?"

"Yes."

"I'm at the strip," he says.

"The strip?"

"The airstrip." He sips his drink. "I help fly the bodies out."

"Oh." I don't want to talk to him. I look at Rizzolo, who is lighting a cigarette. Brinkman sits next to him, drinking his beer. I don't see Wilan.

"You been in a firefight yet?"

"We've been out. Nothing yet," I say.

"Somebody's getting hit up there."

"I know. A Company got into it day before yesterday."

"I heard the rumbling late at night."

"That's when they come out. At night." I turn to Rizzolo. "Where's Wilan?"

"He's shooting pool."

Brinkman orders another beer. The windows are so black, they look like crepe hanging from the ceiling. The music changes to "Sitting at the Dock of the Bay." I finish my beer.

"Have another one, on me," the NCO says. He looks at me, smiling. "My name is Garfield. Bob Garfield." He offers his hand.

"How you doing, Sarge?" I take his hand, grip it. He is almost old enough to be my father.

"I help fly the bodies out," he says. I see myself trussed up in an aluminum coffin, his hands moving it onto a ramp and then into the belly of one of the transport planes. It is a flight I know I will make, and when I think of it, I begin to feel the beer in my stomach.

"It's a rotten job."

I don't like the black windows. Rizzolo moves over to the pinball machines. I watch him putting in a coin, working the flippers. Next to him a marine writhes against the machine there, working the flippers in a frenzy with each ball. He curses loudly when he loses one, bangs the top of the machine, then starts another one.

I take my beer and go over to the machines without saying anything to the sarge. He follows me, stands next to me, watching the ball bounce under the glass. I don't know what to say to him, but I don't want to hear about the bodies.

Wilan comes over and leans on the machine.

"Let's gamble," he says.

Rizzolo finishes his last ball, stands up higher and says, "How?"

"Put money on each ball."

"It's a deal." Rizzolo reaches for another coin.

"You can't use the flippers, though," Wilan says. I hear the NCO laugh.

"What?" Rizzolo says.

"It wouldn't be gambling otherwise."

"You just bet on the roll of the ball?"

"Right." Wilan takes ten dollars out of his pocket and lays it on the glass. "Put your money up."

Rizzolo laughs. He puts a coin in the machine, pushes the button for two players.

Wilan taps the glass. "Put your money up."

"I got it."

"Put it where I can see it."

I feel the NCO raise his glass next to me. I feel sorry for him and turn to see his eyes watching the top of the machine as he drinks. "This ought to be interesting," I say.

He puts his glass down, smiles. I turn back to see the first ball spring around the top rim of the machine. The lights blink. It caroms off wires, bounces around stoppers with numbers, then rolls harmlessly through the idle flippers.

"Three forty-eight!" Rizzolo says. Then he looks at Wilan. "Is that good?"

Wilan moves around behind me to take his place in front of the machine. "That's horrible," he says.

He starts another ball. Both of them scream at it. I watch the ball and I feel someone move, by the door, and I look up, see a marine going out. I look back to the ball, hear a door slam. I see the marine coming back into the room, yelling something. He ducks down toward a table, and I hear a short pocking sound—short and muffled. Glass shatters and everybody goes to the floor. I hit my elbow hard on the wood floor and I hear the NCO go down next to me, hear his bones hitting the floor almost at the same instant. I look around the room at all the black windows and I scream, "Somebody turn out the lights!" The NCO is next to me. I hear him say something, a word like "sock" or "sick," and I turn to him. The pinball is still bouncing around above us, ringing bells, and the NCO lies on his stomach, his hands close up to his sides, elbows up in the air like a man ready to do pushups, and his face white, his eyes staring right back at me. I see a little hole in his left cheek. There is not much blood. He opens his mouth, yawning at me. His eyes move around like the pinball in the machine, around and around. "Sick," he says. "Sick." *He was trying to talk, and that was all that came out. . . .*

"What?" Baldwin stands next to me.

"Nothing."

"You said something about someone trying to talk?"

"No. I was just thinking."

"You all right?"

"Yes."

"Well, pay attention. Didn't you see that customer up there?"

I look and at the front of the store, an old woman studies something on the shelves down there.

"I'm sorry."

"Watch me, I'll wait on her." He moves away from me, walks stealthily down the aisle between the color TVs. He stops halfway to her, turns back to me. He gestures to me with his arm to come on.

I follow him down the aisle, trying to be quiet. I wonder if I should hide behind something, or remain at a distance. He keeps signaling me with his hand to come on. I feel as if he is going to jump her, force her to do something horrible—grab her around the neck, force her head back, and make her eat some terrible fruit. I see his hand turn over flat and signal me to stop. When he is only a few feet from her he says, "Can I help you with something today?"

She looks at him as if he is one of the appliances, a recording in an elevator. She has silver hair piled high on her head, a pair of wire glasses with a gold chain running from each lens down around her wide neck. She wears a thin blue dress which reveals most of the folds in her body. There is a roundness about her I like—something which suggests comfort. She looks puzzled, a frown coming to her face, leaving it, so there is nothing there but a blank stare, then returning again —her eyes moving to the shelves, back to Mr. Baldwin, then to the shelves again. Baldwin leans toward her in the position he took when he stopped.

"Uh—anything I can do?" he says again.

I watch her chin shake as she moves her head back and forth between the shelves and Baldwin. She doesn't know what to say. She picks up a small square plastic device, holds it up to the light from the windows.

"Need a can opener?" Baldwin says. "Let's see, that one is—" He reaches for it, for the tag hanging off it, but she pulls it back, frowns at him.

"Young man, what do you want?" Her voice is deep, like a man who screams for a living. Her eyes look like fried eggs behind the glasses.

"Can I help you?" Baldwin is louder.

She looks at the device in her hand. "How much is this?"

He reaches for the tag, but she pulls the can opener back. She is indignant now, a look of disapproval on her large face—as if he has touched her somewhere she does not want to be touched. "I have to look at the tag, ma'am," he says.

She looks over at me. I look to the floor, out to the windows.

"How much is this?" She tilts her head, determined.

Baldwin speaks very loud now. "I need to see the tag." He tries to be kind, believing she cannot hear him. His hands begin to form signals for her, pointing to the tag, then his eyes.

"Oh," she says, and holds out the tag for him. Both of them study it. At the same time they say, "Fourteen ninety-five." But hers is a question, almost in disbelief, and Baldwin's is a statement.

"Well," she says. She puts it back on the shelf.

"Can I get one for you?" Baldwin says.

"Certainly not." I don't think there is anything wrong with her hearing. She turns to face Baldwin. "Why don't you sell things as cheaply as Reedy's?"

"We're a discount store, but we also have fine products." Baldwin leans on one of the shelves, puts his hand on his hip.

"Fourteen ninety-five." She shakes her head.

"Reedy knows how much his products are worth. So does Mr. Dill."

She smiles, points her finger at him. "Mr. Dill has too many stores, if you ask me."

"There are other can openers here," Baldwin says. He picks one off the shelf. "Here, this one's only seven eighty-eight." He holds it out to her. She waves it away with her hand.

"How come you showed me one that cost fourteen ninety-five?" Her voice is triumphant.

"*You* picked that one out."

The woman shakes her head, begins to turn away. "I'm not going to argue with you." For the first time, I notice a small black bag dangling from her flabby bare arm. "I used to shop in this store all the time," she says when she is by the door. "But you people have gotten greedy."

Baldwin shakes his head.

She raises her arm, the purse dangling at the elbow. "I'll never come back in this place again." She lowers her arm, looks at Baldwin.

"That's OK," he says, loud so she can hear him. "We didn't *send* for you!" When she is out the door he yells, "Old bitch!"

I go back to the counter, listening to him talking to himself as he comes behind me. I don't want to look into his eyes. I'm embarrassed for him.

"It takes all kinds of people to make a world," he says, coming up next to me. I begin to page through the book again.

"And most of them are fucked up," he says. Then he laughs. "That was some lesson, huh?"

"I guess," I say, still looking at the pages in the book.

"Heh. I blew it, you know. I lost my temper."

"I didn't notice."

"No. I blew it." I feel him shaking his head next to me. "I thought she was ignoring me. It didn't occur to me she was hard of hearing."

"She heard you all right."

"Nah. She was deaf as a television set." He laughs again, a short burst. "The only thing I did right was ask her if she wanted that damned can opener."

I pretend to laugh too. He puts his hand on my shoulder.

"Maybe it's a good thing," he says. "You need to laugh some."

"I know."

"One thing to remember. Never argue with a customer."

"OK."

"Even when you know you're right. If I had laughed, said something about 'You can't blame a man for trying,' or something like that —she probably would have bought that seven-dollar can opener."

I look at him. "Really?"

"Yup. People need to feel they've outsmarted you—caught you in your own game. Nobody buys something from a person that proves them wrong about something." He takes his hand away, leans on the counter. Although he has been laughing, his red moustache seems to sag, and his eyes gaze blankly out toward the windows.

"Are you hot?" he says.

"What?"

He looks at me again. "You're sweating a lot."

"I am?"

"You feel all right?"

"I'm fine."

"Where the hell's John?" He walks back toward the front of the store. He stops in front of one of the TVs. "You know? People are really something."

"I know."

"You learn a lot about them in this business."

I think of the old woman, the way the skin shook on her cheeks and her arms, and I feel sorry for her. I cannot believe anyone lives as long as she has.

"Here comes John," Baldwin says. "Why don't you get ready and take off?"

I know he really wants me to go, so I take the books back in the office, sit in the chair by the phone. I don't know Lucy's number, so I call my mother and she gives it to me.

"Are you all right?" she asks.

"Yes."

"How'd it go?"

"Fine."

"I'm coming with Lucy, if you don't mind."

"That's OK," I say, but I'm vaguely disappointed. I don't know what the three of us will talk about.

"You don't have to call her," Mother says. "I'll walk back and get her."

"OK." Then I remember that I left my tape recorder in Lucy's car.

"Mother," I say, after a pause in which I could hear tiny voices crackling somewhere in the line.

"What?" She waits, I hear her breathing.

"I lost the tape recorder again."

"You did?"

"I think Lucy has it." I feel my eyes closing. I think of the eyes on the old woman, seeing the world for so long.

"It's all right, she'll have it," Mother says. "Calm down."

"I'm sorry," I say, and hang up the phone.

PART
THREE

I. DALE

"Before long, it'll be Christmas," he says, drying his hair with a white towel. Anne stands behind him, trying to see in the mirror to brush her hair.

"I used to love September in Illinois," she says.

"It's nice here too." He drapes the towel over the bar which holds the shower curtain. "What're you going to do today?"

"I don't know. I never know."

"Michael going to work?"

"No, he's still only Saturday help."

"Some job."

She puts the brush on the sink, moves to let him pass. "What happened to the job you were going to get?"

"You remember that, huh?"

She looks at him in the mirror. He stands in the hall, outside, but her face is in the mirror, waiting. "Well?"

"I got Michael a job. That's all I wanted."

"So now you don't have to worry about him."

"I worry."

"You haven't said two words to him since he got the job." She pats her hair, then removes the robe. The smooth skin near the top of her thighs shakes, and there is a bruise there. She leans over the tub, turns on the shower. "I hope you saved me some hot water."

He reaches out, touches her. "You're fine."

She takes his hand away. "Not now."

"I like it in the morning."

"You like it all the time."

He laughs, thinks of last night, the warmth of her body, and the icy coldness of the sheets. "You're lovely."

"I'm cold." She gets in the shower. He looks at himself in the mirror, watches it begin to steam up again. "Close the door," she says.

He brushes his hair, thinks of her doing the same thing before she gets in the shower, and laughs again.

"What's the matter?"

"I was just wondering why you brush your hair before you take a shower."

"Gets the rats out."

He wants to look at her body one more time, so he moves the shower curtain aside, sees her standing with her legs slightly apart, her head down, the water running over her breasts. He reaches down, touches her stomach, lets his hand run down to the soft hair between her legs. She doesn't move. He moves his hand, splits the folds there. "I love you here," he says. She puts her hand on his, caresses it as it moves, her head still down.

"Want to get back in?" Her voice is thick.

He steps into the hot water, moves against her, his hand still holding her. She breathes into his shoulder, and he lifts her, holds her up while she balances herself on the sides of the tub.

Later, while they are dressing, she says, "Think Michael heard us?"

"He's probably not even out of bed yet."

"He sleeps later than usual lately." Anne pulls on a pair of white Bermuda shorts.

"Probably a good sign." Dale sits on the bed, watching her.

She goes to the bureau, begins to comb her hair.

"What's all this stuff with Lucy?" Dale says.

"What do you mean?"

"The evening walks and all."

"If you were around once in a while, you'd know."

"I'm just starting to enjoy all this. Don't give me a hard time."

"They're just friends."

"She's a hot ticket," he says, pulling on a pair of socks. "I wonder what kind of friends they are."

"Why do you say that?" She turns to face him. "Does it bother you?"

"No." He shrugs.

"Does anything bother you?"

He looks into her eyes, considers the light there. "Like I said, I'm just beginning to enjoy this."

She moves over in front of him, and he knows she is waiting for his eyes, waiting to ask him something. He studies the shoes he is tying, conscious of her feet in front of him.

"Have you talked to Michael lately?" she says, finally.

"About what?"

"About anything."

He looks at her, then back to his shoes. "I've been busy."

"Why?"

"I've been enjoying myself."

"You were so concerned before. What happened?"

He sits up, looks out the window. Above all the houses white clouds shift in the blue air. All he wants is to be under them, feeling the breezes. "Nothing happened," he says, almost in a whisper.

"He still needs you," she says.

"What do you want? I got him the job."

"And that's it?"

"I can't be hanging around him all day."

She sits on the bed next to him. "You're not listening to me."

"Oh, I'm listening," he says. "I'm listening. What I hear is another plea for returning to Chicago."

"I'm not talking about Chicago."

"Yes, you are."

"I'm talking about your son."

"We're finally beginning to settle into some kind of life here." He looks at her hands.

"You're settling into a life."

"That's what I came here for."

She gets up, moves to the center of the room. He cannot look at her, and the sense of betrayal begins to rise in him again. "I don't have any friends," she says. "I don't have anything to do."

"Jesus," he says.

"You're not thinking of anyone but yourself."

"And who are you thinking of?"

"I'm thinking of Michael."

"Shit."

"He needs to be home."

"This is home."

"Not for him."

He gets up from the bed, walks to the window, keeping her out of his vision. "Is that how you work it?" he says, quietly. "Make love to me, get me softened up for another attack."

"That's not fair."

"I know. So why do you do it?"

"You really don't care, do you?" He hears her coming closer, knows the expression on her face. "You don't care about him at all."

"He's a man. I want to let him be a man."

She is next to him now, her eyes piercing the side of his head. "That's not it at all. You don't care about him."

"I'm not going to change my life for him." He looks at her now. "He's got the responsibility for his own life. And so do I." She turns away, stares out the window. "So do you," he says.

She blinks her eyes, lets out a quiet sigh.

"So do you," he says louder. "If you want to go back to Chicago, then go back. I'm not stopping you."

"Sure," she says. "That's just what Michael needs."

"He's not a little boy anymore."

"He's not right. You know that."

"What do you want from me?"

She returns to the bureau, places her hands on the wood surface, as if she is touching it to see if it is really there. "I know going home probably won't make any difference. I *know* that. But what if it does? What if being home again—"

"Now you're going to start crying."

"I don't know what to do. I don't know what to say to you."

"Don't say anything. Just leave me alone."

"I thought you wanted to be friends with him?"

"The day after I got him the job I knew I couldn't do that."

She faces him. "How? Why?"

"Because he's not Michael!" He yells this, pauses by the window until the sound of it no longer echoes in his ears. Then he says, "I can't be friends with someone who doesn't talk, someone I don't know."

"He talks to you."

"He talks to Kessler."

"He wants to be with you."

"He talks to that fucking tape recorder."

"I can't believe you've given up so easily."

He lets out a breath of air, sits back on the bed. The room is bright with the sun and there are clean shadows everywhere. "I listened to one of his tapes," he says quietly. "I—I heard some things that—"

"You did?"

"Yes."

"Why?"

"I wondered what was on them."

She does not move. He cannot tell if she is breathing.

"Apparently I'm one of the problems," he says, his voice losing its force. "He thought of me when they caught him. It was like I was one of them."

"No."

"Yes. I—I tell you—I—" He covers his face, tries to block out the words, the sounds in the room. "That's why he starts wailing. It's always been when I was around. I remind him."

"I don't believe it."

"Talk to Kessler."

"You've talked to him?"

"I don't have to. I've heard the tape."

He remembers the dark evening room, Michael gone for one of his walks with Lucy—the first walk. Michael went out of the house almost happy, and Dale felt as if everything which had gone before that day had been a drama he saw in a movie, something which troubled him for a few days, and subsided with the passage of time. He walked up to his room, planning to lie on the great bed in there and read, but when he passed Michael's door, he couldn't resist going in. He wanted to see if there was a change there too—if things were somehow rearranged in a pattern he would recognize as normal. There, on the table by Michael's bed, was the tape recorder, with a tape in it. He sat down on the bed, and without thinking, a cold feeling in his stomach, as if he were an intruder in a strange house, he turned the volume down low and played the tape. It was short, described a dream Michael had when he was hit over the head with a rifle butt. "I dreamed I was running from my father. I was a little boy again, running from my father. In the dream, he came over a dune on all fours, like a dog. He tried to pry open my mouth. I screamed." Dale listened, his heart losing blood. It seemed that all he could do was exhale with each of his son's words, and he could not draw in air, make himself breathe. He wept quietly, thinking: *So this is what happens to a man's dreams. The world doesn't really move. It stands perfectly still, watching all the tragedy, like a crowd of people around an automobile accident. And now I understand fatherhood, what happens to it, what it causes. I am Father. Father. And I am Enemy, forcing the child to inhabit Earth.*

He listened to the tape again, felt each word transpire like a gas into all his blood. Then he went downstairs and drank a cold beer, his hands shaking, his eyes cold and alone, seeing nothing but light, yellow light, and shadows in the room.

"He's confused," Anne says now, her voice a soft invasion.

"So you see?" Dale says, looking up. "It wouldn't do any good to go back to Chicago. *I'd* be there too."

"What did he *say* on the tape?"

"I told you. When they caught him, when they hit him, it was me. It was me."

"I'm sorry," she whispers, moving to the bed. She puts her hands on his shoulders. "But I don't think Michael understands all this. I don't think he really feels that way."

"I don't want to be around him," Dale says, tears burning in the corners of his eyes. "It's only time. Maybe time will do the healing. As long as he goes to the job, and keeps coming home, as long as he looks forward to something—" He breaks off, rubbing his face with his hands.

"I didn't think our lives would ever be like this."

He gets up from the bed and goes to the bureau, opens the top drawer, and takes out the telegram announcing Michael's death. He walks to her as if he is in a hurry, trying to keep her from falling. He holds the paper in front of her and says, "Remember when our lives were like this?"

She turns away. "I remember."

"I don't know if I feel any better now than I did then," he says.

"He's alive. He's beginning to adjust to what happened."

"When will he be Michael again?"

"Give him time," she says in a flat voice.

Dale takes the telegram back to the bureau, places it neatly in among the underwear, the shirts and socks.

Anne goes to the door, stares out into the hall. "I think I hear him."

"Don't bother him."

"Maybe if you talked to him about it."

"No. And don't ever mention it to him. Not *ever.*"

She bows her head, leans against the door frame.

"Do you hear?" he says.

"Yes."

"I'll have breakfast with him—if he comes down."

"All I want is for us to be a family again."

He walks over to her, places his hands on her shoulders. "You going to make breakfast?"

"OK."

"If you get bored today, why don't you go walking with Michael?"

"I'm afraid to ask him."

"Ask him."

She nods her head.

"It's not Florida," he says.

"I guess not." She reaches back, touches the hand on her shoulder, then moves out of the room and down the hall. As she passes Michael's door, Dale sees her pause there, lean toward it slightly, then go on.

"Is he awake?" he asks, but she doesn't hear him. He watches her disappear down the stairs.

II. ANNE

In the kitchen, she sets a frying pan on the stove and puts bacon in it, thinking the smell of it cooking might bring Michael down. She stands in front of the stove, waiting for the heat to rise. She tries to remember Illinois at this time of year—the warm air with just a hint of coldness to it, like the sheets under her body at night. If she didn't move in the air, it felt warm; but the wind would rise, or she would walk into the breezes and feel the tattered edges of winter filtering into everything. She liked the bare trees, the early snow, the soft lights in the houses, the wind herding the leaves. Here, it gets cold only at night, and the trees never lose anything, although all the yards fill with white pine needles. So she will miss winter, and Michael coming home, Michael coming in out of the cold air, his face bright and red with the clear crispness of the atmosphere, a crispness which suggested singing and ice-blue evenings in silent snow.

The bacon begins to sizzle. She goes to the window and looks out over the houses at the blue sky, little strips of cloud crossing it like white ribbons. In the distance, where the water must be, tiny black dots whirl and swing, dipping down out of sight and back up into the air again. She watches them, listens for sound in the soft frame of the world. She opens the window, leaning over the table without bending her legs, as if performing a physical exercise to the music which comes to her as the window rises. Above the chattering of the birds, she hears the engines of the town, the radios announcing traffic, playing guitars. The open window is a source of heat, but the air is fresh, smells of pine and salt water. Perhaps it is good to walk in it, to get out by the sea and watch the birds. Stand on the edge of land and look out over the rim of the earth where the blue and indifferent sky turns white, and there are no shadows anywhere.

She returns to the stove and adjusts the heat under the bacon, separates the strips as they begin to curl and go limp. Then she plugs in the coffee pot, checks the bowl to be sure there is coffee there. Dale comes in, picks up the phone, and dials.

"Who are you calling?"

"Eddie."

"Michael up?"

He finishes dialing, nods his head when she turns to him for an answer. "Do try and walk with him today," he says, then puts up his hand. "Eddie, going fishing today?"

She goes to the cupboard above the sink and takes out three plates, walks over to the table, and places them in the sunlight.

"Want me to pick you up?"

She gets the silverware, places it next to the plates.

"All right." He puts the phone back in the receiver, goes to the table. "I'm hungry."

"I think I *may* ask him to go for a walk." Anne turns the bacon, waits for Michael.

"It'll do you good."

"I know."

"What's the window open for?"

"I wanted to see what sort of day it was."

"Hot." He stands up, closes the window. "The air conditioner is on."

Michael comes into the kitchen, dressed in a T-shirt, Bermuda shorts, and sandals. His hair is longer now, but it still clings closely to his head, and he almost never brushes it. He goes to the table, sits across from his father, his head down, his eyes blinking with sleep.

"Morning." Dale smiles, looks at Anne.

"Hello," Michael says. He looks at his plate, pushes it toward the middle of the table. "I don't think I want anything."

"You gotta eat breakfast," Dale says, his voice quiet, almost timid.

Anne takes the bacon out of the pan and puts it on a napkin. The coffee light comes on and she gets two cups, brings them to the table. She wants to go with Michael today, walk next to him and think. But she is afraid to ask him. She looks at Dale, wishes he would suggest it.

"Going fishing today?" Michael says.

Dale nods.

Michael looks at Anne for the first time and says, "Can I just have a little coffee?"

"Sure." She goes for another cup, thinking this is not something they will ever get over. Dale will never be able to forget what he heard on that tape. The thought gives her a cold feeling beneath her skin—almost angers her. If he would only have left the tapes alone. If he hadn't insisted on listening to his son's private fears.

"How's Lucy?" Dale says, suddenly.

Michael stares out the window, seems to nod his head. "Fine."

Anne brings Michael his coffee, places it in front of him, watching his eyes, the slight quiver of his hands. Dale sips his coffee, staring over the brim of the cup at Anne, sharing something silently with her. She is a cook in a coffee shop, and these two men have climbed down off a great blue and white rig, which sits in the parking lot outside like a building, and neither knows the other well enough to laugh at anything. Both of them stare at her, as if they expect her to entertain them. So this is what has happened to her family: a strange and unavoidable evolution, which makes the world another country, and her husband and son idle strangers sipping coffee in a foreign kitchen.

She puts two eggs in the bacon grease, starts them sizzling, then she takes the bacon to the table, puts it in front of Dale.

"Lucy's pretty nice looking, don't you think?" Dale says. Anne frowns at him, trying to convey the question "What are you doing?" without saying anything. Dale stares at Michael.

"I like her," Michael says.

"She likes you too, probably."

Michael smiles at him. "I hope so."

"You understand—" Anne starts.

"You good friends?" Dale says.

"She talks a lot."

"What's she talk about?"

"I don't know. Everything. I feel good with her."

Anne goes back to the eggs, spoons the grease over them. When they are finished, she puts them on a napkin, brings them to the table.

"Aren't you going to have any?" Dale asks.

"I don't think so." Anne sits down next to Michael. "How are you feeling today?"

"Fine. I feel fine."

"Is everything all right?"

"Mother," Michael says, his voice slow and deliberate. "I wish you'd quit asking me that. I'm fine."

"Are you going to see Kessler today?"

"Yes."

"When is Baldwin going to put you on full-time?" Dale says, chewing his eggs.

"I don't know. I'm not doing very well."

"You can't sell very much working only on Saturdays." Dale sips his coffee, glances at Anne, back to Michael.

"I don't know the line yet. I can't concentrate on it." Michael takes the first sip of his coffee, making a sound with his lips that seems so normal to Anne she wants to reach out and touch him, hold him.

"What are you going to do today?" she asks.

"I don't know."

"Are you going to walk?"

"Maybe." He sips again. Dale crunches on a piece of bacon, scrapes his fork along the plate.

"Where do you go when you walk, Michael?" Anne says. She watches the side of his face, his eyes.

"I just walk," he says.

"That toast was the best I've ever had," Dale says.

"I'm sorry," Anne says. "I forgot."

Dale wipes his mouth with a napkin. "That's all right, I didn't need it."

"I'd like some toast," Michael says.

Anne makes the toast, wondering how she can get Michael to let her come with him. She is afraid he will not want her. She does not know what she will do if he wants to go alone. She sees herself retreating to the bedroom again, the house quiet, almost sinister; climbing into bed, lying there watching the window, the bare sky, waiting for all of it to go away.

Dale washes his hands, goes to the back door. "See you," he says, and goes out. She hears the Toyota start, watches a white reflection from it cross the ceiling. Michael eats his toast, slowly, his mouth barely working. She sits across from him, watching the toast disappear, waiting for him to say something.

"Are you all right?" she says, and immediately she regrets it. "I'm sorry."

"Everything's fine," he says.

"I guess I just haven't talked to you for a while, and I want to be sure."

He nods, chews his toast.

"Remember the first time we really talked about it?" Anne says.

"What?"

"When you were in the bathroom with one of your father's ties?"

"Yes." He takes a sip of his coffee, puts the cup down, looking at her now. "What about it?"

"I told you we had to spend more time together."

"I'm doing fine. You've helped me a lot."

"I don't think we've really spent that much more time with each other, though." She stares at the empty plate in front of her, the drying egg, small pieces of bacon.

"I don't mind being alone," he says, a slight quiver coming into his voice. "I like it."

"You do?"

"I'm learning how to make it go away."

"Make what go away?"

"Everything. All the things I can't think about."

"Maybe you should think about them." She sees his eyes widen and she reaches across the table for him, but he sits back. "I don't know. But maybe it's not a good idea to keep it all inside."

"You sound like Kessler."

"Well, he's probably right, son. He's trained to know these things." She withdraws her hand. "If you don't deal with it, it will always haunt you."

He shakes his head, his breathing increases.

"Don't be upset now," she says.

"I feel good when I don't think about it. I'm OK as long as I don't have to think about it."

"OK, OK."

"You and Dad are always making me think about it."

"I'm sorry."

"And Kessler. He won't leave me alone."

"He's trying to help you. I'm trying to help you."

"I don't need to think about it."

"Calm down," she says. "All right. I'm sorry."

He starts to get up from the table and she leans over and touches his arm.

"Don't now. Don't go," she pleads. She feels her voice leaving her, sees the bed upstairs and the window and the quiet house. "I don't want to be alone, just now."

"What?"

"I want you to stay for a while."

"I can't."

"Why?"

"I have to go."

"Don't."

"It's not like before," he says, his voice cracking. She sees his eyes beginning to tighten. "It's not like before."

"What's not like before?"

"Nothing."

She holds his arm, feels the blood pulse there. He begins to tremble, his eyes fill with tears.

"Explain it to me," she says.

"I can't."

"Before what?"

"You're not my mother," he says. It is almost a shout, and the words strike her, pierce all her flesh.

"What do you mean?"

"Leave me alone!" He pulls his arm away.

"Please, son." She feels her own eyes fill and she reaches for him, tries to get all of him in her arms, end this dream, but he gets up, moves toward the door. "I wanted to go with you today. That's all. I wanted to go with you."

"Don't," he says. He stands by the stove, his hands rubbing the sides of his legs. "Don't."

"I just wanted to go with you."

"Don't cry."

"I'm lonely, son."

"I can't now. I just can't." He rubs his cheek, puts his hand back to the stove. He stands on one foot, then the other. "I can't."

"Can't we just walk?" She wipes her eyes with Dale's napkin, tries to stop crying.

"I can't."

"Please. Just a short—"

"No. Not now. Not now." He goes to the door, stops when it is open, looks back to her, his eyes so small he is a child again. "OK?" he whispers. Then he goes out the door, closes it quietly and carefully behind him. She watches him walk down the driveway and on up the street into the white sun.

III. MICHAEL

At the end of the street I watch the cars pass and try not to remember the way my mother looked when I went out. I sit down in the grass and wait. I hear a lawn mower somewhere in the distance. The road is blue in front of me, but down toward the highway it looks white in the sun. The grass is still wet, and I feel it beginning to seep through my shorts. *I can't walk with her. I can't.* I try to see where the lawn mower is. Down the street a little boy plays on a makeshift rocking horse. He rocks back and forth, back and forth, his hair flying. Another boy sits on a bank of grass and watches.

I get up, look back to the house, then walk down to where the two boys are. A little black dog comes out of the yard at me, barking furiously. I stop, look into its eyes.

"Hey, mister," one of the boys says. "Better watch it."

He sits on the bank, looking at me with tiny blue eyes under a lot of blond hair. He is dressed only in orange shorts. The other boy is wearing a red and white striped T-shirt and red shorts. He pulls on the head of the horse, laughing at me.

"That looks like fun," I say.

He looks at the one on the bank, then back to me.

"What's your name?" I ask.

"I'm Batman," he says. The other laughs.

I can't walk with her, not now. She reminds me.

"I'm Robin," the other boy says.

"Batman doesn't ride a horse," I say.

"This isn't a horse, it's a rocket."

"How old are you?"

"I'm seven," Batman says.

Robin gets up, comes down the hill. "I'm nine," he says. "How old are you?"

"Twenty-two."

"Are you a hippie?" Robin asks.

"No."

"Are you a draff dodger?"

I can't walk with her, she looks at me and it's not her, it's not her when I was a boy, and none of this was true.

"Are you?"

"No."

"Well, what are you then?" Batman says.

"I'm just a man."

"Are you a soldier?"

When I was a boy. When I was a boy. She looks at me with fear in her eyes. She's not the same. I'm not the same.

"He's a spy," Robin says.

"I bet he's not."

The dog sniffs at me, its cold nose touching me. It growls, deep inside, under the fur.

"Is this your dog?" I ask.

"Nah. She belongs to my grandfather."

"You don't live here?"

"We live in Maryland," Batman says. "We're visiting my grandfather."

"And grandmother?"

"No. She died."

"I'm sorry."

"Is your grandmother dead?" Robin says.

"A long time ago," I say. "My grandfather, too."

"Don't you have any grandparents?"

"No." I reach down and try to pet the dog, but it backs away, barks again.

"Katie!" Robin yells. He kicks at the dog and she retreats. "I hate that dog," he says.

"You shouldn't kick it. You might hurt it."

"I don't care."

"Do you have a dog at home?" I ask. I see my mother's face on the sidewalk and I stoop down, try to make my shadow cover it.

"Nah, we live in an apartment." Robin says.

"They won't let us have one in the 'partments," Batman says.

"Your mommy and daddy?"

"Daddy doesn't live with us now."

I watch my shadow. A crack in the sidewalk crosses through it, breaks up in the grass.

"Daddy's in the war," Robin says.

I look at the dog, watch it begin to sniff on the sidewalk near me. Batman climbs off the horse, walks through my shadow. *My mother is lonely, she's lonely. I can't walk with her. I can't.* I look at the horse, the eyes of it, then back to the sidewalk.

"Get out of here," Batman says, kicking at the dog again. I trace the crack with my finger, try not to think about their father, the eyes of the horse, my mother's face under the shadow on the sidewalk.

"There's a GTO," Robin says, pointing to a green car which sits in the sun at the corner. The wheels glisten, and when it begins to move Batman says, "Look at that!" It turns the corner and moves by us, the tires making a sound on the road like the growl of the dog.

"You like cars?"

"I want one of those, someday," he says.

"I like Mustangs," Robin says. Then he looks into my eyes and says, "Do you live with your father?"

"I can't walk with her," I say. He frowns, looks puzzled.

"With who?"

"My mother."

"You can't walk with her?" He starts to get hazy, to blur and curl and quiver in front of me.

"No."

"Hey, mister. Are you all right?"

"Everybody asks me that." I watch the shadow, see his moving through mine.

"Come on," he whispers to Batman. "Let's go back to the house."

"What's wrong with him?"

They move away. The dog goes with them, up the bank and out of sight toward a white house at the top of the hill. I stand up, see them moving across the green lawn, looking back at me as they walk. I wave to them, watch them turn away. I walk back to the corner to wait for Lucy.

IV. THE TAPES

Lucy watches a lot of television, so she has a lot to talk about. I don't mind hearing her talk, because it soothes me, helps me not to think about everything. Sometimes I feel like I'm inside my eyes, hiding from everyone.

I walk with Lucy in the evenings, usually, and she talks and I try to remember the world when it was solid—the days and evenings with my father and mother. I can't find them anymore. At night, I lie in bed and try to find them, but they're lost in the white grass, the dead branches. Every now and then I see my mother's face hidden in the winter somewhere, peering out at me through ice, and I try to go to her. I never see my father. I want to see him, but he doesn't appear. Everything moves at night, has force. Sometimes I dream that I'm sitting down somewhere, away from all of it—all the noise, the engines—and I'm able to become what I think about. A fish, or a bird—or a little boy again, in Chicago. When I walk with Lucy and listen to her talk I have that feeling too—I can be what she talks about.

Today, she told me she was glad of our walks, but not to misunderstand them.

"We're friends," she said.

I walked next to her, looking for my mother's face in the corners of the street, trying to be myself before, when there was winter, and cold wind, and there was no war.

In the daytime, I go to the beach and watch the water. I sit there in the sand or on the sea wall and listen to the gulls call to one another, watch them dive to the water for food. The ocean is peaceful—it has a rhythm I like. I want to take Lucy there sometime, but she doesn't like to come out with me when Mother is home alone. She says Mother is lonely and needs her company. My mother is lonely, but—but I can't be with her. I don't want to be near her now. I can't explain it. This morning she wanted to go with me and I told her she couldn't and she started to cry. I couldn't stand to see that. She was ugly. I went out of there pretty upset, but I met Lucy later, and we walked down the street into town, and I felt better. The cars made a lot of noise when they passed so I couldn't hear very well, but I listened to Lucy's voice, the way it sounded with all the engines, and I felt peaceful. I wasn't thinking about anything after a while, just walking and listening. Then I noticed a car beginning to slow down ahead of us, and I realized it was her car.

I looked at her, saw the side of her face, her mouth open slightly, then I turned and saw the car move on down the street.

"That was Ben," Lucy said. She slowed her walk, watching the car disappear into town. "I wonder," she said, then she stopped.

I wanted her to talk some more, so I asked her what she was wondering.

"Nothing. I've got to get home," she said.

"Let's go into town."

"No, we shouldn't."

"Why?"

"I didn't tell Ben we were going for a walk." She bit her lower lip, her brows sinking toward her eyes.

"I don't want to go back."

"Well, I've got to."

"Can I come to your house?" I didn't want to be away from her.

"No." She was very stern, suddenly. I couldn't look into her eyes.

"OK," I said.

She started away from me. I followed her. After a while, she stopped, turned to me. "You can't go with me," she said.

"I want to."

"You can't. Now, you just can't." She walked on, turning her head every few steps to see if I was following her.

I went into town, walked down the street toward Dill's. I thought I might go in and say hi to John and Mr. Baldwin, but when I got to the front of the store, I saw myself in the glass again, and it made me think of this movie I'm in, this part I can't escape, and it frightened me. I felt my hands beginning to sweat. I went by and looked for them as I passed the door, but I couldn't see anything because of the sun, and I was afraid they could see me. I looked for something to do, something to think about. I counted the wires overhead, the poles down the street where they all converged. I noticed the pattern of the bricks in the buildings which lined the street, thought of the human hands which placed them there, neatly, one on top of the other.

I decided to go back toward the water. I walked into salt breezes, back toward home and the water beyond, and then I saw the car again, slowing to a stop next to me. Mr. Houston stared at me, sitting at the wheel with one arm working the window down. I waved to him. He finished rolling the window down and looked at me.

"Where's my wife?"

"She went home," I said.

"Thank you." He rolled the window up and in the same motion stepped on the gas. The car roared away.

I stood there on the street for a while, trying not to think. I knew something was going to change, that whatever it was that made Lucy want to be with me would have to come out into the open, and that I would be the center of all of it. I didn't want to face Mr. Houston, or my mother and father. Lucy cares for me, takes time to be with me when I have nothing to say, when I can't bring myself to talk to anyone. I like the walk. I like her. I need the time with her, whether or not it means anything.

She talks about things I never heard of, but she never says anything that reminds me. The words are peaceful, full of whatever peace she's come to know here. I like to hear them.

I walked past my father's house, on up the road to the highway. I listened to the sound of my feet on the gravel and thought of the little boys with popcorn in their mouths laughing at me on the Fourth of July. That made me think of the woman with the red hair and the fire in Chicago, the crowd standing around watching the house burn down, and the woman lying by the wheels of the car, calling her husband. I wondered what happened to her. I still wonder. I can see the black face now, all cracked and running with blood.

When I got to the water, I was crying. I had control of it, knew I was doing it. I wanted to cry. My eyes burned, and I sobbed loud enough to hear and remember it. This was what I needed, to be a little boy again and have my father change the world for me.

V. MICHAEL

"Not very much today," Kessler says. He gets up and comes around the desk, leans on it in front of me. "Tell me how you feel about Lucy."

"I don't know how I feel."

"Are you in love with her?"

"I don't know."

He folds his hands, crosses his legs. "Do you like her very much?"

"I wish she wasn't married to Mr. Houston."

"Then you love her."

"I like being with her." I watch Kessler's brows, the way they move

175

over his eyes. They have life, are not connected to the skin there.

"And what about Houston?"

"I don't know."

"Was he angry this morning?"

"I don't know. He seemed to be."

"Have you seen Lucy since this morning?"

"No."

He moves over and stands in front of the window by all the plants. He has his hands on his hips, and he stares out at the sky. Orange light crosses the frame of the window.

"Have you had any episodes lately?"

"Fear?"

"Yes."

"Some. I know how to control it now."

"Are you as afraid of it?"

"I'm afraid of what I know."

"Do you think about it?"

"Never."

"Why?"

"I told you."

"Tell me again."

"I'm afraid. I don't like the fear, what it does to me."

He turns around, looks at me over his shoulder. "Can't you put what you know on tape?"

"I've tried. I can't do it."

"Michael, it doesn't help for you to talk into the tapes unless you deal with what troubles you." His brows crawl.

"I've tried."

"You've got to keep trying."

I can't look into his eyes. I try to read the title of one of the magazines on his desk.

"How do you control it?" he says.

"Control what?"

"The fear."

"I read signs, or look at things around me and try to think about them."

"And it works?"

"Yes."

"What about the crying you mentioned?"

"I wanted to do that."

"Why?"

"It felt good." He stares at me, waiting. "It made me feel like a little boy again."

"Why do you want to be a little boy again?"

"Because I didn't know what I know now."

"And what's that?" He turns completely around now, his hands on his hips, his head tilted in the orange light. I look at the small buttons on his vest, count them, *one two three four five six*.

"What's that, Michael?" He reaches up and rubs the back of his neck, waiting.

"I don't want to think about it."

"You have to think about it."

"Why?"

"Because you can't be a little boy again." He says this quietly, like a priest, a thin smile on his face.

"I don't want to be a little boy."

"Yes, you do."

"Maybe."

"You do."

"I don't know what I want. I only know what I don't want."

"I know, you don't want to think about it."

"That's right."

"You've got to do it sometime." His mouth is closed firm now, and the smile is gone.

"Why do I have to?"

"It's the only way you'll ever get past it." He comes toward me. "Come on, it's easy."

"Easy?"

"Easier than you think." He leans on the desk again. "I know you were a prisoner, that you were not fed, that you were—"

"Stop it." I put my hands up, cover my ears. I close my eyes but I can still see him standing in the thin image of Sergeant Hall pointing a gun, screaming at Caswell. It's the beginning. Mortars explode in my eyes, making only light and smoke.

"Michael?" Kessler says.

Caswell tells Hall to fuck himself. I see his lips move, but I can't really hear him. Kessler puts his hand on my arm. Caswell tries to get closer to the high part of the wall and Sergeant Hall pushes him away, kicks him with his boot. "Get back!"

"What?"

"Get back. Spread out!"

Kessler takes his hand away. "Go on, go on."

Caswell screams. A door opens, a woman's voice says, "Is everything all right in here?"

"Get out!" Kessler says.

"Spread out, damn you!" Hall screams. The door closes. Kessler moves, I hear his clothing rustle like the leaves on a tree. Caswell sprawls on the ground behind me. I look at Hall, see him yelling, and I open my eyes. Kessler sits at the desk, his hand up to his chin, watching me.

"I can't."

"You're getting there, don't stop."

"No. I don't want to."

"What were you remembering?"

"The beginning."

"The beginning of what?"

"Everything. Everything that happened."

"Tell me."

"I can't." I feel my eyes trembling.

"What if I leave the room, you talk into the tape."

"No."

"I'm trying to help you, but you've got to try harder."

"I want to go now."

He reaches into his pocket, pulls out a handkerchief. "Here, wipe your eyes."

"Thank you." I brush the cloth over the tops of my eyes without closing them, then I wipe my cheeks. Kessler sits behind his desk watching me, swinging slowly back and forth in his swivel chair.

"Do you talk to Lucy about all this?"

"No."

"Not ever?"

"I don't talk to anyone about it."

"Do you feel all right now?"

"Yes."

"Do you want to go?"

I nod. He swings the chair around, looks at the calendar on his desk.

"I'm going to be out of town for the rest of this week."

"Good."

"What?"

"Nothing." I don't ever want to come back here. He forces me to think about it.

"Can you come back on Saturday?"

"I have to work."

"How's that going?"

"Fine."

"You like the work?"

"It's OK. Can I leave?"

"Come back on Monday."

"All right." I get up, start for the door.

"Don't forget the tape recorder," he says. He holds it up to me. "No wonder you keep losing it."

I take it out of his white hands, notice the hair on his knuckles. "Make a lot of tapes for me while I'm gone," he says.

I go out of the office and past a quiet secretary, who watches me as if I have stolen something. In the street I think of Lucy, wonder if she has called. I walk through the grove back to my father's house.

VI. DALE

Dale reaches out and turns off the radio, sits back and listens to the sound of the car rushing through the wind. He is tired, holding the wheel as if without it he could not remain erect, thinking: *Perhaps this is what I should recall as a good day—one I should try to copy. I made love in the morning, had a good breakfast, then went to the sea. Eddie was in a good mood, was willing to laugh. The red tide is just starting, so the beaches do not smell yet. A day I should copy. Except I am the enemy. The enemy.*

The sea wall was comfortable, and he caught four rather large grunts. Eddie caught six, including a red snapper. The fishing kept Dale's mind off the gathering memories of all his private crimes—his twenty-year reign as king and torturer to his son. In the last few weeks, since he heard the tape, he has had plenty of time to accumulate all the scenes, all the small, loud dramas which changed a day, or an hour, in Michael's life. Michael is gone from him in the same way the infant ceased to exist—there are only pictures to remind him. He cannot hear the voice, the crying. The years with Michael fade suddenly into motion like a silent movie, a trembling of hands. *And what is punishment?* he thinks. A form of tyranny, a minor torture. Yet what can a father be?

When the boy, the child, carries in him all the murderous genes of the race. I will teach you what is right, what everyone records as necessary and decent—to hold in what the body wants, what the mind cannot refuse. I will change you with anger and pain, form you because I am stronger and I know what the world expects. An act of love? Those people who held him, wouldn't feed him—what did they want to change in him? Were they capable of love? Perhaps human love is nothing more than a subtle, indefinable form of abuse. An oppression born out of weakness in the soul—out of the private wishes of human will. To be able to make someone like you are—to recreate the self in another body.

No. It was not a good day. He concentrated on the warmth of the sun, the breezes from the ocean, the gulls high among the clouds, and the quiet lapping of the water against the sea wall—a calm day, with good air, and the line moving in the water—and in all the reflected light he saw Michael crawling in the high grass, running in mortal fear from what he thought was his father.

He steers the car onto his street, the street of his home, his wife and son. Something in him relishes the smoothness of the steering wheel, the incessant whir of the tires under the car. He does not want to leave this quiet cocoon, but the black driveway approaches, and he pulls into it, sees Anne standing on the front porch, her arms folded, watching the car, and there is a look on her face that scares him. He stops the car halfway up the drive and waits for her to walk over to him, all the time thinking: *Something's wrong, something's wrong.* When she is near him, he looks into her eyes and says, "What's the matter?"

"I'm not sure," she says. Her voice is strange, like a recording.

"Is it Michael?"

"I don't want to talk about it out here. Come inside." She starts back up the walk. He gets out of the car, follows her.

"Tell me, what's wrong?"

"It's Lucy."

He goes up the steps, follows her into the house. After he closes the door, Anne says, "Ben just called."

"What?"

"Lucy hasn't come home."

"It's only a little after five."

"He said she should have been home hours ago." Anne still has her arms folded, and she rubs her elbows with her fingers.

"Well, what are you so upset about?" Dale wants her to say what she is thinking, to get the fear out into the room.

"He said he saw her with Michael this morning."

"Oh." He looks at the curtains by the window, the white light outside.

"What do you mean, 'oh'?"

"Just that I understand why you're upset."

"Are you thinking what I'm thinking?"

"I don't know what to think." The idea runs in his head, won't stand still in the light, but he recognizes it, and knowing what it is he cannot remember anything else. "Is Michael home?"

She looks surprised. "No."

"Do you know where he is?"

"That's what I'm worried about. I think he's with Lucy."

"You do?"

"Yes. Of course." She goes to the dining room table, sits on a chair there, her arm resting on the table. "Tell me what you're thinking."

"What if—" He stops, can't finish it. He sees Lucy's lifeless staring face mingled with dirt and grass, and Michael standing over her.

"What?"

"What if something's happened to Lucy?"

Anne turns away. "Stop it."

"Isn't that what Houston's thinking?"

"How do I know?"

"What did he say?"

"He was worried. I thought you'd gotten over that?"

"What?"

"You know." Anne puts her hand up to her forehead, lets out a loud breath of air. "I wish Mike were home."

"Is he late?"

"A little."

He goes to the table and sits next to Anne. Although he is near enough to hear her breathing, he does not touch her. He studies the fine texture of her hair, trying to imagine what they will have to do when this is over, when what has happened becomes words that drop out of someone's mouth.

"Think I should call Mr. Kessler?" Anne asks.

"What for?"

"Michael had an appointment there this afternoon."

"He must have made it. Don't they call when he misses one?"

"I don't want him to get involved with her," Anne says, striking her thigh with a small fist.

Dale puts his hand on her shoulder. The skin feels cold, slightly damp. "If that's all you're worried about, if that's all that's happened, I won't be too crushed by it. I—"

"It wouldn't be good for him."

"If it happens, it happens."

"He would be hurt."

"It's the world, honey. Things like that happen. If that's what's going on, it might help him." He begins to hope for it, to pray silently that Anne's fears are accurate.

Anne buries her head in her hands, shakes her head.

"Are you crying?"

She raises her head, looks back at him, her eyes blank and without light. "No. I'm just tired. And worried."

"Don't be." He gets up, goes to the phone. "I'm going to call Houston."

He lets the phone ring several times but there is no answer. He puts the phone back in its cradle and returns to the dining room.

"No one there."

Anne goes to the window, looks out.

"See him?"

"Yes. He's coming through the park."

"Is—"

"He's alone." She goes to the door, opens it, and stands behind the screen watching Michael approach the door. "Hi."

Dale hears Michael say something, a vague and strained response. He goes to the living room, stands in front of the couch, trying to decide what he should be doing when Michael comes in. He looks for a newspaper, but there isn't one. He sits down, then gets up, just as Michael comes through the door. Dale looks into the face of his son and sees that he has been crying again. Something has happened. He has done something. Michael stands next to his mother, his hands in his shorts, his head down. Anne touches him, moves him back so she can close the door. She never takes her eyes off him, and he keeps staring at the floor in front of him. Dale falls on the couch, air escaping from him like a soul, and Michael looks up, tries to say something.

"Are you—" Anne stops, looks at Dale. Then she says, "Not a good session?"

"No." Michael almost whispers.

"Where's Lucy?" Dale says, watching Michael's face, looking for something there.

There is no change in expression. Michael says, "I don't know." Then, he raises his head. "Did she call?"

"No," Anne says.

There is no sound in the room. Dale cannot make his mind stop, and the silence begins to gather force, as if there is something outside the room which only silence will keep out—something evil. Dale tries not to think at all, tries to let the moment pass. He refuses the image of Michael which keeps forcing its way into his skull. Then he sees the veteran there, the one-armed veteran, drinking a beer and saying, "Shot four people, shot four people, shot four people."

"What's the matter?" Michael says.

"That's what we were wondering," Dale says.

Anne waves her hand, moves Michael further into the room. "Were you with her today?"

"This morning. Why?"

"What did you—" Dale can't force the words out of his mouth. "When did you leave her?"

"It was early. What's wrong?" Michael looks at Anne, then back to Dale. "Is something wrong?"

"She hasn't come home yet," Anne says.

Dale gets up, walks toward Michael, who backs away, his eyes widening. A line begins to form in his forehead. "What's the matter?" Dale says.

"Nothing."

"Why are you backing away?"

"When you got up, it reminded me of something."

"What?"

"I got scared."

"Why are you scared?" Dale is almost paralyzed in front of his son, waiting for him to say something which will destroy all their lives, forever.

"What's the matter?"

"Nothing," Anne says. Then she turns to Dale, tries to move him away. "What's got into you?"

Dale moves her hand away gently, says, "Let me handle this."

"Handle what?" she says.

"Why are you scared, Michael?"

"I don't know. You got up suddenly."

"And?"

"I just remembered something."

"What?"

"Dale, stop it." Anne touches his arm again. Dale moves away, circles into the dining room, conscious of Michael revolving like a statue on an electric pedestal.

"I'm not mad, son. I just want to know what happened today."

"I went for a walk with Lucy. But she couldn't stay with me."

"So what did you do?"

"I kept walking. I went down to the water."

"What happened to Lucy?"

"She went home."

"You're sure."

"Yes."

"What did you remember that scared you?"

"It was when I was a boy again."

"Again?"

"Yes." Michael still has not moved. Dale sits at the table, crosses his legs.

"You didn't see Lucy again today?"

"No."

Dale covers his eyes with his hand, sees the veteran there, laughing, and quickly he puts his hand on the table, stands up. "I don't know what to think."

"What's happened?" Michael says.

"Mr. Houston called," Anne says in a quiet voice. "He's worried about her. He said he saw you two out walking this morning."

Michael shakes his head, an involuntary movement which imprints in the center of everything Dale remembers. Then Michael's hands come up, as if he is counting something in the air. "She's not going to call me tonight, is she?" he says. His voice quivers, and Dale cannot make himself look at his son.

"She might, when she gets home," Anne says.

Michael goes out of the room, up the stairs, his head still shaking. Something is going on in there, something Dale does not want to exist, but that he must know.

"That was the most ridiculous display I've ever seen," Anne says.

"What?"

"You know what."

"Tell me."

"If you think your son's a murderer, why don't you call the police?"

"He knows something—"

"You can all go looking for the body together," Anne whispers violently.

"You saw him."

"What was I supposed to see?"

"When people get like him, they do things they're not aware of."

She goes to the television, snaps it on. "Here. Maybe you can find a plot to fit what's going on in your head."

"It's Michael's head I'm worried about." He goes to the telephone, tries Houston's number again. Anne seats herself on the couch, watches the television with unseeing eyes. Dale hangs up the phone, returns to the living room. The television's white light makes shadows on Anne's face. There is no sound.

In bed, later, Dale cannot sleep. He watches the shadows on the wall made by the moon—sees maps there, tries to find a city, a harbor. Anne sleeps next to him, her breathing a steady reminder of the rhythms of time. Lucy did not come home, and Houston was frantic. Michael did not come out of his room, not even for dinner, and there was a scene on the back porch with Houston demanding to talk to him, and Anne telling him to go home, to stop worrying. Dale stayed in the kitchen, listening, believing that events were falling together the way water runs through channels and crevices, seeking its level ground. He knew the meaning of the world then, understood what people meant when they said "as events unfolded." But he could not make himself open Michael's door. Houston went home, said he would come back tomorrow. He would call the police. "Something's screwy," he said. Dale saw him through the window, struggling to get over the fence, an old man for whom all things were an ending of some kind. It is sights like that which make eyes boil with knowledge and fear.

A breeze rises outside, and the shadows move. Is there a body out there, the cold skin covered with dew? He said he was walking with her, that she wanted to go home. He was afraid of something. He was upset. Houston saw them walking. During the day.

Anne shifts in the bed, lets out a soft moan. She is dreaming something—perhaps an end to all this. Her body is warm against him and he thinks of the years he has enjoyed that heat, sought it in the cold sheets of Illinois winters—the house breathing, and a whir of traffic outside; the cold wind tripping over the eaves of the house, making a sound like the howl out of a cold human throat. And Michael asleep in the next room—a boy, a child who by being alive made the ice winters bearable, almost pleasant. Through all the years Dale saw his son as the source of something he had never been able to put into words; something in Dale's unconscious perceptions of the world. A sense of the inexorable nature of things, but also of the possibilities in all of it. A child, an opening through the black trap in which everyone must abide, and from which there is no escape. A small light. Something minute which was, in its own way, lasting.

And Houston said, "There's something screwy." *Something screwy.*

Tomorrow, he thinks, *there will be police. What will Michael do then? How will he answer the questions of a total stranger?*

Michael. Where is he? What happened to the boy, the young man who visited all of Dale's years? What goes on in the mind when it can't escape its own shattered and fibrous dreams?

Dale turns in the bed, tries to find a position which will let him sleep—dream something else. He hears the voice of the veteran, "Killed four people, killed four people," until his eyes ache with it. Michael should have been left in the hospital, among people of his lasting and furious dreams. He is helpless. His life only the ache of an exposed nerve.

The moon suddenly disappears, and the room darkens—the city on the wall fades. He sits up, pulls the sheet up to his chin.

"What's the matter?" Anne says.

"You awake?"

"I am now."

"I'm sorry."

She rolls over on her stomach, raises her head above the pillow to look at him. In the darkness, he cannot see her eyes. "What's the matter?" she says again.

"You know."

"Would you stop worrying about it?"

"I can't help it."

"Go to sleep." She puts her head down on the pillow, turns away.

The moon returns to the room. He sees her hair spread out on the pillow. He reaches out, touches the crown of her head. "I love you," he says.

"And I love you. Now sleep."

"I'm going to get him out of here early tomorrow."

"Why?"

"I have to talk to him. If he's done something, I want to know about it first."

She turns to him again. "You're being silly."

"I have to know."

"If you had any faith in him, you'd already know."

"Like you do."

"Yes."

"You saw him in that hospital. You've seen him around here when he goes off."

"Stop it."

"You didn't see him on the fishing trip."

"Now just *stop* it." Anne's voice is loud.

"There's something screwy." Dale is conscious of the night, and wants to explain something to all the darkness. "That's what Houston said. He's thought of it too."

Anne turns over, a sulking and emphatic movement which forces him to look at her.

"I can't help how I feel," he says.

"You know what happened to me this morning?" She is calm now, almost peaceful.

"What?"

"I asked Michael if he would let me go walking with him. And he said I couldn't." She pauses, her hand playing with the sheet in front of her. "And you know why he didn't want me to go? He said there are things he doesn't want to think about, and we—he said 'you and Dad' —we force him to. We make him miserable."

He looks back to the wall, waits for her to finish.

"And then he said, 'You're not my mother.' "

"What?"

"That's what he said. I'm not his mother. And it occurred to me today—I had a lot of time to think about this. I was so hurt at first, I couldn't stop crying. But it occurred to me that I really am not his mother. Not the mother he remembered when he was in Viet Nam. In a way, we are as changed by all of this as he is."

"Well, how can we be the same?" Dale says, reaching for her hand. "He won't let us."

"This isn't his home. He came back to a strange place, and you and I are strangers to him."

"Now we're back to Chicago." He takes his hand away.

"We came here to get over Michael's death. But he's alive."

"So?"

"We're spending a lot of time trying to get over *that.*"

"There's more to it than that. It's not just that he's alive, but that he's not Michael anymore. Not anyone. Not—"

"He's not Michael because we won't let him."

"What are we supposed to do?"

"Listen to me for a minute." She sits up next to him, adjusts the sheets around her.

"I'm listening."

"I think he needed to come back to the things he dreamed of when he was a prisoner. He came back here, and we were living it up here in the sun as far as he knew. He knows we thought he was dead. As far as he knows, we were well rid of him." Her voice trembles slightly at this.

"He doesn't think that."

"Let me finish." She brushes her hair back, takes a deep breath. "This is not what he thought he would come home to. This is just some other place. And we're just other people. He knows more about people now than you or I will probably ever know. And since he's been here, we've spent all our time checking on him, asking him how he is, if everything's all right."

"After that episode the second week, it's no wonder."

"And he hasn't had a chance to adjust to us. We were so glad to have him alive at first—now, I think he believes we are afraid of him."

"Maybe we are."

"I'm not. I was, but not anymore."

"So what do we do?"

"We let him be the Michael he is now. That's all we can do."

"How do we do that?"

"Stop worrying over him. Stop suspecting him."

"That doesn't help him face what's going to happen to him tomorrow, if Lucy doesn't show up somewhere—breathing."

"She'll show up." Anne settles down into the bed again, pulling the sheets up over her shoulder. "It might be better for him," she says quietly, "if you did take him with you early tomorrow. Don't force him to go. But if he wants to, go ahead and get him out of here. I don't think I want him around if Lucy doesn't get back, and we have another visit from Mr. Houston."

"I'll have to get him up."

"OK. That would be normal. We've been wrong to wait for him to come out in the mornings anyway."

"You don't think anything happened to Lucy?"

"I don't think *Michael* did anything." Her voice is muffled by the

188

pillow now, and he knows she will be asleep soon. "Do me a favor?" she says.

"What?"

"Don't quiz him. Leave him alone."

Dale lies down, puts his head into a cold pillow. He reaches for Anne and pulls her body against him. "I'll try," he says.

VII. ANNE

She leans on the stove, smoking a cigarette, and watching out the back-door window for Mr. Houston. The sun is getting high over the houses, and Michael and Dale have been gone for more than an hour. They went out the front door, quietly, Michael following his father like a pet. He said nothing to her, not even good morning, and Dale watched the phone in the kitchen as if he had put a timer in there and then forgotten when he set it to go off.

When she went in to wake Michael, he wasn't asleep. She saw his eyes as soon as the door was open, and he said, "What's the matter?"

"Your father wants to take you with him today," she said.

"Where?"

"Fishing."

He turned over in the bed, groaned something into the pillow.

"What?"

"I don't want to go anywhere with him."

"Why?" She went to the bed, stood in the pink light there which leaked into the room from the rising morning.

"He thinks I've done something wrong."

"How do you know?"

"You saw him last night."

"I think you should go with him."

"Did Lucy come home?" He turned over again, faced her.

"I don't know."

He put his hand up, pushed his sparse hair back off his forehead. Anne moved to the head of the bed, touched his hand. She wanted him to notice her, to look into her eyes and know her—know how nothing which went before, or might come after, would ever alter the love she held in her body like an unborn and lasting child. "You are my child," she said. He looked at her eyes, seemed to see something there which frightened him.

"I'm sorry about yesterday," he said.

"I understand," she whispered, stroking his hand, trying to smile.

"Do you think I did something to Lucy?"

"No. No one thinks that."

"Houston does." He looked away.

"You heard him?"

"Yes."

"Lucy will come home." She took her hand away, folded her arms in front of her.

"And Dad thinks so, too."

"He isn't as sure as I am, perhaps."

"Is that why he wants me to go fishing?"

"I don't think he wants you to be around when Houston comes back, asking a lot of questions." She leaned down then, tried to look into his eyes. "You don't need some stranger asking you about such things. We know that. Your father is thinking of you."

"He is?" His eyes seemed to recognize something on the wall—a shadow of a breeze, or the white light from some moving reflection.

"I think you should go, son."

"I'm supposed to work this afternoon."

"A Friday?"

"But I'll go, I'll go. If he wants me to." He would not look at her, and the thought that he was lying about work made a shadow in her mind which seemed to withdraw all the heat from her. She felt a shiver near the base of her neck.

Even now, watching out the window, she feels the cold pockets of fear in her veins. He was lying, and it was so easy. He didn't even think about it. Of course he has lied before—she is sure of that—but never so easily. And he backed out of it immediately, agreeing to go. It was all so silly, Dale wanting to get out of the house before the phone rang, and Michael not wanting to go with him. So why would he lie, if he was going to go anyway?

She puts out her cigarette, lights another. She has let her coffee get cold, but she sips at it anyway. She does not want to maintain this vigil much longer, but she is afraid that if she goes back into the other rooms of the quiet and empty house, the sound of someone knocking on the door will scare her.

She goes to the sink, rinses her cup. Through the window over the sink, she can see the back fence and the Houston yard beyond. She cannot see the back door to the house from here, so she returns to the door. When she looks out the window there, she sees Houston coming across the lawn toward the fence, dressed all in white, his gray hair lifted by the breezes into stiff pointed shapes on the top of his head. He climbs the fence clumsily, his hands shaking.

Anne opens the back door, walks out onto the porch to meet him. "Heard from Lucy?" she says.

"No." He walks on toward her, his eyes without expression.

"Not even a phone call?" She feels silly for saying this, but she wants to stop his approach, which seems so full of purpose it scares her. He comes up the steps, stands directly in front of her.

"I want to talk to Michael."

"He's not here."

"He's always here."

"No. He's not." She tries to smile. "Michael told us all he knows."

"I want to hear it from him." He moves to go past her.

"Don't," she says.

"Don't what."

"Don't think what you're thinking."

"I want to talk to your son. Are you going to let me?"

"He's not here, Ben. I wouldn't lie to you."

"When will he be back?"

"This afternoon."

"I'm going to call the police."

"You haven't called them yet?"

He looks down at his feet, out into the yard. "No."

"Why?"

"I thought she might come back this morning."

"Ben, I thought you—"

"She's got to come back," he says. His eyes grow smaller, he reaches out to the railing of the porch with a gnarled hand. "I don't know what I'll do if anything's happened to her."

"Has she ever done this before?"

"Never."

"Not ever?" Anne thinks of Lucy's first husband, the time between when she left him and the divorce.

Ben seems to realize that she is thinking this. He looks into her eyes and says, "Not to me."

"I think you should call the police."

He starts back down the stairs, shaking his head. "I guess I will."
When he is in the yard, he turns back to her. "I didn't want to do that."

"Why?"

"It's like admitting something's happened to her."

"Lucy can take care of herself. I don't think anything's happened."

"What if they find her?"

"You want to find her."

"What if they find her in a—in a—" He breaks off, his voice only
a weak note of high music dying in the sun. Then he says, "Michael
doesn't know anything?"

"Honest, Ben. He told us she went home after she saw you in the
car."

"But I came right home, and she wasn't there." His voice gets
stronger. "I know he knows more than that. He didn't get home until
late. He must know something. He must."

Anne goes down the stairs, walks into the grass in front of Houston.
She reaches out, touches his arm. "Look, I know how you must feel, and
I want you to find her. But you have to trust us, Dale and I, to question
Michael. He's not very stable right now—not—"

He takes her hand away gently, without anger. But his eyes are
fierce now, and they won't let her look away. "That's what I'm afraid
of," he says. "That's what I can't get out of my mind. That boy of yours
is not right."

"He's not sick that way." Her voice trembles slightly. "Not that
way at all."

"How do you know?"

"I just know."

"But how? It happens, you know. It happens." He shakes his head
again, backs away. "It happens."

"If you say the wrong thing to Mike, he'll have another—another—"

"Another what?"

"You'll upset him."

"Upset him? My wife is missing!"

"Please, trust me."

"If I can't question him, the police can." He turns and walks back
to the fence. She watches him struggle back over it, his head high in
the air. When he touches ground on the other side, he looks back to her.
"Where'd he go?"

"I think you should go ahead and call the police," she says.

He nods slightly, returns across his yard to the house, disappears in the foliage there by the patio. Anne goes back into the kitchen, her hands shaking, and lights another cigarette.

VIII. DALE

"You're pretty bored here in Florida, aren't you?" Dale says. He looks out to the bay, and beyond that to the sea. He has in his mind a sense of drama, of scene. Michael sits next to him, swinging his legs, staring down at the water. They are on the sea wall, and Dale holds a fishing rod in his hands as if it is something he found there after sitting down. The line runs limply out into the water. Michael has not said anything except in answer to questions, and the ride to the sea wall seemed endless. Now, Dale wants him to say something, watches his son's mouth, waiting for an answer, his eyes beginning to burn with the sounds of the water on the wall and the gulls overhead. "Aren't you?"

Michael looks at the sky, back out to the water. "I'm OK," he says.

"What are you thinking about?"

"You remember when I was a little boy, and you helped me save enough pennies to make a fifty-cent package?"

"No."

"You did."

"Is that what you were thinking about?"

Michael nods, takes a deep breath. "I never did spend that money."

"Why are you thinking about that?"

"Last night, I looked for it."

"For the package?"

"I couldn't find it anywhere."

"What did you want that for?" Dale watches Michael's legs, the thin blond hair on the calves, matted with sweat. They are the legs of a man, a full-grown man, and he swings them like a child, hitting his bare feet on the hard brick wall.

"I don't know."

Gulls whirl and swoop above the blue water, white fragments of cloud whirling in the wind. They make high sounds, and Michael's feet rhythmically hit the sea wall.

"Stop that," Dale says.

"What?"

"With your feet. It bothers me."

Michael watches his feet slow to a stop, as if he cannot control them any other way.

After a pause, Dale says, "I should have called Eddie this morning."

"Why?"

"I told him to meet me this morning here."

Michael frowns, looks into Dale's eyes. The sun makes a ribbon of clear light on the corners of Michael's eyes, and Dale studies only that, waiting for his son to say something. But he turns back to the water.

"I thought it might be better if only you and I fish," Dale says.

"How long do we have to stay here?"

"What do you mean?"

"Are the police coming to the house?"

Dale does not want to look at Michael now. There is a tone in his son's voice that seems almost playful, but that suggests something else —something born out of knowledge and calm resignation.

"Why should the police come to the house?" Dale says, after a long pause, his voice careful and even.

"To ask me about Lucy."

The name Lucy echoes in Dale's heart. He holds the fishing rod tightly in his hands, waits. Michael touches the sides of the wall, his face without expression.

"I wish I could find that package of pennies," Michael says.

"What about Lucy?" Dale tries to concentrate on the blue water.

"Maybe I put it in a secret box somewhere."

"What about Lucy?"

Michael looks at him. "Nothing."

"Why should the police ask you about Lucy?"

"That's what's going to happen."

"How do you know?"

"I know."

"Tell me about it."

They are looking at each other now, and Dale sees in the eyes of his son a penetrating and organic refusal—a complete separation of mind and spirit, one human being from another.

"What's the use?" Michael says.

"Tell me."

"You won't believe me."

"Try me." Dale's heart crawls in his chest, he cannot catch his breath.

"What should I say?"

"Talk to me about it."

"I don't want to."

"I want to know. If you've done something, I want you to tell me."

"If I've done something?"

"Yes."

"Why are you so afraid of me?"

"I'm not afraid of you."

Michael lowers his head, seems to let something out of his body, grow shorter as if a soul has left him without anything in the center.

"Lucy and I went for a walk," he says. "She saw Houston in the car, and she said she had to go home."

"Go on."

"That's it."

"What happened then?"

Michael's face turns red, then seems to fade into the landscape behind him. Dale cannot concentrate on the blurred features, washed out like a mistake in a meticulous watercolor. His hands grip the rod.

"What do you want me to say? That I killed her?"

Dale closes his eyes, tries to put all the colors where they belong, rearrange the blurred landscape in front of him. "I don't want you to say that if it's not true."

"I killed her, Dad."

In Dale's eyes, Michael runs across a long gray lawn, tiny, wearing shorts, a high blue and red kite hanging in the sky above him like some terrible predatory bird. He comes laughing, to hug his father, his feet stirring the tall gray grass, his hair trailing high in the wind—a boy, a child.

"Don't you want to say anything?" Michael says.

There is a pause. The gulls click their bills, cry out to the still air and the tumbling sea.

"I told you what you wanted to hear."

"Is it true?" Dale hears his own voice as if it were a recording. He opens his eyes, sees a fly leaving Michael's cheek.

"She went home. I didn't see her again the rest of the day."

"Did you kill her or not!"

Michael's eyes widen, his brows begin to twitch.

"What did they do to you?" Dale nearly screams this.

"I don't want to talk about it."

"What did they do to you? You haven't got a mark on you!"

"You're yelling at me."

"You need someone to yell at you."

"No, I don't."

"Tell me what they did to make you capable of putting me through this."

"Through what?"

"You son of a bitch." Dale looks right into the eyes of this man, this person who plays such cruel games. "You son of a bitch!"

"I was captured."

"I know that. Do *you* know what they did? I mean, was it a drug or something?"

"I don't want this," Michael says. His eyes are clear and dry, but he takes short deep breaths, and lowers his head.

"Don't start crying, for Christ's sake."

"I'm not crying."

"Is there anybody else in the world this has happened to?"

Michael puts his hand up to his face, covers his eyes.

"Stop crying, goddamn it. We won't talk about it."

"I can't tell you about it yet. I get scared when I think about it."

"I don't know what to believe anymore. What do you get scared about? Lucy? Or the war?"

"I'm sorry. I don't like being afraid."

"What are you afraid of?"

Michael looks up to the gulls. Dale studies the side of his face, the green crystals of his eyes.

"I have a goal, Dad."

"What are you afraid of?"

"I know what I want."

"OK. Tell me that. What do you want?"

"I want you to—I want—" He breaks off and begins to sob.

"For Christ's sake!"

"I want to go home again. I want to be a little boy." He lets out a cry, as if he is calling to the birds.

"Tell me about Lucy."

"I didn't do anything."

"What are you afraid of?" Dale takes his arm, squeezes it. "Tell me."

Michael looks at his father's hand, then out to the sea.

"Tell me." Dale shakes him. "I'll get it out of you somehow even if I have to—"

"I'm afraid of *you!*" Michael screams.

Dale blinks, shakes his head. "Me," he says, quietly. Then he stands up on the wall, raises the fishing rod over his head. "Goddamn!" he screams, throwing the rod out high over the water. The line curls and shrinks, the rod sinks into the water almost without a splash. Dale turns and walks back inland, toward the houses and shops, away from the murmuring water and Michael.

IX. MICHAEL

The thing didn't even make any noise when it hit. It just turned the water aside and went under. My father is gone. I've stopped crying, but I feel cold inside, and my arms ache. I watch the birds for a while, feeling sorry for my father. I notice the curvature of the long horizon, and think of the great ball that is earth—the speed of it. I think of the word "teeming." All this life, flailing away in biological confusion. Everything seems distorted, twisted. How can anyone see order in it?

The gulls dive for fish, and behind me are buildings and monuments and parking lots which were scratched out and molded by the world's most predatory and snarling animal. I know that's what I am. A beast that chatters.

It's extraordinary that my father's fishing rod disappeared so silently. He threw it high over my head and I watched it fly. I didn't see him leave. I can't get along with him, I'm afraid of him. I'm ashamed of him. No. I'm ashamed of myself. He thinks I've done something horrible. So I probably have. I shouldn't have lived. I shouldn't have come here.

The water is clear under my feet.

In my memory is fire, burning me, and a leap into the sea. An imaginary fire, but it burned me just the same. I remember it. I saw my flesh turn black. Like the woman next to the car calling her husband.

Every morning I wake up holding on to myself, and every minute of the day is a surprise to me. I concentrate on each physical act, as if I might forget to put on my shoes. I know where all food comes from, and when I eat, I can feel its progress through me.

Always in the back of my mind is the fear. I can't stop thinking about it. Kessler says not to think about it. "Go on with life." He says the word as if it were a sentence. LIFE. "You came back alive. Stop thinking of yourself as a casualty."

Below me, in the colorless water, I can see something round and full of the colors of the spectrum. I watch it moving slightly in the rough sand, and then I turn onto my stomach and let myself down into the water. It's cold on my bare legs, and I ease down until my feet touch in the wet sand. The water is up to my waist, and merely cool now. I move my hands around in it, think of the peace, the incredible silence under the sea.

This is where all of us began. We are all saltwater beasts who, for some reason, inhabit land. A different beast. Not insect. Not animal. Not fish. The product of some evil chemical, some poison that evolved into a terrible bundle of fibers and nerves, crawled up on land into the atmosphere, mixed with the light. I think of crowds of people celebrating New Year's Eve in New York, and in the same instant I see clearly all the little tiny scrambling men hurling shells into artillery pieces; I see all the man-made smoke and noise; I see Caswell squirming on the ground as if he were an insect on a pin. And I know how perfect it is that "die" is a verb.

I sink down to my knees, the water rising to my neck just under my chin. It is cold again. The gulls cry discontentedly above me. I feel the breeze rising. I go under the water, eyes open, and I see the wall draped with green algae, my hands out in front of me, white and unnatural. I feel the water in every pore, and I squat there by the wall, light and relaxed. To stay down, I have to move my hands so the algae stirs, breaks away. I can't see clearly any more. I don't even think about air. I don't feel anything yet. My lungs begin to shrink, very slowly, at first, then more rapidly, until I think they will disappear. The water darkens above me suddenly, and I look up, see a shadow there broken by the water's surface. I think it is my father, so I look for the round colorful object I saw moving in the sand, but I can't see it anymore. I rise up out of the water. I can't see very well, but as I rub my eyes, I hear the figure say, "Where's your old man?"

It's Eddie. He stands on the wall staring down at me. I feel like an insect he has discovered among his tulips.

"He just left."

"What are you doing down there?" he says. His voice is loud, suspicious.

"I was looking for something."

A breeze strikes my back and I suddenly feel chilled. I begin to shake.

"Where'd your old man go?"

"I don't know." I really get cold now. I can't keep my head still.

"You're turning blue."

"I'm cold," I tell him.

"It's hot as hell out here. You should feel good." He doesn't offer his hand. I take the top of the sea wall in the palms of my hands and pull myself up. Water runs down my legs, drips off my nose, out of my hair.

"You don't know where he went?" Eddie says. He seems embarrassed, standing there beside me. He wears gray coveralls and brown work boots. He hasn't shaved, and his face looks as if it has been etched out of some stubborn metal.

"I wish I had a towel," I say.

"It's warm."

I do feel the sun. I will be dry soon enough, and then I will stop shaking. Eddie stamps his foot and makes a clicking noise with his mouth, like one of the gulls.

"Goddamn it," he says.

"I don't think my father will be fishing today."

"Why?"

"He won't be fishing."

"Why not? He said he would."

The sun is beginning to take me now, and I feel the shaking begin to get smaller, to reduce itself in its conical way back to the center of my heart.

"Is he mad because I was late?" Eddie's voice is almost timid.

"He's mad at me."

"What'd you do now?" he says, more confident.

"He got mad and threw his rod out there," I say.

"Out where?"

"Out there. In the water."

"What?"

"It didn't even splash hardly."

"What kind of crap—" He stops, considering. Then, "What sort of games did you pull on him this time?"

I turn to see his eyes staring at me as if he knows something about me I don't want him to know. He waits for an answer, but it takes me a while to realize what he said.

"You ain't sold me that bill of goods, boy," he says. His voice has no tone. I keep my eyes on the water while he breathes behind me, his eyes fixed on the back of my head. I feel them there as if they give off heat. We stay that way for what seems like a very long time while the wind whispers to us and the gulls dip and cry out above the water.

"You know what I think?" he says finally, in the same toneless voice. I sit as perfectly still as I can, try to hide my breathing. I feel him move, and when he speaks again his head is down close to me, right next to my ear. "I think you're a goddamned fucking coward, that's what I think."

I don't look at him. His face is right there with those eyes in it, waiting for me to do something. He straightens up, finally, and speaks down at me again. "What do you think of that?"

"Nothing," I say to the water.

"You and your father are really a pair," he says. "He moans because you've come back a loony. You act like the war was some personal insult to you—something designed to make your poor miserable goddamned coward life unbearable." His voice rises. I feel his head next to mine again. "Two boys. *Two boys* I lost in that war. Ask your father if he ever heard me moaning about it."

"I'm sorry," I say. I try not to see him. I feel his breath on my cheek, hear the air going in and out of him.

"Two boys," he says again, quietly. "You couldn't stand in their shit, much less their shoes."

"I'm sorry."

"Fucking coward." He straightens up again. "Tell your old man I'll do my fishing with someone else from now on. I ain't that goddamned lonely."

I turn over again on my stomach and slide back down into the water. I do it in one motion this time, slowly, without looking at him. I will wait here until he leaves.

I watch his shadow until my lungs begin to shrink again, then I pull myself along the sea wall. I hear him hollering something. The water is cool, full of algae now because of the rooting of my white hands. I move faster, down the wall, away from Eddie. I let the air out of my lungs and the bubbles rattle inside my head as they rollick to the surface. My eyes begin to feel terribly dry; in all that water my eyes, open and unblinking, feel as dry as if I have sand in them. My chest begins to collapse. I raise my head up slowly out of the water, take in air and go down again. I do this quietly, like an alligator. I keep moving along the wall. I feel seaweed around my feet, my waist. I pull it down off me, unwrap it, let the water hold me.

I stay that way, moving along the wall, rising for air slowly, so I make no sound. Eddie is gone. The indifferent sky is all blue, not a cloud anywhere. I begin to lose sight of my hands, the wall. My eyes burn. It is more of a problem than my need for air. Each time I go down, I stay longer—waiting to be pulled up out of the reeds, the green water, and punished for everything. . . .

. . . Caswell. I crawl back to him, try to pull his knees down. I see the roof of his mouth, his teeth, in a scream so close to the ground it raises dust and chips of grass. He coughs, his mouth open wide. I think he is going to vomit. His mouth closes, then opens again. I touch his knee, move his leg down away from his body.

"Get the fuck away from him," Hall screams. He points the pistol at me now, waving it toward the line. "Get back up there and start firing."

"You shot him!"

"He's a fucking coward!" Hall waves the gun. "Get away from him, or I'll shoot you too!"

"You shot him," I scream. "You shot him!" I want everyone to hear: Brinkman, Rizzolo, who was dead when we got here, the Vietnamese.

I put my hand on Caswell's ankle. I put my hand on Caswell's ankle, look into his face. It is me, it is me, my face. I scream, crawl into the grass toward the ditch. Toward water. I want to become a fish, hiding in the reeds. . . .

. . . A fish. I must get back to the sea. Only the sea is peaceful. I do not have to talk. I do not have to think.

I rise up again for air, surprised to see Florida, the blue sky, the gulls high overhead flying in peace. I let myself back down. I can stay here if my hands will let me, if I can learn to use the air in the water. I don't want to be a person anymore. I think of the crowds in New York again, the people all over the streets in Chicago, and the men scurrying around the artillery, breathing smoke.

I think of Kessler, Lucy. Who can I tell all this to? Somebody needs to understand I am not sick. I am only afraid when I am in the light, in the air. I want to find Lucy, bring her back. Explain to her.

I stand up into the blue air, climb up over the wall and walk on the gravel road into sand and toward town. I walk inland. Cars pass. People yell at me, honk the horn. I walk along the highway, down to a grass field, then into a small neighborhood full of white houses with orange roofs, and blue shutters. I see clear drops of water running down each knuckle. My hair clings to the top of my head like a hat. There is no breeze anymore. I can hear the engines of the city.

I walk along a blue street, past black driveways. A woman screams. I look for her among the houses. I see a small child running across a white lawn, long blond hair bouncing into green foliage, a hedge. I hear another scream.

I cross a brown dirt road, walk into a grove of pine trees. A soft rush of air, carrying the odor of food, brushes my face like a sheer curtain. I follow a path up a steep hill, toward bald and thinning trees, where the sun makes thin bony shadows. On the other side of the hill I see a park. There are swing sets, seesaws, monkey bars. Two women push swings with tiny green and yellow bundles in them. I walk along the edge of the park, hear the women yell something at me. I watch them take their children out of the swings, move toward a black shed on the other side of the park. I walk back into a grove of pines, thinking about a tree's occupation of land, and how perfectly intelligent it is. They don't ever have to move. Only human animals move trees.

I emerge from the grove and realize I am standing on the corner where I saw the green GTO Batman was so impressed with. I cross the street, look down to where my father's driveway curves down the hill toward the road. I do not see his car. I walk up the street to where I talked with the two boys, but I don't see them anywhere. Perhaps they went back to Maryland where they do not have a dog, and where they must wait for their father who is in the war. There is no one in the long, uphill yard when I pass, but near the house, sitting in the white grass, I see the little wooden horse Batman was riding.

Another car passes, slows down as it does. Someone yells at me from one of the large white houses on the hill. I get to the corner, walk down Lucy's street. I hope she is home. I want her to be home.

I look back into the sun, and lose sight of the world. I watch my feet moving on hot asphalt, then gravel, then asphalt. Then I am on grass, warm dry grass. My feet are white in green soft grass. I watch my toes in it, look for the street again. There is a concrete surface next to the grass and I move to it. I walk up steps, stand in front of a yellow door. Lucy must be here. I open the screen and knock, but my hand doesn't make any sound. I try again, and this time the door comes open and I walk in.

The house is full of captured sunlight, and all the chairs are empty.

I hear a noise in the back of the house. I recognize the bookshelf against the far wall, go over to it to look at the titles and wait for Lucy. A shadow crosses the floor in front of me and I look up, see Mr. Houston standing there by the kitchen entrance, his hands shaking.

"Is Lucy here?" I ask.

He puts his hands out in front of him, moves toward me with his mouth open, his face shaking. "You get out of here!" he yells. His hands are strong and cold on my arms.

"I was looking for Lucy."

He looks at my feet, then pushes me back toward the door.

"Is Lucy back yet?"

He holds me against the wall by the door. "What have you done to her?"

"I just wanted to know if she was back."

"Where did she go?"

"I have to talk to her."

He takes my arms, pushes me out the door. When I am outside, his hands withdraw back through the door.

"Hey!" someone yells behind me.

I turn to the street, see a police car slowing down as it passes in front of the house. Another one is parked against the curb.

I must get back to the water. I see a policeman getting out of the car by the curb.

I run toward the street, and he starts running to cut me off, to keep me from the water. I stop, and he slows to a walk.

"Take it easy, fella," he says, coming toward me.

I back away. I have to get around him. I can see the blue water in a distant haze behind the policeman, who is still moving, his hands out away from his sides. Then I see another policeman moving around to my right, some distance away.

"Take it easy now."

I move to the left, very slowly. If I move slowly enough, they may not see me. Both of them come closer.

"Hold on now," the first one says.

I know I will not make it. I run toward the side yard, see a tree looming in front of me. I hear them coming behind me, so I climb the lower branches of the tree, pull myself up and away from them. They gather at the base of the tree, looking up at me.

"Come down out of there, son," one of them says.

I watch a small crowd begin to gather, listen to them yelling at me.

X. ANNE

"What happened?" she says when Dale comes through the door.

"That's it!" he says.

"What happened. Where's Michael?" She follows him through the small dining room into the kitchen.

"I'm finished with him!"

"Stop yelling. Tell me where Michael is."

"I don't know, and I don't care." He paces back and forth in the yellow square the sun makes on the floor.

"Calm down," she says. "Tell me what happened."

He stops, looks at her. "He told me he killed Lucy."

"What?" Anne feels her blood turning to cold air. "What?"

"That's what he said."

"He—he—" She takes her hands and turns them over in front of her, then folds them together. "He said—he—"

"In the same breath he told me he didn't do anything."

"He said he didn't do it?"

Dale puts his hand up to his forehead, rubs the skin there. His voice is quieter now. "I don't think he knows whether he did or not."

"What?"

"It's just possible he told me he did it just to hurt me. To scare me." He starts to pace again.

"Tell me what happened."

"I don't want to talk about it."

"Don't be angry at me."

"He's not my son anymore."

"Where is he?"

Dale waves his hand, a gesture which looks like he is throwing something away, something stuck to his hand.

"Where is he?"

"I left him there."

"Where?"

"On the sea wall where we fish."

"So you left him alone out there again." This is a statement, as if she is saying something she predicted long before. But it had not occurred to her. She did not think he would leave Michael again, run away from him.

"Did Houston call the police?"

"He said he was going to. I haven't heard anything."

"No one's called?"

"No."

He turns away from her, walks to the counter by the sink and leans forward on both hands.

"What are we going to do now?" she asks, quietly.

"I really don't know. And you know what? I don't think I care anymore, either."

"He's your son."

"No, he's not. He's not anyone I know."

"He's been through so much." She looks out the window on the back door, sees the fence, Houston's yard.

"Everybody goes through a lot."

"Not what he went through." She moves across the room to where he stands, looks at the lines in his neck and by his eyes. "We don't know what they did to him."

He turns on her, waves his finger in her eyes. "There's not a mark on him!"

She blinks, looks at his hand, then back to his eyes. "You don't give him—"

"He's not even sure himself what happened to him."

"You shouldn't have left him."

"I didn't leave anybody I know. He's not anybody I know."

"Stop it! He's Michael, your son."

"No. He isn't anybody."

"He's Michael now. *Now.* Not the one you remember." She strains to hold her anger. She is afraid, and she is conscious of every nerve in her skin. Her hands are sweating.

"He's not anybody!" He screams this and Anne looks to the kitchen window.

"I don't care who hears us," he says in a normal voice. She sees sweat around his red eyes.

"Calm down. You'll have a heart attack."

"I would like to know what they did to him." He says each of the words separately and at short intervals.

"He doesn't remember it," she says, angry now.

"He knows. He knows."

"How can you be so sure?"

"He knows what happened to Lucy, too."

"Nothing happened to Lucy."

"She's missing, isn't she?"

"Dr. Kessler says—"

"Fuck Kessler!"

"Not so loud." She nearly screams this.

"Fuck him!" He yells so loud she feels his breath in the room. She wants to leave, but he stares at her, waiting. "Did it ever occur to you," he says slowly, "that Michael has it made?"

"What do you mean?"

"He lays around here, collects his four hundred bucks, or whatever it is, and we feed him, pay his way everywhere. He doesn't have to worry about survival. He's got it made."

"Are you finished?"

He raises both arms, hollers it out. *"Got it made!"*

"He's trying. At least he's trying."

"He's probably killed some young girl, and you say I've got to try."

"Stop it!"

"I'm not going to sit here and wait for the police to come pounding on the door trying to find him."

"What are you going to do?"

He moves toward the door. "I'm going to see old man Houston."

"Don't do that."

"Why?"

"He was here today. He's afraid."

"I don't blame him."

"If you go over there you'll only cause trouble."

"For who?"

"For your *boy!*" She cannot get the scream back. The room seems to withdraw all of its sound.

After a pause, Dale says, "So you think he's done something, too."

She does not know what to look at. Everything in the room, including Dale, seems to catch her eyes, fix them into place and produce nausea. "I don't know. I just don't know." She feels herself beginning to cry, so she turns away, first to the door, then to the stove. Dale walks into the living room. She stands by the stove and braces herself with her hands. Her eyes are closed, and she inhales deeply, tries to stop the tears.

"I thought you understood," she says.

"What?" he calls from the couch where he has seated himself. She sees him rooting through the newspapers on the coffee table. She walks into the room and stands in front of him.

"What are you going to do?" she asks, when he does not look at her.

"I'm going to read the paper."

"What are you going to do?"

"He's getting out."

"I won't let you drive him away."

"Then you can go, too." He picks up a section of the paper, his hands trembling. A car passes outside, its tires buzzing on the pavement like a wood saw.

"I *will* go," she says with determination.

He waves his hand at her. He is hidden now, by the newspaper. She sees the senseless headline "LOMBARDI HAS CANCER."

"Was he crying?" she asks.

"I don't want to talk about it anymore."

"What did you say to him?"

He turns the page, snaps the paper between his hands. "I didn't say anything to him," he says quietly. "Michael did all the talking."

"You'll kill him," she says, and she believes this.

"For Christ's sake!" he says. She watches him hit the table with the newspaper, get to his feet, pause, and then walk out of the room through the kitchen and out of the house. She sits on the couch, hearing Michael's breathing against her chest late at night, long ago, his voice full of tears, saying, "I had a bad dream." She sees the smile on his face in the dream she had, his small body under the wheels of the car, and she begins to cry again. She cannot make herself stop, and in all the labored breathing of it, she sees her son, her boy, a helpless and strange young man, alone in the angry world.

She walks to the kitchen, takes a paper towel and wipes her eyes. Dale's car is not in the driveway. She cannot go and look for Michael, nor can she stay in the house and wait. Maybe her son will now be among the missing. Lost somewhere on earth, remembering his private terror. He must come home. If he must leave, then she will go with him. They will both go back to Chicago, live among the gray buildings until he finds peace, his peace.

Outside, the sun is alone in the sky, and it makes shadows among all the houses. Children play on tricycles, run through fenced yards making daylight noises, and Michael, by himself, continues his dangerous journey. When will he come home, come back? When will he ever not be haunted by everything he lived away from home, away from her?

She tries to busy herself in the kitchen, but there is nothing she can make herself do for long. She starts a pot of coffee, then turns it off, thinking that coffee would only make her sick. She moves into the living room, sits on the couch again. She pulls the gauze curtains back, watches cars pass, people walking in the park. She rests her head on the back of the couch, closes her eyes, tries to see Michael when he was a child coming to her with all his successes, all his failures, his eyes wide and large, reflecting a light which used to give off heat, warm her at the center of everything she knew.

When she opens her eyes, it is still very bright, and the appliances whir in the kitchen. Her head aches, as if there is pressure slowly building inside. She lets the room come into focus, realizes she is listening to loud radio messages echoing outside, and the voices of people yelling something she cannot understand. She gets up, rushes to the kitchen, looks out the window on the door at the Houston house. A crowd of people are gathered at the base of a tree in Houston's side yard, raising their arms, yelling at a figure who is perched in the tree, swinging his legs. It is a naked man. She starts to turn away, go back into the living room, when she recognizes Michael.

XI. DALE

He has checked all the rooms, looked for a note on the door, the kitchen table. The house is empty and silent, except for an eerie ticking noise in the foundation. He stands in front of the couch, looking out the front window. He is calm now, after having several beers at the Holiday Inn. He went to Eddie's house first, but there was no one there. So he drove into town, looking for Michael along the street as he went. He drank by himself, trying not to think, but hearing the argument with Anne, Michael's voice saying, "I killed her, Dad," over and over until the sound and confusion of it forced him to move. He went out into the street, tried to find a newspaper, a headline telling the story of his son's crime. If there was a crime. He was not sure. This kept his mind working. It is what works on him now as he watches the breezes move the trees in the park across the road, watches the shadows shifting on the sand, thinking: *Why would he say, 'I killed her, Dad'? Why would he say that? If he has killed her, I want to put him to sleep, finish this.*

The thought creates something in the back of his throat, and he lets out a short cough, putting his hand up over his mouth. "No," he says out loud. "No, please." Then he returns to the kitchen, looks once again for a note—something to tell him what has happened. He studies the phone, as if looking at it will force it to ring. He does not know who he should call. The police? "Hello, I think my son might have been arrested today, and I was wondering—" Houston? "Did they find Lucy's body?"

He gets a beer out of the refrigerator, walks back into the living room. He sits on the couch, putting his feet up on the table, thinking: *The only thing to do is wait. I will wait.* He puts his head back and closes his eyes. He wonders about Anne, where she has gone, if she is with Michael now. Or if perhaps she has gone looking for him, and nothing has happened yet. *Nothing has happened yet. Even if he has been arrested, he's only a suspect. The only evidence is that Houston saw them walking that morning. He saw them walking. They were together, then Lucy is missing. Michael is not right. Not right. He's been in the hospital, here and in his last year in the service. A Viet Man, Viet Nam veteran. Violence. A prisoner. When he comes in I will hear him. I will hear them when they come home. Home.*

When he does hear something it is nearly dark. He sits up, listening, for he cannot remember what it was that awakened him.

"Anne?" he says.

There is a light in the kitchen, cigarette smoke swirling under it. "Anne?"

"I'm in here," a voice says from the kitchen.

The windows are gray and outside the cars pass with headlamps clear and distinct. Dale's neck is stiff, and his legs seem electrified, the bottoms of his feet soft, conducting hot current up through his ankles. He walks slowly into the kitchen. "What're you doing?" he says, rubbing his eyes.

"Thinking." She is dressed in her blue sun dress, sitting at the table holding a cigarette. A pack of Marlboros lies in front of her, a blue lighter neatly on top, and the ashtray next to her hand is full.

He stands at the stove, letting his eyes come fully open, trying to think of something to say.

"When I came in I thought you were dead," she says. Her voice is subdued, and there is something in it he doesn't recognize; a resignation, perhaps. She has made her mind up about something, and there is no hint of emotion or animation in her words. "I stood there in the living room looking at you and I didn't remember you. Couldn't think for a minute whether or not I knew who you were. I watched your face, listened to your breathing, and realized—" She pauses, takes a long time putting the cigarette up to her lips, her eyes staring through the smoke at something over the sink. "I realized that you really are somebody else. A man I met twenty-three years ago with a life—" She stops again, flicks the ash on the cigarette into the ashtray. "A life totally separate from mine. Separate and different."

He stands by the stove listening to her, watching her smoke. He is afraid to ask her about Michael, and he doesn't know what to say. He will let her finish because he does not like the sound of her voice.

"I realized you're just another man. Someone I live with," she says slowly. "Not really family at all except by legal paperwork. You're not related to me. I don't belong to you in any biological sense."

She puffs the cigarette, then, blowing smoke, looks at the filter, studies it as if she is preparing to disassemble it.

"You're still angry?" he says.

"No."

"Then what's the matter?" He feels a quiver in his voice when he says this, and he takes a deep breath, waiting for what she will say.

"Who said anything was wrong?" She looks at him. He cannot bear the detachment he sees in her eyes.

"Where's Michael?" he asks.

She looks away again. "Asleep."

He watches her put out the cigarette, pick up the pack, and withdraw another one. While she lights it, he notices a fly swirling around the light over her head, sees it come to rest on her hair, then rise up dizzily into the air again, circling the light. Anne draws on the cigarette, inhales deeply.

"How long have you been doing that?" he says.

"What?"

"Sitting here smoking one after another."

She points to the ashtray. "You're the detective in the house. You figure it out."

"Look," he says. "I'm sorry. I was mad. I didn't mean what I said."

"You said so much. So very much. Are you sure you didn't mean *any* of it?"

"What's happened?" He hears his voice die in the room. She does not answer. He watches the fly eddying through the thin rising white smoke under the light. Anne stares at something on the far wall. She will not look at him.

"Where'd you go?" he says, finally.

"You mean you don't know?" For the first time there is tone in her voice, and he is conscious again of the airless beating of his heart. "Oh, I had a time," she says. "I had just a fine time."

"What happened?" He tries to look at her, but she is only a blur across the room. He hears the meticulous fly bump against the light.

"You just did wonders for Mike."

"He talked to you about it?"

"No."

"Well, what then?"

She puts her head down.

"Tell me what happened." He wants to go to her, but he is afraid of the tone in her voice. When she begins to cry he is helpless. "He's all right, isn't he?"

"Go away," she cries.

"What's the matter. Is it Lucy?"

"Just go away." She holds the cigarette over the ashtray, her hands trembling. "Leave me alone."

"If something's happened, I want to know about it." He begins to pace, unable to go to her. He cannot make himself stand still and watch her cry. "You've got to talk to me about it." He stops by the sink, leans on the cold porcelain, runs his hand up over the top of his head through his hair, trying to think of something which will get her to stop crying, get her to tell him what has happened. "Is it Lucy?" She does not answer. He moves again, across the room to the counter and the stove. Then he says, "If you won't tell me, maybe Michael will."

She suddenly sits up, her eyes wet and red. He moves to the door, stops there to look at her, waiting for her to say something. They stay that way for a moment, then she says, quietly, each word dropping from her mouth like a stone, "You stay away from him. Do you hear?" Then she screams, "Stay away from him!"

He does not know what to say to her. He watches her lips, the hair in her eyes under the light, the smoke in wreaths around her head. Then he says, "He's my son, too." He walks out of the kitchen, heads for the living room and the stairs. He hears her get up, stops by the dining room table. The room is dark. He waits for her there, thinking: *He's my son, too. He's my son, too.*

XII. MICHAEL

I hear my mother scream at him, then the house is quiet and I wait in the dark. I'm afraid. My father will come to my room, turn on the light, and take me from the bed. Crickets and night moths sing outside. I can't hear any engines—no trains, no jets, no cars. The world is still, except for its insects, the faint rumbling of the sea, and the last breath of the moving trees. I have never been so conscious.

Something moves downstairs. I hear my mother say, "No," losing breath as if in a struggle. They are coming for me. The layers of my skin separate, fill with cold weightless fluid. My hands sweat.

It is dark. My eyes are alone and separated in the black air. I listen for their steps, for the movements of those other bodies toward me, toward my black space, my silent, cold cocoon. It is the anniversary of my death, a soundless, primitive celebration. I remember so much now, without effort. Without pain. It is as clear to me as a name I have suddenly remembered—a name I had forgotten. A name I could examine in darkness, seeing clearly all its attributes, its characters, but failing some-how to pronounce it. I lived in a hole in the ground for forty-one days and nights. The darkness is all I remember. At first, just the darkness—but there's more. I was wet and cold in the beginning. Afraid. Then I was not afraid anymore. I was angry, living the punishment in a luxurious privacy of hatred. I made my fingers explore the soil around me. I ate some of it, thinking I would die. I was someone else, assuming shapes the way some fish change colors—aching to survive. I wanted to tell someone about Caswell. I wanted to kill Sergeant Hall. *Kill* him. I ate more dirt. I would eat anything, anything at all. I became nothing. Then, a land mine. Tortured explosive, waiting to be tripped. Send fragments of myself into all the air, thick as smoke. Fall like rain. Make wounds.

I could not move my legs. I sat in urine. I wept. I couldn't feel or hear anything anymore. And thatch above me came off at night. Hands pulling it away, voices laughing. Some nights I could see the moon shining through the thatch, through the overhanging trees—the moon, so solid and normal, that shone over Boston and Chicago, made tiny patches of glorious light on rivers and lakes. The moon so perfect and safe, hanging in the universe like a street lamp on a clean boulevard somewhere else in the world. The moon that shone on my father, on his section of the curving earth. I cried out without words, begging in no language.

And they came for me.

They came for me, laughing and talking in their grunting, serious language. Even the laughter sounded like part of their conversation, as if it communicated something more than mirth. I could not understand statement, or command, or even question. I made sounds out of my throat which seemed to come from somewhere in my body—as if each cell cried out on its own against this death, this accumulated dying.

Hands took hold of me. Took hold of me.

A sound at my door removes the blankets and sends shocks to my hands.

"Leave me alone," my father says.

I hear my mother whispering. I know her desperate hands are holding him away.

I get out of the bed, stand by the window. The door opens. I cannot see my mother.

"Michael?" he says.

"Yes?"

"You awake?"

"I'm here." I do not see my mother. He stands in the yellow frame of light in front of the door. He is black. I can't see his face.

"Can I turn a light on?"

"Is my mother crying?" I say.

He turns the light on and my eyes seem to fold in on themselves.

"You're up," he says.

"Where's my mother?"

"Where is she?"

"Is my mother crying?"

" 'My mother'? Since when do you call her that?"

"Where is she?"

"She's in the bedroom." He lowers his head, steps to the side out of the door frame. He comes further into the room. "She's mad at me because I want to talk to you."

"Why?"

"She's afraid I'll do something—I'll say something to upset you."

"What do you want?" He's not looking at me. He places his hand on the bureau by the door.

"I just want to talk to you, son. Can I—can I do that? Would you mind if we just talked?"

"OK."

"You're not mad at me, are you?" He looks at the floor in front of him.

"I don't know."

"I'm sorry about this morning."

"OK."

"I didn't mean to upset you."

"OK."

He turns his head back to the door. His hands try to find someplace to hide.

"Can I sit down?" he says.

My mother suddenly stands in the door frame, holding a handkerchief to her face. He turns to her.

"We're just going to talk," he says. He touches the door.

"Leave the door open," I say.

He looks at me, his mouth open. Then he lets go of the door, and sweeps his arm toward the center of the room. "Come in then," he says. He is getting angry.

Mother takes the handkerchief down and looks at him. Her eyes seem yellow and overexposed. "Please let him sleep," she says.

"I want to talk to my son. He's wide awake, standing up by his bed. He says it's OK if we talk. Right, Michael?" He turns to me.

"I don't know."

"Leave him alone," Mother says.

"Can we talk or not?" he says to me.

"What do you want to talk about?"

"I just want to know what happened today. If it's not too much."

"Please, Dale," Mother says. She is crying. "Please."

"Get out of here!" She jumps back, moved by the force of his voice. He pushes her all the way out and slams the door. I hear her call my name.

"Now!" His voice is exploding in the room. "Sit there on the bed and listen!"

I sit on the bed, holding my mother in my eyes. He walks around in front of me, as if he is looking for something on the floor. I wait. Then he says, his voice not as loud, "What did you do today?"

"I went to the Ben Franklin store," I say. I try not to cry. The room is foreign to me. I must be dreaming this in a cafeteria somewhere.

"What Ben Franklin store?" he says. "There's no Ben Franklin store in—"

"I got caught stealing."

"What were you stealing?"

"A slingshot."

"A slingshot?"

"Yes. And a man caught me."

"What man?"

"The manager."

"What was his name?"

"I don't know."

"What were you doing in—what store did you go to?"

"Ben Franklin."

"What Ben Franklin?"

"The one on Kedzie."

"What are you talking about?" He comes toward me, whispering.

"I told you."

"Tell me what happened today," he says. He breathes in front of me, his eyes beginning to shrink. "Does it have anything to do with Lucy?"

"Lucy?"

"Michael," he says. I feel his breath. "I'm not going to take much more of this. You hear?"

"I didn't go to school today."

"You're not in Chicago!" he screams, takes my arms. "Listen to me." His eyes are coming out.

"I'm sorry, Dad," I say. "I'm sorry."

He screams again. "Where are you! Michael! Where are you!"

I try to break away, but he holds me, his eyes beginning to fold in the heat.

"I'm sorry, Dad."

He pushes me and I go down, hear my bones against the floor. I try to get under the bed, but he pulls me up, holds my arms pinned to my side, screaming, "You want to be afraid of me? Be afraid of me! You want to be crazy? Be crazy!" I am a doll, a mannequin. He tries to say something, then he throws me down on the bed. "I'm sick of it!" He goes out of the room and closes the door. . . .

. . . The bowl in my hands is full of urine. It comes down at me from outside where the heads are. I see four heads. They grunt and shout. I drink the warm sour fluid. The heads laugh. Behind them I see the moon shining in the trees. I choke. I can't make anything but my hands move. My skin is cold. The dirt around me shifts, crawls on my skin. A head shouts down at me. I drink again. My face makes a noise, a shudder like a horse. The heads laugh. It is real laughter, with tears. Some of the heads roll away. The moon seems to wink at me. There is sand in my hair. I hear someone crying. Someone weeps, begs. I try to scream. I don't know what my hands are doing. The skin comes off my feet, my legs. One of the heads lets an arm down, tries to grab my hair. It pulls my ear and I stand up, feet sinking. My head comes through the rim of the hole and I am above ground. They are staring at me. Only my head sticks out of the ground. One of them shouts at me. I feel my body begin to shake. Someone is crying again. I try to talk, but all I can say is "the the the" over and over again. No one can hear me because of the crying. I can't make other words. The heads laugh. One of them grunts something, then rises up in front of the moon, moves over to me. He puts his bare foot under my chin, pushes my head back. The others laugh. I try to laugh, too. If they would be friends with me. I am not an enemy. I am a person. I scream this, but no one hears it. The sound disappears in the trees. The crying gets louder. The laughter stops. I hear them breathing, and the insects begging in the forest. The toes move from under my chin. He yells something. I think of my father. He yells again, reaches down, pulls my hair. The crying stops. I close my eyes. I hear him rise, fool with his pants. *My father takes off his belt. I'm sorry. I'm sorry.* I feel it on the top of my head, warm down the sides of my face, my neck. I try not to breathe. The laughter begins again, echoes out into the night like the cry of wild birds. *I'm sorry.* I'm sorry. A hand pushes me down. I try to scream. I can't get angry anymore. I can't get angry. My feet crumble beneath me. Hands move grass, thick grass over the moon. It disappears. The heads grunt quietly now. I think of death instead of sleep. My stomach churns, collapses. I choke. In between breaths I give up something wet and thick. It steams on my knees. I'm behind my eyes. I watch the hands close out tiny flecks of moon still above me. I come out of here when there is no moon. They move me at night. They change places with me hanging from a pole. A bamboo pole. My head dangles, I am the genitals of a four-legged animal. My head moves through the damp green grass, the thick wet foliage. It's quiet now. I want to lie down. My neck holds everything up. It's thin, only a trembling thread. My body shakes, agitates the dirt. I hear snoring. I hold my breath, try to pass out. I beg for death. This is where I end up. I end up here. The insects cry above me. I try to think of my father. My father. Nights in the tent, telling stories. His laugh. I wonder what he is doing now. If he is awake. He's in the world with me, doing something, breathing, right now. *My father.* When they come for me I think of him. I think of him. Someone starts crying again, whimpering quietly. I want my father to come and get me now. Forgive me, I think of him when they come. It is a punishment. I am punished. If he would come and get me. If he would get me. *I can't sleep, want to talk? think mom wants to come out here with us sometimes? I can't sleep, want to go in the house, son? I'm sorry.* I hear a noise above me. The thatch moves. My hands come up over my face. Something's moving above me. I'm afraid to open my eyes. It's quiet again. I look up. There's nothing. Only the disintegrated moon. *I can't sleep my father laughs here like this. See? he punches holes in the lid of the jar with a screwdriver everything's got to breathe son I touch the sides of the jar watch the bugs slip down fall on each other go get the hammer we'll have this thing up in no time his fingers tap the wood soundlessly we've got to build it sturdy so no one can come and get us I can't sleep* It is so completely dark my eyes ache for light. I try to feel my legs. Insects crawl in the wet dirt. I listen for movement above earth. My heart breathes like the tiny pulse of all the whirring insects. Someone grunts and they start talking again. The voices sound like the rattle of some weakened electric motor. I hate them again, hate their talking like the squeals of a trapped animal. I wonder what they talk about. I am only a few feet away, waiting to die. One of them will do it. He will stop talking and come over here, a breathing creature carrying fluid and sinew and thoughts, and he will see me die in the nerves of his head. I can't remember how I came to be in the earth waiting for them. They look at me as if I am something furry they found in the grass. I hate them *put a little grass in there with them son they eat too I don't want to take the lid off the jar* because they will come for me again. They hit me on the back of the head when they caught me and I went out of the world someplace. I want that death again. *you're killing them so? you're killing them don't they're just insects son they'll survive I can't sleep want to go inside? do you? I'll stay if you do my father laughs* then pulls away the thatch. There's a head in front of the moon. I can't see its eyes. A voice says something to me. Gentle, almost kind. I don't understand it. It says the same thing, a little louder. I try to talk. Please let me die. I struggle to stand, but the voice stops me. *want to go in or not?* Yes I do. Oh yes I do. Yes yes I do. I want to go in now. I want to go in now. I hear high, gurgling, birdlike sounds. The head watches me, almost as if it is listening. It looms over me, staring with eyes I can't see. I want to go in now. OK? Let's go in. The head says something again, seems to wait for an answer. I'm sorry. I hear more talking. A cloud covers the white moon. They want to play with me again. . . .

XIII. ANNE

She sits on the bed wiping her nose with a Kleenex. "He was arrested today," she says. Dale stands by the door shaking his head. "He broke into Houston's house, and he was—" She breaks off, crying.

"Finish it," Dale says in a flat voice. She feels him next to her.

"He was running around without any clothes on."

"Jesus!"

She gets up, goes to the closet, begins pulling out dresses.

"What are you doing?"

"I'm getting out of here."

"No, you're not."

She looks at him, at a face she does not know.

"Don't," he says.

"I'm taking him out of here." She throws two dresses on the bed, returns to the closet.

"You won't solve anything that way."

She continues to throw dresses on the bed, and he begins to pace. She moves to the dresser, takes clothing out of the top drawer, in a hurry now to get this over with. To get out of the house and out of Florida.

"Where will you go?"

She cannot look at him. "I don't know yet."

"Why are you leaving?"

"You really don't know?" She does look at him now.

"I'm sorry," he says, his voice rising. "I didn't know about today."

She begins on the second drawer, pulling things out now as if they are burning.

"Michael thinks I'm the enemy," he says, his voice trembling.

"You are."

"No."

"You caused this. *You!*" She throws a bra onto the bed. She is not crying anymore, although her head aches and she feels as if there is something in her ears, something muffling all sound.

"Tell me the rest of it," he says. "At least do that."

"OK," she says. "If you want to know." She stops by the dresser, leans on it, thinks of Michael surrounded by all the uniforms, the gray metal desks and brown wooden chairs which squeaked when people moved in them, the typewriters clacking, telephones ringing—the image of Michael's face in the midst of all that, looking innocent and afraid, almost foreign. "They put him in a cell. They gave him a sedative and put him in a cell. Naked."

"I swear I didn't know he would—"

"He cried. Almost as if he knew he failed."

"I'm sorry."

"So am I," she says. She reaches under the bed and gets the suitcase.

"What about Lucy?"

"I thought you knew what happened to her."

"What?"

"You were so sure. Don't you know?"

"What?"

"Michael dragged her off and cut her pretty little throat," she whispers, as if she is confiding in him. She wants to ridicule him, make him suffer. Just now she is as close to hating him as she has ever been.

"Do you know what happened to her?" His voice is louder.

"No. And right now, I don't care." The suitcase is full before she looks at him again. He stands in the door frame, his hands in his pockets, watching her with a puzzled look, as if he is trying to figure some mathematical problem in his head.

"Do you have any money?" he says quietly.

"I have some."

"Are you going to take Michael with you?"

"Yes." She closes the suitcase, snaps it shut. A sound rises from Dale's throat, forces her to look at him. He has his hands over his face, pushing the skin high on his forehead.

"Don't give up now," he says.

She takes the handle of the suitcase, holds it tightly in her hands, trying to make the day retreat. "I thought we were getting somewhere," she says after a pause. "I thought we were working it all out."

"We still can," he begs. "I lost my temper. I was hurt."

"It's too late," she whispers.

He shakes his head, looks at her with weak, yellow eyes. "Honey."

"Why did you *do* it?"

"I was hurt. I couldn't forget what he said on the tape."

"So you wanted to hurt him?"

"I didn't think of it that way."

"But you did hurt him."

"I yelled at him."

"You were feeling sorry for yourself."

"I guess."

"And now Michael will probably have to go back in the hospital."

"Anne, when he told me he killed Lucy, I felt my heart move. Then he said he didn't. I was so frustrated." He folds his hands in front of his face, as if he is praying to the overhead light. His eyes shine, reflect in soft infinite patterns the light—as if it emanated from the intricate glass like substance of each cornea. She cannot make herself look away, but she sees herself from a distance, staring at him, and she wants to move—get out of that room. Somewhere in her dreams, she is running in the darkness under the stars. She wears a white dress and the night breezes, carrying salt air, and the odor of green pine, caress her figure, move the dress out into the corners of this framed picture like the white feathers on a great winged creature—a bird, an angel. She is free, running without effort. She mingles with the cool air, her body only vapor, a cloud, white under the black dome of night. She will assemble in a bead of water, resting on the smooth-textured, deep green bed of a leaf, and in the morning, the sun will rise in her.

"Please don't leave," he says. "Wait till tomorrow."

She puts the suitcase on the floor, walks by him and into the hall in front of Michael's room. She edges the door open, sees Michael lying on the bed asleep, his hands moving slightly, as if only a single nerve refuses to sleep. She hears his breathing, a quiet and rhythmic whisper, and she cannot wake him. Dale comes up behind her, puts his hands on her shoulders. She turns the light off, closes the door.

"I'll leave tomorrow," she says with determination, taking his hands off her as if she is discarding a towel. He steps back, leans on the wall. "Tomorrow."

"OK," he says. "I can't stop you."

She walks back to the room and closes the door.

XIV. DALE

My father, he thinks. *What did I think of him when I was a boy? I loved him, thought he made the days and nights for his own amusement. And I am the enemy to my son? When he was in their power he thought of me? Power. I was a giant to my son, and I had power, sheer force to make him do what I wished. I did not often need violence.*

He leans back in the chair under the kitchen light. Outside, the lights of the town slowly diminish as more and more individual human souls prepare to rest. Soon, only the streetlights will break the solid darkness. In the glass of the window he sees his tired face, the light making shadows under his eyes. It is a visage like a death mask.

And she says she is leaving. Taking Michael with her.

He gets up, goes to the back door, opens it quietly. He goes out and down the stairs, turns left and walks out to the garden. It is overgrown with weeds, stands out of the normal grass like the wild hair of the hopelessly insane. He stands in the grass, looks out over the houses for the moon, Michael's moon. An airplane drones overhead, and a chill breeze rises against him, as if the airplane has disturbed the air over these quiet houses. Down the street, a car negotiates a turn, the tires squealing.

When I was a boy, he thinks, *the city made noises which frightened me. I went to my father, and he held me against his chest—I remember the rising and falling of his chest as he snored next to me—and I was safe. Safe. If Michael would come to me. If he would come to me. Maybe I didn't take enough time with him when he was a boy. I should have listened to him when he wanted to talk. I always had something on my mind. Something else. There was time for him, I made some time for him. A man can't give up everything. Not everything. I had to live, too.*

He hears the voice of his son in the center of his brain—the child's cry of delight, of mischief and fear—and he listens to his own voice saying, "Not now, son. Not now, son."

He looks up to the window of Michael's room, tries to visualize the grown man sleeping in there—the grown man who remembers stealing something from the Ben Franklin store in Chicago when he was ten years old; the grown man who believes he is that boy. It is an episode Dale cannot fully remember. Something he let out of his mind with the passage of time, and he does not know what he said then. He must have yelled at the boy, punished him in some way. And where is the Michael of all the years in between?

The airplane is gone now, although the sound of it still echoes across the sky. He walks back to the porch, turns and studies the house beyond the back fence, the house of Lucy and her husband. It is dark over there, but he knows the old man is probably not asleep.

He walks back into the house, closes the door quietly behind him. He turns the light in the kitchen off and walks to the couch in the living room, settling there as if he has been drinking. When cars pass, waves of light cross the ceiling above him.

Somewhere in the night behind his eyes there is a scream. Lucy is there, holding a drink in her hands. Ben laughs. "What happened?" a voice says. Another scream. Lucy turns milky, like chalk soaked in water. When Ben touches her his hands get her white skin on them. *Why are we sitting here? Where's Michael?* Anne pours a drink, sits next to Lucy. *I'm not going anywhere. Anne, where's Michael?* Ben wipes his hands on the furniture. He studies the fingers. Dale looks at his own hands, expects to find a tiny element burning in each fingernail. He groans, tries to show his fingers to Anne. He can't make any sound. Anne laughs at something Lucy has said. Lucy drips white liquid like sweat, it gathers in beads on her brow, her hands. *Where's Michael?* A little boy comes into the dark circle where they all sit. He carries something in his hands, something wet and small. *What is that? Leave him alone,* Anne says. *What is that? Stop it. I want to know what it is.* Lucy laughs, her teeth gleaming. *Stop it. I want to know what he has.* Michael doesn't move. His head is larger than his body, much larger. It seems to grow. *Give me that.* He backs away. Anne picks him up, puts him out of the circle, sits down again. *There, now we can talk.* Lucy nods her head, glares at the floor. Dale tries to scream. A voice echoes in his head. Lucy opens her mouth and the ringing of a phone begins behind her teeth. She smiles. The ringing continues. He reaches for her but she moves. The ringing gets louder, begins to separate into solid and distinct sounds. Then it is just a telephone ringing and he cannot see anything anymore. He listens to it, tries to make his eyes come open, hears someone on the stairs, moving down into the room and past him. The ringing stops just as he opens his eyes.

Anne is in the kitchen saying something into the phone. He gets up, lets his eyes clear, tries to hear what she is saying. When he cannot make it out, he gets up and goes to the dining room, stands by the table there just out of the frame of light from the kitchen.

"I'm glad to hear it," Anne says. "OK. Thanks for calling."

He waits, but she does not hang up the phone. She stands with her back to him, leaning on the wall, nodding her head.

"That's all right," she says. "I understand."

He watches her, his heart beginning to move in his chest.

"No. I'll call her tomorrow." She nods her head again. Then, "Thank you again," and she hangs the phone up without looking at him.

She turns off the light, walks to the back-porch door, stares out the window there.

"Lucy?" he says.

"Yes."

"That was her?"

"No. It was Ben. Lucy is home."

"She's there? There in the house?"

"Yes."

"What happened?"

"I don't know. Something about her former husband."

"She went back to him?"

"He came and got her." Anne stares out the window. He wants to go to her but he is afraid, he doesn't know what she is thinking, why she won't look at him. "He was violent. Took her to Georgia. Apparently it was an ordeal."

"She's all right."

"Yes." She reaches in her robe, pulls out a cigarette. The flare of the match illuminates her face momentarily, but there is nothing there, nothing he recognizes. In the darkness again he watches the coal of her cigarette make red lines in the black frame of the window.

"I feel so silly now," he says.

"I wonder how Michael feels." She draws on her cigarette; the coal brightens her face. She leans on the door now, her face turned to the side.

"Anne, I don't know anything else to say, but I'm sorry."

She waves her hand.

"I understand now," he says. "I didn't before. I was angry and hurt and—like you said—I was feeling sorry for myself."

She doesn't say anything. He watches the coal of her cigarette move in the air.

"I'll love him, if you'll let me," he says.

"I don't know anymore."

"I understand now," he says again. He knows he must put it into words, he must tell her what he has come to know without any thought, any language. "It was only power Michael was afraid of. Not me. Power."

"What do you mean?"

"He was in their power. They controlled his life the way a parent does. You see? It wasn't me." He feels his voice beginning to break. "He isn't afraid of me."

She lowers her head, seems to grow shorter.

"Honey?"

"Don't."

"Let me try."

"Leave me alone."

"Let's go upstairs. Right now."

"Why?"

"I want to look at him. That's all. I won't wake him." He moves toward her. "OK?"

"He has to go back to the hospital," she says without tone.

"Maybe not." He cannot get strength into his voice.

"We've lost him again."

"He was upset. I was yelling and everything." He puts his hands in his pockets, leans against the stove. He is only a few feet from her now. The coal brightens, goes dim. He hears the rush of air from her lungs.

"Our baby," she says, her voice rising. She cries in the darkness by the door.

"I'd like to come to you," he says.

"What?" She wipes her eyes.

"Can I come over there?"

The coal makes a trail in the air, a wave of her hand. He walks over to her, puts his arms around her. "Let's go upstairs. See if he's awake."

"Let him sleep."

"He may be awake."

She moves her head in the hollow of his shoulder. Her crying is quiet now, almost the slight murmur of a bird.

"OK?" he whispers.

She nods her head against him. They walk together up to his room. In the hall outside his door, she whispers, "Don't wake him." She has stopped crying. He starts to edge the door open, when he hears Michael say, "I want to go in now."

He looks at Anne, who seems to be studying the crack under the door. She moves away, goes to the bathroom to throw her cigarette away. When she returns, she does not touch him. He reaches for her, pulls her to him.

"Did you hear that?" he says.

"Yes."

"Is he dreaming?"

"I don't know."

Michael says again, "I want to go in."

Dale opens the door. Michael lies on the bed, his legs pulled up to his chest, his head moving back and forth on the pillow.

"Michael?" Dale says.

"I think he's asleep," Anne says.

"He's dreaming."

"I'm sorry," Michael says.

Dale goes to the bed, Anne next to him, hesitant, almost holding him back. "If he's dreaming we should wake him," he says.

"I don't know."

"Michael?" Dale says. He reaches down, touches his son on the shoulder.

"What?" Michael whispers.

"Are you all right?"

"Yes."

"Were you dreaming?"

"Yes." He rubs his eyes, moves back on the bed.

"It's all right, son." Dale reaches out. "It's all right."

"I won't steal anymore, Dad." His eyes are empty, without light. They are the eyes of a fish. Anne sits on the bed, puts her arms around him.

"Go back to sleep," she says.

His eyes get wider. Then he starts to breathe fast, closing his mouth as if to gulp the air. "I want to go in, now," he says. "It's too cold out here, Dad."

Dale kneels in front of him. "Oh, my boy."

Anne looks at him, her face expressionless.

"I'm sorry, Michael. I'm sorry," Dale whispers. He touches Michael's arm. "I'm so sorry."

Michael's chin trembles; he fights back tears, breathing deeply. "I want to go in, *Dad.* I want to go in now."

Dale takes his son in his arms, holds him, looking in Anne's eyes, her dark brown eyes. She tilts her head, a puzzled look on her face, as if she is discovering something the world does not know. Dale nods. "We'll go home," he says to her.

"Dad, I want to go in," Michael says. "OK?"

"We'll go in, son," Dale says, looking still at Anne. "We'll go in. We'll go in."

Bausch, Robert
On The Way Home